Also by Mary Tannen

SECOND SIGHT
AFTER ROY
EASY KEEPER

Edith Seagrace has come to New York City from a small upstate town. She has landed an internship at Ubu, the magazine that first sparked her girlhood fantasies of the literary life—and she has lucked into an apartment as well. She and her roommate, Clarence, are dizzy with delight: at last, the beginning of Real Life...But with so many stars in her eyes, Edith doesn't notice the frenzy her arrival has created. Her new boss, her eccentric neighbor, Ubu's editor-in-chief...all are drawn to Edith for their own secret reasons. And Edith, unwittingly, is about to become a lightning rod for the lost dreams and desires of this band of lonely sophisticates. With deft wit and stylishly drawn characters, Loving Edith evokes the enchantment of a New York summer, the endless possibilities of life at twenty-one—and the fleeting, brilliant allure of a second chance.

"Highly charged and entertaining... Ms. Tannen...takes her readers nimbly through this bustling narrative, aided by a pinpoint accuracy in describing the behavior of her New York sophisticates. She treats them and their foibles with admirable ease, managing to laugh at these eminently fallible people without ever being mean to them."
—The New York Times Book Review

"Lots of charm, plus the taste and feel of a New York summer."
—Cosmopolitan

"*Loving Edith* is at once a '90s period piece, instantly as identifiable as a Lalique vase or Tiffany lamp—or a *New Yorker* cover. Many enchanting passages leave the reader smitten."

—*Philadelphia Inquirer*

"Sharply observed, engagingly witty and decidedly knowledgeable about the world it depicts...a romantic paean to a city that still beckons outsiders as the ultimate in glamour and worldly appeal."

—*Cleveland Plain Dealer*

"Tannen doesn't miss a step in this gracefully conceived gavotte."

—*People*

LOVING EDITH

Mary Tannen

RIVERHEAD BOOKS, NEW YORK

Riverhead Books
Published by The Berkley Publishing Group
200 Madison Avenue
New York, New York 10016

Riverhead hardcover edition: May 1995
First Riverhead trade paperback edition: June 1996
Riverhead trade paperback ISBN: 1-57322-544-4

Published simultaneously in Canada.

The Putnam Berkley World Wide Web site address is
http://www.berkley.com

The Library of Congress has catalogued the Riverhead hardcover
edition as follows:

Tannen, Mary.
Loving Edith / by Mary Tannen.
    p.   cm.
ISBN 1-57322-008-6
I. Title.
PS3570.A54L68   1995   94-43796   CIP
813'.54—dc20

Printed in the United States of America

10   9   8   7   6   5   4   3   2   1

For my mother

CONTENTS

LOVING

EDITH

THE STRANGE ATTRACTOR

LULU IS ENJOYING A SOAK IN THE BATHTUB OF HER ROOM in the König von Ungarn in Vienna. She's put in a double helping of the bubble stuff that came gratis in a stoppered glass bottle —none of those cheesy foil packets for this hotel!—and has fashioned herself a bubble helmet and enormous foamy breasts. She wants Larry to come and see. "Larry!" But he's on the phone, making notes, doing deals. She raises herself so she can see in the mirror and does some cavorting, Marilyn-type moves—hands on breasts, licking lips, then shaking her head so bubbles fly. Larry will love this. Larry loves her, adores her. Which is why she came along for the first part of his trip, even though she has important projects of her own back in New York.

She slides into the water and allows her hair to float on top like a mermaid's. If the bubbles die before Larry can tear himself away from the phone, she will be like this when he comes in, hair like seaweed, a Botticelli Venus rising from—well, not rising, lying in—the foamy surf. A smile playing on her lips. A smile that is still young, but no longer girlish. She has matured. She has done well. She is entering a new phase.

In New York it is six hours earlier. Desert Ray will have arrived—yesterday or the day before, Lulu isn't sure. Ray is awake, most certainly. Out doing—what? Lulu tries to conjure an image of Ray, what she looks like now, what will attract her in the city, what will repel her. How she is likely to begin her day. Coffee and muffin? Granola and yogurt? A cigarette? Lulu hopes not, although if she does smoke, it's probably just a phase, one she'll give up, as Lulu did. Lulu always imagines Ray doing what Lulu did at her age, which might be completely wrong. Lulu lacks information. She and the doctor agreed that it would be less painful if she didn't know what was happening, day by day, week by week, year by year. That way Lulu could get on with her life. When Ray turned twenty-one, a meeting might be arranged if it were agreeable to both. Ray had to want it as well, had to agree.

This meeting seemed so far in the future when Lulu and the doctor made the plan, that Lulu didn't think she could bear to wait so long. She might not even be alive! And then, suddenly, there was a letter from the doctor, saying that the twenty-first birthday was imminent. So soon! Lulu had always imagined that by the time Ray was twenty-one, Lulu would have achieved certain things. She expected that she would be an older, settled woman, not still young, still exploring possibilities, still on the point of setting out. How could Lulu have a child who's twenty-one?

She called the doctor to postpone the meeting for six months, maybe a year, until her life had taken on some shape, some density, the gravitas appropriate to someone with an adult child. The doctor didn't understand what the problem was. Lulu didn't want to go into detail. The doctor said that Ray was planning to come to the city anyway for the summer. The news that her child was actually approaching, had made plans, however accidentally, to come to her, lifted Lulu's heart and then it seemed easy. Wasn't Lulu taking over Molly's loft for the summer—and Molly's brother's, Reggie's, loft above it? Ordinarily Lulu is lucky to find a spare bed where she can sleep. Now fate had handed her a whole extra place, one which she could generously give over to Ray. Lulu made phone calls. Reggie didn't mind. Molly was intrigued. The doctor was puzzled: Wouldn't it be better just to give the child Lulu's phone number, and they could meet for lunch if they wished? Lulu insisted. This way she could choose the moment when she would reveal herself to Ray. And there would be a whole summer to get to know each other.

As she has many times before, Lulu mentally goes through her wardrobe, planning what she will be wearing the first time Ray sees her. She looks good in that dress Larry bought her for the trip. But maybe a dress is too frivolous. She should be outfitted for work when she and Ray first meet. The first time is very important. It could skew Ray's impression forever, one way or the other. If Ray were to know certain things about Lulu, she might form a negative opinion. A negative on top of a negative.

Many children hate their mothers for giving them up. Studies have been done. A lot more is known, things that weren't known, or at least Lulu didn't know them at the time. But how could she have done otherwise? Lulu always stops at this question.

Once the doctor had taken the baby in his arms, something was set in motion. Lulu signed papers and walked away as if in a trance. Only later did she try to get her baby back, but then it was too late. The doctor showed her the papers, explained the law.

Edith! Why do you call her Edith? she asked the doctor. She is Desert Ray. Lulu named her even before the midwife cut the cord that connected them, body to body. Desert Ray. How could he take that name and leave a stodgy one in its place?

Confidence and optimism are dying with the bubbles. What kind of person will Ray be? A person named Edith, possibly very foreign to Lulu. A person who calls the doctor's daughter "Mom." Lulu hardly remembers the doctor's daughter, only that she didn't seem to approve of Lulu, might even have been afraid of her. What has she told Ray about Lulu, about the circumstances of the birth and adoption?

When Lulu heard Ray was coming to the city, she felt that blood was drawing her, that Ray desired this union as much as Lulu did. But what if something completely different is bringing her? Maybe she has a boyfriend; maybe she has a job. Maybe there is something else, something the girl cannot see or name, that is compelling her to come—a strange attractor. (Lulu thinks that's the term astronomers use to describe an object they cannot see, but whose presence they divine from the way other objects are drawn to it, screaming through space toward its invisible center.) The city is full of strange attractors. Perhaps Lulu, with her needs, her plans, will be only an annoyance, a hindrance to her daughter, an obstacle in her path.

Lulu has a vision of her baby Desert Ray turning head over heels on a trajectory through cold, starry skies. Larry calls from the other room, "Are you okay in there?" She plunges underwater to still involuntary moans, and curtail a descent into darkness that she cannot afford. Only her rich friends can indulge themselves in despair. Lulu has to be up. It is her obligation. Larry didn't bring her all the way to Vienna on a first-class flight so she could be depressed over something he doesn't even know about. Her body floats like a corpse in the River Ganges, waiting to be reborn.

"Lulu?"

She surfaces, gathering bubbles to her breasts. "Larry," she sings. "Larry, come in this instant!"

EDITH SEAGRACE, SQUEEZED INTO A SMALL ROOM WITH three other applicants, is considering their feet, or shoes, to be exact, which seem to have been issued from a single source, a dispensary for bulky black oxfords. Edith has seen such footwear at Grimsby College (on a few disaffected art majors who threaten to transfer), but neither she nor Clarence, her roommate, guessed that they would be appropriate, even mandatory, for the interview, and that the brown loafers she and Clarence decided would look "young but not jejune, serious but not stuffy, practical with a touch of class" were screaming out the shameful truth that two days ago she stepped off the bus from Compton Falls never having been to New York before except on class trips, and that she had to ask directions twice just to get to the *Ubu* offices on Union Square—in short, that the feet in these loafers have led her to the wrong place, where she can never hope to fit in, and from which she will be ejected as soon as Geraldine McGarry, who arranged the interview and has seemingly forgotten about it, sees her and realizes the mistake.

While Edith has been pondering shoes, the other applicants have been getting acquainted, no doubt becoming friends for life as they have so much in common, beginning with their choice of footwear. Of the two females, the one in the long flowered dress who doesn't shave her legs but is wearing her mother's real pearls is Peyton Peaslee. The other is Kylie Lemon. It took Edith a while to figure out what was wrong with Kylie's face: She hasn't any eyebrows. It makes her look as if she's walked through a fire. Peyton and Kylie took Edith in at a glance and decided that she was invisible. The male, Ben Griffin, made eye contact and said a word of greeting, but Edith was too cowed to respond with anything more than a mumble. Now he's chatting with Peyton and Kylie, who have so many mutual friends that Kylie says it's "really weird" they've never met before. They are all waiting for someone called Henry, and there's a subtle competition over how well they know him. Kylie rashly reveals that her dad called Henry and set up the interview for her; Peyton coolly lets slip that Henry called her and suggested she come in for a talk. Ben starts drumming on the arm of the wooden bench with some pencils he found on the table. He flips one in the air and catches it again. Kylie nearly exchanges a glance and smile with Edith over this, but looks away in time.

Edith supposes that Henry is listed on the masthead. It's done alphabetically at *Ubu,* without title or rank. In principle it's democratic. In reality it prevents outsiders from knowing who does what at the magazine, prevents them from addressing manuscripts or résumés to the right person.

Edith planned her summer around working at *Ubu,* assumed that she simply had to walk in and demonstrate that she didn't have two heads and the position would be hers—after all it is a nonpaying job, an internship they call it—but now she despairs.

Reality is running counter to expectation. Edith got it completely wrong, down to the way the reception area looks. She pictured a large carpeted anteroom furnished in sleek international style, polished and bright like *Ubu* prose. In this case reception area is a misnomer, implying as it does acceptance, possibly welcome. This is a waiting room, as impoverished as the one in her grandfather's clinic in Compton Falls. Her grandfather at least provides distractions for the anxious visitor: a bubbling aquarium, a rack of magazines. Here there isn't even a copy of *Ubu,* just a wooden bench and two chairs. The receptionist (again the wrong word; try *attendant* or *guard*), a man in a black silk shirt who sports a topknot of dreadlocks, sits behind a wooden barricade and what looks like a transparent bulletproof shield. In the short time Edith has been in the city she has noticed that taxi drivers, postal clerks, and sellers of subway tokens keep such shields between themselves and the public, but she is surprised to see one here.

"Henry!" Kylie squeals, jumping up so fast that she hits herself against the arm of the chair but appears not to notice. Edith wonders if Kylie is accident prone, and tries to imagine what sort of mishap would have caused the loss of eyebrows. Kylie propels herself toward a short, elegantly dressed man who has just emerged from behind the barricade. He's bald but with a face as unlined as a baby's. He administers kisses to Kylie's flushed cheeks, at the same time holding her slightly away from him. Peyton stoops to receive Henry's busses; Ben gets a manly handshake.

"Well, let's take you first, shall we, Peyton?" Henry guides her through the door by placing his hand on the small of her back. "How are you finding Princeton?" he asks before the door closes. Kylie bites at a cuticle. "Her father's really rich," she says to Ben. Ben resumes his drumming.

Edith, on the other end of the bench, might just as well be a pile of dust in the corner. She felt Henry's blue eyes skim past and rule her out—Henry, keeper of the gate, granter of favors. Should she introduce herself when he comes back? For all his air of being everyone's favorite uncle, despite his cherubic baby face, Edith feels he could be cruel to someone without connections or the right shoes or her mother's pearls slung casually over a thrift-shop dress, to someone who doesn't belong.

Edith selected Geraldine McGarry's name off the masthead because her grandfather said he thought it had been there a long time, years, and that McGarry must be important by now. And McGarry had written a cordial letter in return, sounding intrigued by Edith's tale of having first read *Ubu* in the waiting room of her grandfather's clinic. What if McGarry is a nobody on the staff, who sits in an airless room correcting spelling and putting in commas, someone at whom everyone laughs behind her back, which is why she was so gracious in her letter—much too nice, Edith realizes. McGarry's probably cowering behind a stack of manuscripts hoping Edith will go away.

McGarry as Edith pictured her was tall, slim, *urbane* (a word Edith loves), a woman in every way unlike Edith's mother, Carolyn, who was appalled when she discovered her eleven-year-old had graduated from reading *Highlights for Children* to *Ubu*.

But it was Edith's mother who'd originally drawn her attention to the magazine. Carolyn had been replacing periodicals in the rack. "Why do you subscribe to this one, Dad? No one reads it," she'd said. The other magazines were dog-eared and scattered around the room, while *Ubu* stood on the shelf—three months of issues—the pages as crisp as the day they'd arrived, as if they'd been sprayed with repellent. Because it had literary merit, Grandpop had said; he read it when he had time.

At first Edith only looked at the pictures: fashion shots of long-legged women striding through bombed-out urban land-scapes, or leaning on crates in vast unfurnished rooms with white curtains billowing at open windows. She began reading the fiction to find out what the pictures meant, but the fiction offered other mysteries. Finally she tackled the reviews and articles, reading every issue front to back, trusting that what was strange would become familiar, that the effort would be worthwhile, that *Ubu* would eventually give up the password into a parallel universe, one that she couldn't see but into whose force field she felt herself being drawn. Edith located this universe in New York City, a mythical place she cobbled together from the pages of *Ubu*. The few times she went to attend a play and shuffle through a museum in a carefully shepherded group of schoolchildren, she discounted what she saw as being not the real city, not its inner chambers, but a narrow path outsiders took around its fortified walls.

Now she's here, or at least at the portal, hammering to be let in. She and Clarence, her best friend at college, had decided that this was the summer he was not going to work for his father's construction company, Earl Hennessy and Sons, and she was not going to help her grandfather in the clinic. They were going—in the words of Clarence—to strike out for the great metropolis and seek their fortunes. They spent so many hours rehearsing how they would tell their families, how they would counter objections (because their families' strong and vociferous objections were a given), that they never got around to discussing logistics, such as where they would live, or what they would do for money.

Spring came even to Grimsby College (which Clarence maintains is still locked in the last ice age), and they hadn't yet announced their plans. Clarence decided to do it over the phone. Edith went back to Compton Falls. It would be best to tell

Grandpop and Carolyn simultaneously. Ever since Edith's father died when she was very young, she and Carolyn had lived with Grandpop. Even though it was understood that Carolyn was the decision maker as far as Edith was concerned, Edith knew Grandpop had an influence, and that he almost always took her side.

Dinner was hamburgers, peas, and mashed potatoes. Edith was already memorizing the menu so she could report back to Clarence, underscoring the utter conventionality of Carolyn's cooking, to explain why, of course, there was no way Carolyn was going to let her live in New York City. (Carolyn has a theory that communities with populations over ten thousand lose their moral glue and become sinkholes of depravity.) Edith could feel her plans, and her will to fight for them, sliding away. She had almost resigned herself to failure when she announced her intentions. Carolyn fulminated, as Edith had expected, but Grandpop didn't even murmur a syllable in Edith's defense. He was silent, seemingly lost in some other concern. Grandpop's indifference hurt Edith more than Carolyn's predictable outrage.

She returned to Grimsby in defeat, only to find that Clarence had triumphed. As he put it, he had ridden right over his parents' objections, dazzling them with his cogent arguments, trapping them in the coils of his impeccable logic. Coils of logic? Never mind. She and Clarence spent several days discussing Carolyn's overprotective attitude toward Edith, speculating that it might have sprung from the death of Carolyn's husband at such an early age, or even from the circumstance of having adopted Edith after so many miscarriages.

After a week or two Grandpop called to say that Carolyn had come around. Edith could spend the summer in the city, and by the way, Grandpop just happened to have an artist's loft in which they could live rent-free, in exchange for stretching canvasses and forwarding mail. An old classmate—no, the *son* of an old classmate from Harvard—had offered it.

Unlikely, improbable, unbelievable. Even Clarence knew that "Marcus Welby," as he called Grandpop, was not the type to have a connection to an artist in New York. Clarence and Edith spent several days convincing themselves that it was possible that Grandpop could have a friend Edith didn't know about, had never heard mentioned. And in due time Grandpop produced an address and keys.

Just before Edith left for the city, Grandpop handed her a check for four thousand dollars.

He'd insisted on driving her alone to where she could catch the bus to New York and, as she was getting out of the car, he presented what he called a "grant." It was a shocking amount. In Edith's family money was hard-earned and even small purchases were weighed and debated. For what? A grant for what? "For life studies," he said. "Look around and learn." And then he did something even more unexpected: He gave her the name of the woman who'd given birth to her. He scribbled it on a prescription pad, hurriedly, as if someone might see and report to Carolyn. "She used to live in New York. You might run into her," he said. The bus pulled up, so Edith didn't have a chance to question him further.

On the long ride to the city she fingered the paper in her pocket, but it wasn't until the last hour of the trip, when the sun had finally left the sky and she'd had to turn on her light to see, that Edith finally read the name: Lucille Arslanian. It seemed familiar, as if she'd heard it said one time in a conversation that had stopped just as she entered the room, or as if she'd read it somewhere, maybe on an envelope stuck inside a drawer. The name—like information about sex—had been withheld because Edith was a child. But now she was twenty-one, and the secret had been revealed.

Since no one had ever spoken directly to Edith about her mother, Edith had had to fill the vacuum with what she learned from rumors, from scraps of information that drifted her way. Edith was ever on the alert for these, but they were meager, sketchy, for although Compton Falls is a town where everyone talks about everyone else, and Edith, by virtue of the time she spends helping out in her grandfather's clinic, hears more than most, Lucille Arslanian is a name that wasn't likely to come up. She seemed to have appeared from out of nowhere. She stayed long enough only to give birth, and then vanished, perhaps into that same unknown place from which she'd come.

New York City. Now Edith knew. She could look up the name in the phone book; she could telephone, make a lunch date, or—safer, because you never know—she could go to the woman's address, find out what kind of a place it was, hang around outside, waiting to see her from a distance. Edith had no doubt that she would know instantly who this woman was. Instant recognition, although Edith had never seen a picture, never heard a description. Because Edith carries her genetic imprint. They would both have the same eyes, or hair, or the same smile or walk. Edith would recognize herself in this woman. It could be, should be, like coming home. Mother and daughter reunion. Or it could be devastating. This is why Edith has not looked for the name in the phone book. She has not even told Clarence.

The paper remains in Edith's blazer pocket. She touches it as she would a good luck charm, watching Henry usher Ben, the last applicant, out the door. Evidently Henry's given everyone an internship; the interviews were only formalities. Edith rises, determined to introduce herself to Henry, when the outer door opens and a woman enters as if no one is there at all, only obstacles she must go around. She's tall, slender, middle-aged. Her smooth dark hair is streaked with silver.

"Geraldine, how is he?"

"Hello, Henry. I'll tell you later." Henry steps aside, but Edith, feeling this might be her last chance, pushes forward. "Ms. McGarry? I'm Edith Seagrace. We had an appointment?"

Abruptly, Edith materializes. As if she has eaten a piece of the magic mushroom, she grows until she fills the room so that McGarry and Henry must step back to take her in. McGarry's gray eyes widen to decipher the information that Edith's appearance presents to her. "From Compton Falls," McGarry says, almost to herself. Edith curses her loafers, her schoolgirl blazer. But Geraldine McGarry is holding the door open for her, not the exit but the entrance, past the barricade. Edith puts her hand in her pocket and finds the paper. As she passes before Henry, she feels a flash of something like triumph or vindication.

SITTING AT MARTIN'S DESK, GERALDINE IS ON HER SECond cigarette after having had a glass of sherry. Colleagues passing on the way home for the evening have been puzzled to see her here, and smoking, of all things, which Martin strictly forbids in his office as he claims the smell never leaves, that on damp days he still catches whiffs of Nadja's Gauloises from twenty years ago. Does this mean Martin isn't coming back? Is he more incapacitated than they've been led to believe? No one stops to ask; Geraldine commands respect but not affection, as Martin has always delegated the unpleasant tasks to her. For instance, it was Geraldine who had to do the firing when cutbacks were necessary two years ago. She did a brilliant job of culling and saved the life of the magazine, but it cast her even further into the role of villain, Evil Prime Minister to Good King Martin.

Although this has been Martin's office for nearly twenty years, tonight when Geraldine walked in to get something—she's forgotten what—it seemed the way it was when Geraldine first came to work at the magazine, when Nadja presided. Nadja had come from Paris, fleeing war and Fascism, making a last stand for artistic freedom in New York City. The emigré atmosphere still lingered a quarter of a century later. Courtly European artists and writers would wander the halls, settling in sometimes for months to write long pieces that few had the patience or background to read anymore. The Europeans seemed ancient to Geraldine, although they were probably contemporaries of Nadja, who was sixty, like Martin is now, a mere dozen years older than Geraldine. Not so old. Back then Nadja probably considered herself in her prime.

Geraldine stubs out her cigarette and is getting up to refill her glass when Henry comes in. They're both embarrassed to be found in Martin's office, like siblings catching each other in the parental bedroom. Henry says he's looking for something Martin wants him to bring over this evening.

"Oh, you're going to see him—"

"He asked—"

Until now Geraldine has been the only one permitted to see Martin. She suspects that Henry bullied Martin into letting him come; she also doubts that Martin has asked to see anything pertaining to the magazine, but Geraldine says nothing about this. Not wishing to seem the kind of middle-aged woman who prefers to drink alone, she offers sherry. To her annoyance, he accepts.

Now that they are seated in a simulation of comradery opposite each other on Martin's shabby mismatched sofas, Geraldine sees too late that she has played into Henry's hands. He wants information on what possessed her to hire an intern. The internships are Henry's private fief. He awards them to sons and daughters of influential people, thereby insinuating himself into their families. Geraldine says it's time the magazine opened up a bit, drew in some new blood. Why shouldn't a kid from an obscure background be given a chance—Henry interrupts. Geraldine needn't apologize; he doesn't blame her for falling for a pretty girl.

Geraldine lights another cigarette and settles behind a cloud of smoke. Last year she became involved with a well-known lesbian writer, Ryo Yamanaka. It lasted only six weeks but it was a highly visible affair, as is everything involving Ryo. When it was over and Geraldine came to her senses, she was wildly embarrassed although it didn't matter professionally, and Ryo is notorious for seducing straight women. Henry, an avowed homosexual, enjoys tweaking Geraldine on this. Let him think she hired the girl because of sexual attraction. If only the explanation were that simple.

"So how's Martin, really?" Henry sips at his sherry.

"You'll see for yourself, Henry. I'll be interested to hear how you find him."

"Just tell me, is he awful-looking? His mouth isn't twisted, is it? I couldn't stand to see that."

"He had a heart attack, not a stroke. And it was a mild one. He's the same only—diminished." Geraldine stops herself. She doesn't want to discuss Martin behind his back, especially not with Henry. "Maybe he'll be different with you than he was with me. It's a good sign he's asked to see you."

"I kind of forced myself on him, actually. I got Florence to ask me to dinner—" Too late he puts the glass to his mouth to hide an involuntary smirk. He knows Geraldine will be jealous and hurt that she, a much closer and older friend than Henry, gets summoned to the house in the morning like a secretary or errand boy, while he wrangles an invitation to dinner. Geraldine's pride would never permit her to manipulate friends in that way. Pride and decency, virtues that were drummed into Geraldine while she was growing up, are useless in the life she leads now. Worse. They're impediments.

She permits herself the satisfaction of staring at Henry's fat buttocks as he leaves. Henry has his suits altered to cover this defect, but no matter how smoothly and artfully the fabric falls (the jacket never comes off even on the hottest days) everyone notices and it torments him that this is so.

She pours another sherry and lights a last smoke. It's time to reflect on what she's done. Why did she even answer the girl's letter when a brief rejection would have sufficed: "We regret that all internships for the summer have been filled. Thank you for your interest." She answered because the coincidences struck her immediately and viscerally: the age of the letter writer, the name of the town, the fact that her grandfather was a doctor—how many doctors could a town of that size have? It amazed Geraldine that the details of an event she shrugged off as an annoyance at the time could have become incised in her memory. In twenty years she'd never called to mind these bits of information, and yet there they were, preserved like flies in amber. The whole drama of it must have had more significance for her than she realized.

Could this be Lucille's child? she asked herself. Suspicion took over: Had Lucille put the child up to writing the letter? Geraldine decided to take the risk and answer; she had to know.

Then came Martin's heart attack and she forgot everything. Suddenly today the child appears with a face wrested out of time—Lucille at twenty—yet altered by Martin's eyes, not as they are today, protected and diminished by glasses, but as Geraldine had almost forgotten they were: bright, opening wide to include everything at once. Unusual color, greenish-blue with spots of gold.

Geraldine watched through the interview as the girl's face went from Lucille to Martin back to Lucille. The high forehead was Lucille's; the eyes of course were Martin's, but they had an almond shape like Lucille's—a hint of the exotic there; wasn't Lucille part Armenian? The nose was long and thin with some of Martin's patrician arch but the lips were full like Lucille's. (Martin's mouth is thin, making him look a little pinched.) Edith's hair is curly and thick like her mother's but light, a sort of gold color that brings out the flecks in her eyes. (Geraldine has seen pictures of Martin's mother; her hair was blond.) And the girl moves like Lucille, from the pelvis out; Martin holds himself stiff and walks from the knees down.

The girl must have thought Geraldine's questions oddly personal, but Geraldine had to find out what the girl knew. Astonishingly little as it turns out. She must know she's adopted; they all do these days, but other than that nothing. She didn't know Martin's name, hadn't been to the city ever on her own. Her adoptive mother (father's deceased) must have kept her close to home, uninformed, unenlightened. Now the child has broken out of the protective shell. She has come as unerringly as a Monarch butterfly who, with the approach of autumn, flies to ancestral wintering grounds in the Yucatan, and with no more awareness than the butterfly of what compels her. It would have been easy to put her off course, and yet Geraldine threw open the gates and shooed her inside. Why? Residual Catholic guilt? After all, Geraldine did try to arrange the annihilation of this creature when it was in its pupal stage.

Lucille had been Nadja's protégée. Nadja, in the manner of European Surrealists, had a passion for the American naif. While Martin preferred bright young sophisticates from good Eastern schools (he'd hired both Florence—from Smith—and Geraldine —from Wellesley), Nadja brought in the wild cards. There was a ranch hand from Wyoming who contributed poetry, a primitive painter from the Ozarks who designed a series of covers. And one day there was Lucille the flower child. She claimed to have lived a summer on the streets of San Francisco and hitched across the country. Her clarity of skin, height of forehead, delicacy of wrists, gave an impression of good breeding, whatever that meant. Surely a street-dweller, a hitchhiker would have been rougher, coarser. Nadja didn't care if Lucille was genuine or not; she loved the presentation, the package. She began taking Lucille around to openings with her, dressing the girl in clothes Nadja would "borrow" from designers.

Naturally it caused resentment. Geraldine realizes how much only now, looking back. Florence was jealous because until then Florence had been Nadja's favorite. Florence had laughed at Nadja behind her back and claimed to be revolted by her attentions, but she couldn't help resenting the way Lucille preempted her place, and while Florence had kept Nadja prudently at a distance, Lucille had no compunctions about taking anything Nadja offered, from clothes to—there were rumors—love. What galled Geraldine was how Lucille nabbed all the plum assignments and how like a happy child she would dash them off, leaving Geraldine to fix up grammar and check accuracy. Often Lucille's pieces would be silly but they had a certain panache, a quirkiness; they fit into the magazine yet preserved an individual style. They caused comment. Martin also resented Lucille. He pretended to enjoy her spirit and humor, but he couldn't forgive her for being Nadja's discovery, not his.

Geraldine still doesn't know if Lucille suspected the envy she inspired. At times it seemed she knew and was laughing at all of them. At other times Geraldine was equally certain that Lucille suspected nothing, that she considered it natural for Nadja to shower her with favors and for everyone else to be thrilled for her. Lucille believed people gave out of their own inner goodness, which was convenient because then she didn't have to worry about giving back.

When Lucille came to Geraldine and Florence, shut the door to the office they shared, and told them that she was pregnant, Geraldine wasn't sure if Lucille was confiding because she trusted them or because she wanted to get them to do something for her. At first Geraldine had to force back a smile because she knew Nadja would never forgive Lucille. Geraldine inquired about the father, thinking it would be one of the oddball artists or musicians Lucille hung out with. Instead Lucille named Martin. Geraldine assumed Lucille was lying to deflect Nadja's anger onto Martin.

Geraldine found a reputable New York gynecologist who would perform the abortion. Florence helped with money. They were both going to escort Lucille after work. But when the day arrived Lucille wasn't in the office. The letter came about a week afterward. She'd gone to a commune in upstate New York, where she would have her baby . . . beautiful people who'd taken her in; she hoped Geraldine wasn't angry. All these years Geraldine has remembered the postmark: Compton Falls.

Geraldine and Florence discussed driving up there and talking Lucille into going through with the abortion. At least they should warn Martin. But in the end they did nothing. Things went back to the way they'd been except that Martin and Florence began seeing each other and within six months announced their engagement.

After the marriage there was a financial crisis at the magazine. Nadja was forced to retire and Martin took over. Florence resigned, which left Geraldine as Martin's main confidante at the magazine, his second in command in the subtle way that things arrange themselves at *Ubu,* for the magazine shuns titles and hierarchy. All is fluid, democratic.

It was around that time that Geraldine saw Lucille again, on the street, by chance. Lucille threw her arms around her, said she'd been thinking of her, what a coincidence. It seems she was going to have a show with some of her fellow students at Parsons —she was in art school now—and maybe Geraldine would like to come. It would mean so much to get a mention in *Ubu*. Geraldine asked what had become of the baby. Lucille said she was living upstate, being cared for by the daughter of a doctor who'd been kind to Lucille. Geraldine did not attend the show. Some time later when one of the younger writers came to Geraldine, wanting to do a piece on an artist called simply Lulu, Geraldine recognized Lucille in the photo and killed the idea. She never told Martin any of this.

Geraldine tries not to let her personal feelings enter into decisions she makes for the magazine. But in Lucille's case, she felt she had to insulate Martin, protect him from her. It wasn't that Lucille was evil—at least Geraldine didn't think she was. But Lucille had a way of insinuating herself into another person's life.

She was wormy, like Henry. You never could tell what she was after until she had it. Geraldine is just the opposite, blunt, straightforward. Lucille's charms always left Geraldine cold. In fact, they aroused her antipathy.

She'd expected to feel the same about Lucille's daughter. She'd set up the interview cynically, expecting to observe this phenomenon and send it on its way. But something happened. The girl has a freshness, an openness that is very pleasing. Her candor reminded Geraldine of herself. There seemed to be a link between them, as if they'd both been raised in that absurdly old-fashioned way in which you are taught always to tell the truth, keep your socks straight, brush your teeth, and give a day's work for a day's pay. Perhaps Martin's good, honest genes neutralized Lucille's artful ones, or more likely the doctor's daughter who raised Edith had kept an eye out for Lucille-like tendencies and nipped them in the bud.

Geraldine found herself offering the girl an internship. She was powerless to do otherwise, because the girl trusted her to be fair. Edith in all innocence had chosen Geraldine as her protector, and Geraldine found she couldn't refuse.

The cleaning people are coming in. Geraldine doesn't like seeing them face-to-face—the people who empty her wastebasket, who wipe hairs and flakes of skin off the surface of her desk, who wash out the glasses and replace them in the cabinet. They know all about her and she knows nothing of them. She would never have a person clean her apartment, but here it's out of her control. As she packs to leave she feels the effect of the sherry. She forgot to eat today, except for a miserable fat-free bran muffin at Martin's. She'll go home, sleep off the alcohol, and do her work later.

. . .

"You told me Ninety-fifth between Third and Lex." The taxi driver, a dark head behind the murky protective shield, sounds both defensive and wary. Geraldine wonders how often he's had a passenger become irrational, even hysterical. She sees immediately what happened: She gave Martin's address by mistake, which explains why they are speeding up Third Avenue leaving her own street far behind. Too late to turn back. She'll drop these things off at Martin's tonight and save time tomorrow.

It's only when Florence comes to the door, wearing a silk knit tunic over tights, high-heeled sandals, lipstick, makeup—hardly what one wears at home while tending a sick husband—does Geraldine remember Henry. Florence—shushing the dog, a big slobbering thing that barks every time Geraldine comes—says don't be silly, of course Geraldine's not interrupting. They've just finished dinner. Why doesn't Geraldine go up and join them. Florence is making decaf.

"Don't tell them I'm here." Geraldine puts a hand on Florence's arm. "I really came to drop things off and have a chat with you."

"How nice." Florence takes her into the kitchen, where the remains of dinner are still out, and fixes her a plate without asking. She pours them each a glass of Chardonnay and sits at the table opposite Geraldine. It is officially understood that Florence and Geraldine are best friends, but actually they never see each other outside Martin's presence. They tried getting together for lunch a few times after Florence left the magazine, but their interests soon diverged so widely—Florence went back to school to become a psychologist—that they found themselves searching for topics of conversation. And, then, somehow Geraldine couldn't forgive Florence for conducting extramarital affairs right under Martin's nose. Martin didn't seem to mind, but Geraldine did. In those years—Florence's heyday—when there always seemed to be some writer enthralled to Florence, Geraldine could almost not bear to look at the woman. It was an effort to be with her in a large gathering; one-on-one would have been impossible.

What a relief that those years are behind them now, and Geraldine can look on Florence as a friend once more. It turns out they have quite a few topics on which they can converse: theater, books, films, politics. Geraldine, warmed by the wine, looks fondly on her old friend across the table and regrets, fleetingly, that they ever let Martin disrupt their sisterly twosome.

From upstairs comes the combined and familiar laughter of Henry and Martin.

"Isn't it wonderful? It's the first time he's laughed since—" Florence stops.

"He *should* be seeing other people. It's strange, the way he's been keeping to himself. It makes for uncertainty at the magazine," Geraldine says, very generously she thinks. After all, Florence can't be blamed for letting herself get bamboozled by Henry.

While Florence takes coffee upstairs, Geraldine goes to the garden for a smoke. This block of low town houses backs onto another similar one, enclosing a long strip of contiguous gardens. Open windows release sounds of silver against china, the chink of goblets coming together in toasts, laughter and conversation. Some dining is going on outdoors, heard but not seen behind fences and hedges. Florence has lived in this house all of her life. She inherited it from her parents. Geraldine is still in the first apartment she found when she came to the city. Then she was thrilled to get it: a fourth-floor walk-up with separate bedroom and kitchen, two windows. Unfortunately the increase in her salary came after real estate prices went skyrocketing, and Geraldine can't bring herself to pay the exorbitant price that even a slightly bigger and nicer place would cost. Geraldine will probably die in that apartment unless she goes to a nursing home first because she can no longer climb the stairs. The moon is up, just appearing over the high-rises on Third Avenue, shining on white flowers Florence has planted in big terracotta pots. Geraldine rarely sees the moon in the city. It's as if it has come only here, for the private delectation of the happy souls who dine and drink and laugh. . . .

Florence thinks Geraldine may be weeping; she isn't sure and she knows Geraldine would not want her to see, so she says, "Oh, there you are!" and goes back to the kitchen for the wine and glasses, giving Geraldine time to recover just in case. As a therapist, Florence encounters tears daily, but they unsettle her outside the sanctioned confines of the office. She has never seen Geraldine do this before. What if it's over some lesbian affair? Florence is very liberal about homosexuality—as a therapist she has to be—but when Geraldine fell in love with Ryo Yamanaka, it made Florence queasy. She and Geraldine had been so close when they'd worked together at *Ubu,* out to cultural events in the evenings, or just sitting up half the night, talking over a bottle of wine. What if Geraldine had been a lesbian all along, secretly desiring Florence as a sexual partner?

There's a slight tremor in Geraldine's hand when she takes the glass, but her voice, after a curative drag on her cigarette, is calm. Geraldine is speaking about someone they knew years ago. Florence interrupts: "I haven't thought of her in ages. There was something—some business with Martin, wasn't there? Oh,

24

yes—she claimed he'd gotten her pregnant. And you and I went scurrying around to get her an abortion. And we never told Martin because we knew it would upset him." Florence laughs. The idea of Martin getting anyone with child strikes her as funny. Although Martin did make Florence pregnant once by accident not long after they married. He talked her into getting an abortion because Florence was thinking of going back to school, and Martin didn't want to be any more dependent on her parents than they already were. Florence never managed to conceive after that. Years later, Martin confessed that he had never really wanted children. When Florence told him that he should have informed her of that before they married, he looked surprised and said it had never occurred to him. He'd vaguely hoped that they wouldn't have children, but he'd also expected that they would.

"As it turns out Lucille was telling the truth. I saw their daughter—Martin and Lucille's—today in the office." Geraldine's voice slices into Florence's thoughts. But it can't be true. Florence tries to imagine Martin's face merged with Lucille's and finds she can't remember what Lucille looked like. Florence doubts if she'd know Lucille if she walked onto the terrace this minute.

"Come down to the office and take a look," Geraldine says.

"You hired her?"

There's a lull, as if the people in their dining rooms and on their terraces have suspended conversation to hear Geraldine out. She fumbles for her Marlboros, thankful for the dark, that Florence can't see her neck and cheeks getting splotchy. It strikes Geraldine more forcibly than before that she has done a very odd thing. She wonders if she's going through another mental crisis, like the one she had after Ryo broke up with her. Only this time there doesn't seem to be any external cause. The weeping before, whatever was that about? Maybe she's going through the change of life and this is the first sign. Florence is encouraging Geraldine to consider the possibility that she made a mistake: She couldn't clearly remember what Lucille looked like; for some reason she convinced herself she saw Lucille's face on the girl.

"This thing with Martin is a strain on all of us," Florence says. "I find myself going over things that happened years ago. Odd memories pop up—it must be having the same effect on you."

That must be it, they both decide, gratefully, gracefully.

When Florence shows Geraldine out, they hear Henry still talking upstairs, no doubt exhausting Martin. "Tell him to go home," Geraldine whispers to Florence, and they kiss each other on the cheek.

Geraldine stands under the outside light, listening to Florence bolt the doors from within. Why did she capitulate so easily to Florence? Why didn't she insist that the girl has Martin's eyes, that the evidence demands recognition? Because then Geraldine would have had to explain why she let the girl into the magazine, into their lives, and the answer to that is something Geraldine could not begin to explain to Florence. How could she say that the girl seemed to understand that Geraldine was a person of honor, that she would do what was right? Florence, for all her charm, abilities, her talents, does not subscribe to this same code. For Florence, morality is an elastic concept: Whatever is good for Florence seems the honorable thing. She's not predaceous like Lucille, but then she's never been as hungry as Lucille. It will be interesting to see how Florence, who has everything, reacts to Edith, who has nothing—only her rightful claim to Martin.

A man walking on the sidewalk glances down at Geraldine

standing by the door and quickly looks away. She closes the gate with a firm click.

It's not for Geraldine to argue the girl's case, she thinks, heading up the street in search of a taxi. The fact is the child has come and all of them—Geraldine, Florence, Martin—are going to have to acknowledge her existence.

THE HEAT

FOR CLARENCE'S BIRTHDAY EDITH IS TREATING HIM TO lunch at the Caffé San Marco on West Broadway. She pictured them outside—Clarence thinks it's the height of sophistication to have a glass of wine at a table on the sidewalk—but that was before the heat set in. While waiting for Clarence, Edith does try sitting out for a moment to see how bad it would be. Even in the shade of an umbrella she can feel heat radiating up from the pavement and off the side of the building. The air buckles, making storefronts across the street appear to be melting. She watches a figure shamble by disguised in a fuzzy dog costume, white with black spots, a Dalmatian evidently—something Clarence will be sorry he missed. A man and woman stop in front of the restaurant. He has his suit jacket over his shoulder, his tie loosened.

The woman is in a long light skirt and top, with espadrilles and bare legs, like someone at a resort who flings clothing over a bikini to go to lunch. A straw bag, the kind that could hold a book and towel for the beach. Long hair in a bushy ponytail sticking out from under a baseball cap. Fortyish, with the look of someone who's managed to avoid the rules. She senses Edith studying her and regards her full in the face. Edith changes her focus, pretending to be intrigued by something far in the distance.

"You've got to be kidding. It's a furnace out here," the man tells the woman and they go inside. Edith follows, taking the table next to theirs in the dark interior cool as a cave. She hopes Clarence won't be too late because she has to get back to work.

She's enjoying the internship. Of course, it's fairly mindless —replacing paper in the fax machine, retyping manuscripts, filling in at the receptionist desk—but she likes the atmosphere, the energy created by intelligent people working toward a common goal, the sense of elitism (usually a pejorative term but different somehow when one has been magically admitted to the group).

"I feel more at home here than I've ever felt anywhere," Edith said. It came out spontaneously one evening after work as she sat chatting with Geraldine in her office. Geraldine has gone out of her way to make Edith comfortable by introducing her around and letting her in on the workings of the magazine, its history and culture. Edith meant the remark as a compliment to Geraldine, but instead of pleasing it seemed to disturb. Geraldine lit a cigarette and drew herself back into the smoke. Does Edith sometimes feel out of place? she asked.

How did she know? It's spooky, how much Geraldine seems to sense about Edith. Edith was so amazed and excited to have

someone who understood her, that she told Geraldine everything
—how out of place she feels at Grimsby College, working hard
in the premed department, but with no idea of why she's there.
She can't remember making the decision to be a doctor. It's as if
she's being carried along on an invisible track. "Sometimes I see
Edith Seagrace printed on a class list, or something, and it looks
like someone else's name. I never told anyone this except for my
roommate, Clarence—I mean—it's crazy, isn't it? But you understand. You understand so much about me. That thing about
past lives—I don't believe it or anything, but it's strange, isn't it?
It's almost as if you were my mother in a past life."

Edith's words exactly. She must have come across as some
flaky New Age loser. Geraldine stood and looked out the window, although there was nothing to look at. Was she laughing at
Edith, or had Edith hurt her feelings—maybe even insulted her?
Edith blabs everything to Geraldine, but Geraldine is careful
about what she tells Edith. All Edith knows—that Geraldine is a
lesbian who lives alone—she's learned from office gossip.

"You have to get the puttanesca. The way they do it here is
fantastic." Edith has been eavesdropping on the next table, although eavesdropping is hardly the term because the woman, at
least, clearly doesn't mind being overheard. "I'm going for the
lobster ravioli, but you must have the puttanesca if you've never
had it before, and the focaccia. They make their own and it's the
best."

Edith believes that if you're going to speak loudly enough for
everyone to overhear, you have an obligation to be interesting.
The woman seems to subscribe to this theory. Now she is
describing in detail a man she's become involved with. "When he
sees me on the street he stretches his arms out wide and folds me

in like egg whites into whipped cream." Her companion mumbles something about marriage. "He's asked me in a half-assed way." They laugh.

Enter Clarence, with that new scurrying walk he's picked up since he came to the city. "Have you been waiting long? Oh God, I hope not. I met someone on the street from Upper Darby, can you believe? From my class in fucking high school. Oh my God. He's like: 'Uh, Clarence?'—well, you see the way I look. . . ." Pink denim short shorts, yellow undershirt. Cowboy boots. Earring. Clarence has stolen the show. Now the couple at the next table are looking at Clarence and Edith. "The weirdness of it all is I just started in talking like I was back on the football team, just one of the guys, and in the meantime I'm standing there dressed like a flaming faggot."

"Maybe you should tone it down, Clare. It's kind of over-the-top, you know what I mean?"

"That's why I'm here, so I can be queer," Clarence says, sitting opposite her.

"I didn't mind waiting." Edith leans forward, lowering her voice. "This woman at the next table—"

"I know her. She lives in our building."

"She does?"

"I think so. Anyway, she came in like yesterday, I think? I was just going to work and a limo pulled up—"

"A limousine?"

"It was probably rented. They do that here. She looked like she was coming back from a trip somewhere. She had suitcases. I was going to help her, but she just hefted them—she's stronger than she looks." Clarence ponders the menu. "What are you having?"

"Well, she says the puttanesca is the greatest, and the focaccia, although she's having lobster ravioli. And you have to order a glass of wine, because it's your birthday and you're my best friend, and if it weren't for you, we wouldn't be sitting here, all cool and sophisticated in TriBeCa."

At the next table the food arrives. "I can't stand it. I have to have some of yours right away, it's so good." She reaches across and helps herself to a forkful of her companion's pasta. "Mmmm! Oh, my God, you're going to love it. It's like having an orgasm!"

"I'll have the puttanesca," Edith tells the waiter, which makes Clarence choke on his water and send it spraying across the table.

"I can't believe you ordered that with a straight face," he whispers. "Little Edie Seagrace, goes to the big city and first thing you know, she's ordering orgasm for lunch."

Edith kicks him under the table, although she asked for puttanesca just to amuse him. She regrets it when it comes—dark, thick, oily, composed of unrecognizable ingredients with a musky aftertaste of something she doesn't like. At least Clarence is happy with his primavera, the white wine. Even the linen napkin pleases him.

The man at the next table leaves for the men's room. The waiter comes to clear but the woman stops him, takes her companion's plate, and finishes what's on it. She eats hurriedly, all the while watching the men's room door. She licks her own fork, then his.

"Maybe she's on a diet and can't control herself when she gets around food," Edith says.

"She'll be sucking the spots off the tablecloth next."

The woman insists that her companion order the tiramisù. He has just a bite, and she finishes the whole thing. He picks up the check. "I should get this. I invited you," she says, but makes no further effort. He says something about how it's his pleasure. As they leave the woman turns and meets Edith's stare.

"That was kind of awkward. She must have known we were watching her. But if you put on a show, you have to expect it. I guess I should have said something when I came in, or at least nodded. We're going to be running into each other all summer," Clarence says.

"Oh, you think she recognized you."

"Sure. What did you think?"

"I don't know. It was strange, that's all."

"Next time I'll introduce myself."

"Oh don't do that," Edith says quickly.

"Why not?"

"I don't know. She just seems like a leech. Like you might not be able to get rid of her."

"I thought she was neat. Kind of used up but still in there swinging. Anyway, if she lives in our building, we're not going to be able to avoid her."

"I'm going to try."

MARTIN WAS A SICKLY CHILD. NO ONE KNOWS THAT about him; even he had forgotten how he used to lie days and weeks in bed with terrible colds. Once, he had pneumonia and missed almost a month of school. When he was finally well he refused to go back, afraid the others would have learned so much that he would be left hopelessly behind. His mother tutored him at home and of course he came out at the head of the class. He was an only child; his mother may have let him stay home more than he should have; he was company for her. Now as he lies in bed, he remembers those days of sleeping and waking, hearing his mother running the Hoover, the boy delivering groceries, the telephone ringing from the table in the downstairs hall, life going on at a distance from the sickroom which was an island set apart.

Set apart and dedicated to the healing of the patient. No one understands this, especially not Florence. He had to fight to get the phone taken out of his room and now she wants to put it back, "just for Bruno," who's been calling daily, when Bruno is the last person Martin should be speaking with.

Bruno pays the bills. He's the son of Magnus Monk, who rescued the magazine from bankruptcy years ago. But Bruno doesn't understand, as Magnus did, that the magazine wasn't built to make a profit. It was underwritten from the beginning by wealthy patrons, friends of Nadja, who set up a trust fund.

In '73 the blue-chip stocks that the trustees in their conservative wisdom had bought began to weaken, while at the same time the magazine, having failed to catch the wave of the seventies, was losing relevance and subscribers. With the encouragement of the trustees Martin began looking for possible investors and came up with Magnus Monk, who'd built a huge publishing/entertainment complex in Germany and was ready to invest in the States. Magnus wanted the magazine for the prestige and contacts it would bring to his company; the magazine could lose money until Doomsday for all he cared.

Nadja was still in charge then, and, although she had no other investors in mind, she was adamant against letting Monk buy controlling interest. She claimed Magnus's father did business with the Nazis during the war, said she had established the magazine as a haven from Fascism and that Magnus would subvert the mission of *Ubu,* the mission of surrealism. This put the trustees in a quandary. The choice came down to letting the magazine go under with Nadja at the helm or persuading her to retire so Martin could take over and sell to Monk. Nadja did not go gracefully. She was still involved in a lawsuit with the magazine when she died of a fast-growing tumor. She never forgave Martin.

With Nadja gone Martin was able to weed out a lot of deadwood, writers past their prime who expounded on topics no one was interested in anymore. Martin brought in the kids, let them write about what was happening. As far as surrealism, Nadja had been right: About all that was left from that movement was the name of the magazine, *Ubu.* But surrealism had never really caught on in the States anyway. The culture's too practical, too materialistic, as Nadja would say. Martin went after advertisers aggressively, something Nadja had never done, and actually brought the magazine to where it was no longer a literary magazine, but a mass-market publication, right up there with *Harper's* and *The Atlantic Monthly.* He beefed up the fashion section, made it less arty, more consumer-oriented, figuring that fashion could run payback articles while the rest of the book remained pure. It was an innovative idea, one that enabled the magazine to actually make money. Magnus was delighted but he never forgot that he hadn't bought *Ubu* for that purpose.

Now Magnus is growing roses in Swabia, and son Bruno, with his Harvard MBA and his spreadsheet mentality, is running the show. He wants to discuss how advertising pages are down, how the balance is slipping into the red. When Martin was at his desk in his office, he was able to jolly the younger man along and remind him that Magnus hadn't bought the magazine as a cash cow, that other publications were suffering as well, that it was an industry-wide recession. But it's hard to get the right tone in your voice when you are supine in bed.

The dog is barking, the doorbell ringing. It's Henry coming

for a "working lunch," his idea. Martin moves with caution to a sitting position and picks up the manuscript he put aside hours ago.

Henry brings the contamination of the city in with him. Heat emanates from his chunky body along with the smell of the streets, everything Martin has been trying to shield his heart against. Henry pulls a chair up to the bed, and Martin retreats into his pillows.

Until recently Martin enjoyed Henry's energy and intensity. Geraldine never liked Henry, never would, but Martin always defended him. Henry wrote the first big story on AIDS before *Time,* before *Newsweek.* His story on transvestites won an award (probably belated recognition of the prescience of the piece on AIDS). "He's hungry. He's not afraid of getting dirty," Martin once told Geraldine. "He's greedy and he'll drag us down into the dirt with him," Geraldine countered.

Is it Martin's illness that makes Henry seem pushy, or has Henry turned it up a notch? Martin thinks Henry was this way before the heart attack—leaning on Martin, invading his turf, which could have contributed to the deterioration. Outside influences permeate the core, the vital organs, something Martin never appreciated before.

Henry wants to discuss how to get more advertising pages. He thinks the magazine should start a new campaign geared to advertisers and hire a new agency to come up with a fresh approach. "The reality is the last campaign was stodgy and arrogant. We need to convince advertisers that we are relevant today."

"Henry, don't you have enough to do with what goes into the magazine? Why are you getting mixed up with that crew down in advertising?" Editorial and advertising are kept strictly

separate at the magazine, church and state. Only Martin is supposed to be able to talk to both. Except for the fashion department, there's none of that overlap that other glossies are guilty of,
where a good portion of the stories are paybacks to advertisers.

"I'm only trying to save the magazine, Martin."

Save the magazine. Didn't Martin once say something like
that to Nadja? His heart kicks sluggishly in his chest. Martin
takes Lopressor, a beta-blocker, to keep the heart from overdoing
it—no more than a hundred beats a minute, which still seems
like a lot—but sometimes he thinks that it skips a beat or two.
Someone should be monitoring it. There should be a device that
records Martin's heartbeats back at the hospital where it can be
watched by a trained technician. Certainly such a device exists.
There must be all kinds of technology that Martin isn't aware of.
Health has never been one of Martin's interests. He always left
the medical stories to Henry.

FLORENCE IS IN THE KITCHEN, PUTTING TOGETHER SOME
plates for lunch. She hopes Henry won't mind the nonfat cottage
cheese and water-packed tuna. Martin has become a fanatic about
cholesterol. She frowns to hear their voices; Martin's sounds
querulous and negative pitted against the freshness, the insistence
of Henry's. "He can't keep up anymore," Florence says. She's
begun talking to herself; a few times it happened on the street,
remarks that catch her by surprise. She doesn't know what to
make of it.

"Henry, you're in for a treat. High-fiber, cholesterol-free
lunch. I hope you're fond of bean sprouts." Florence comes in,
carrying a tray.

"I can't get enough of them," Henry says. He helps set up
the table by Martin's bed. Are those age spots on the back of

Florence's hands? She looks worn, worse than Martin in a way. Well, she is getting older, isn't she? Florence dazzled Henry when he met her for the first time at a dinner party here. The guests were a mixture of young and old, celebrated and obscure —an important male expatriate writer sitting next to an emerging female performance artist, that kind of thing. Florence made certain that everyone had a chance to show off and find connecting threads. At the end of the evening, Henry felt part of an enchanted web, and Florence was the benevolent spider who had spun them all into her magic.

"You're not eating with us, Florence?" Henry asks.

"I'm trysting in the kitchen with a contraband provolone. Ring if you want anything." She indicates a little brass bell in the shape of a girl in a hoop skirt, her long hair flowing to her waist.

"Charming." Henry picks it up.

"It was Mother's," Florence says. "She actually used it at the table when we had help. I found it again when Martin decided to become an invalid."

Henry turns the bell around and sees the face of a wrinkled hag. He looks to Florence for an explanation but she's left. Henry sets the bell down with the face turned away. Martin, who had slumped back in his pillows, straightens himself to get his food. His hair has flattened in the back and is sticking up on top. *Bed head,* Henry thinks against his will. He wants to be sympathetic, but the truth is he's offended by the enthusiasm Martin is displaying for his cottage cheese and tuna while Henry's talk only made him bored, or worse, annoyed, as if Henry were a fly that had gotten into his room, a fat insistent buzzing insect. Henry expected Martin to rise above his illness, not succumb to the narrow egotism of the invalid who has no interest beyond his own bodily functions.

Last night Henry had dinner at the Palm with Bruno, and a nightcap at the bar of the Plaza Athenée, where Bruno is staying. Talk came easily, talk about making the magazine more current, taking it into the millennium. This morning Henry went into work elated; he was eager to share it all with Martin. It's only now in this shut-up room with the air conditioner droning that Henry realizes what a difficult and delicate conversation this might be.

"A night on the town with Bruno. Must have been fascinating. Did he talk about Maximizing Earning Potential?" Martin has captured Bruno's slight accent, and Bruno *is* overly fond of MBA-ese.

"You know, I don't think we've been giving the guy enough credit, Martin. He does come up with some interesting ideas."

"I don't want his ideas. We have ideas. I want his money. Magnus understood his purpose. He wouldn't have been so crass as to even have an idea."

"Yeah, well, Magnus had all that postwar guilt of his generation." Henry chases a cherry tomato around his plate. "Bruno's a pretty hip guy. He knows the scene in Berlin. There's a lot of energy—"

"Come on, Henry. He's a technocrat, a bottom-line type. Profit and loss."

"Since when did you become averse to making money—" Henry's voice hangs in the air. Martin's eyes are closed; his hand is on his chest. "Are you all right, Martin?" Martin's eyelids flutter. "I'll get Florence!"

Martin stops him at the door. "I thought it was a fibrillation, but it seems to be beating normally now."

Henry's own heart is pounding. If Martin had had another heart attack, if he had vomited, if his eyes had rolled back in his head, Henry would not have wanted to see it. He stays poised in the doorway, afraid that Martin might have another spell.

Martin takes off his glasses and lays them on the bedside table. Henry looks away so he won't have to see Martin's naked eyes, slightly bulging, green amphibian irises with yellow flecks, and whites with broken capillaries that give Henry the willies. But Martin's eyes are closed. He speaks to the ceiling in a flat sick voice. "It's very tiring always to be monitoring it, worrying if it's doing its job. No one really cares but me. Everyone wants things back to normal, but I have to concentrate on staying alive. My cardiologist doesn't really know. He talks in terms of percentages. Eighty-percent chance of full recovery, he says. It's easy for him. But what if it's the other twenty percent? What then, Henry? I need more facts. I need the latest research, the latest methods."

"I thought you were seeing one of the top guys—"

Martin waves a long, pale hand. "He's smart but he's busy, you know? I feel I don't qualify. I'm not glamorous or sexy enough. A mild myocardial infarction he calls it, as if it's beneath him. He likes massive coronaries, something interesting and complicated. They're like all of us. Doctors aren't different."

"What if I put one of the kids in research on the case? Get the latest stuff on heart disease—"

"That's a start, I guess. Talk it up with Stuart or Anita. They might do a story on it. I mean it's topical, relevant."

Relevant for the geriatric crowd, hardly a hot demographic, Henry thinks. As if Stuart's going to drop his story on TB, or Anita is going to get off infertility to do something about heart attacks. Martin's out of touch. All he can think about is his heart. It's as if he just discovered he had one.

As Henry is leaving, Florence catches up with him in the hall.

"You look dejected, Henry."

Henry takes out a handkerchief and blots his forehead. "It's hard, you know, seeing him like that. It must be worse for you." The dog, panting, leans heavily against Henry's leg. The smell of its breath rises in an unseen cloud. Florence has her hand on the door but seems reluctant to open it.

"The worst is that he doesn't have to stay in bed. He's supposed to be back at work. That's what Tom—his cardiologist—says, but Martin won't."

The dog lets some saliva drop onto Henry's trousers. He reaches for the door, but Florence's hand is still on the knob. Awkwardly he takes her hand, which she interprets as a signal for an embrace. She hugs him, clinging, as if he were a rock in a turbulent flood. But Henry isn't a rock. He manages to reach around her and open the door. The heat bursts in upon them. "I'll do what I can," he says.

AFTER A DAY IN WHICH THE SUN STOOD STILL OVER THE city, blasting into the narrowest alleys, lacerating macadam streets until they oozed with open blisters, it is finally giving up. Low-lying clouds of dubious composition ignite in its dying rays and glow in a chemical rainbow of hues: methyl violet, lithium-chloride red, chrome-oxide green. The river, pushed by the incoming tide, stirs and disgorges a feeble breath that carries odors of dead fish and diesel fuel. Lulu, walking down Hudson Street, hair crammed into a cap to keep it out of the way, feels the draft on her neck, turns her face to the river and smells ocean.

She went home after lunch and slept most of the afternoon as if she were in the tropics, she told Larry when he called from

Budapest. Lulu lived once in Bahia and once on Ibiza. She knows how to work in the morning and far into the night, reserving the torpid afternoons for sleep. Larry wanted to know why she didn't just go out and buy an air conditioner or move into a hotel until the heat wave was over.

She was inventive in her reply. She never lets her wealthy friends—even Larry—know that she is poor. Destitute. If they realized they would come rushing to her aid, but after the flood of beneficence there would be a gradual seeping away. Her poverty would discomfort; she would become an obligation instead of a friend, and eventually only a guilt-provoking memory.

She's the friend who's always available to stay in the house in Malibu and supervise renovations, to take off for St. Bart's and help a person forget whatever. Lulu's friends understand that they will pay her way, but they never wonder—and Lulu wouldn't want them to—how she lives when she isn't with them.

Any time Lulu has acquired money it has been like finding a little pot of gold, not like earning wages for work. She's had a few small parts in movies. Once, she lived with a musician and they cowrote some songs; occasionally a royalty check arrives from those half-forgotten tunes. She applies constantly for grants and sometimes one comes through.

Lulu is an artist. She talks about her "work" as if there were a large warehouse somewhere filled with objects she has fashioned, but she does installations mostly, multimedia stuff. Once she did an earthwork on landfill that later became Battery Park City. There isn't much left after one of her shows in the way of objects a collector could buy.

When friends ask why she's spending the season in New York of all places when it's supposed to be the hottest summer of the century, Lulu answers that she's putting together an installation, which is true, although she decided to have a show because the place she found where she could stay rent-free for the summer was in the city. After Lulu moved in, she found an empty storefront on Grand Street only slightly out of the gallery district. The owner, Joshua Montero, wants to rent it but hasn't found a tenant yet. Lulu let him look at her scrapbook of reviews of shows she'd done in the past and told him she'd like to mount an installation in the space. Montero's a little rough, raised in the Bronx, Jewish mother, Puerto Rican father, but young and street smart. It wasn't hard to charm him and, really, what does he have to lose?

So when Desert Ray first meets Lulu, she will see her living in Molly's nice loft (Ray doesn't have to know, right away, that it isn't Lulu's) and putting together a one-woman show. Lulu wouldn't have minded if Ray had been around to witness Lulu arriving from the airport in Larry's limo. But she wasn't. How long will it take before Lulu and Desert Ray meet? Should Lulu leave it entirely to chance or should she cook up some story, knock on the door and introduce herself? Maybe she will, after she's given herself a few days to get over the jet lag. She looked like such a wreck when Richard took her to lunch, but he didn't seem to mind, and she managed to keep him entertained.

This evening Lulu has equipped herself for work. She's carrying two plastic garbage bags, heavy red rubber gloves, and a three-foot-long, half-inch-wide metal pipe, her "garbage wand," handy for poking into trash cans, warding off rats, and, if the need arises, defending herself from other garbage raiders. There's a team of homeless people living by the waterfront who systematically go through the neighborhood trash. As soon as Lulu told them she wanted only the three cans in front of a particular building, they left her in peace. It's the freelancers who might be a problem—amateurs, hungry interlopers looking for half-eaten sandwiches.

She is delighted to see that all three battered galvanized pails are filled to the top with shiny black plastic bags. She carefully unties the first. There, like a little pot of gold left just for her, is a neatly reclosed container of Chinese sesame noodles, better than half-full. She goes after it greedily, holding the container close to her mouth and scooping noodles with her fingers.

Clarence, on his way to Maude's where he works as a waiter, recognizes her. He's determined to introduce himself and get over the awkwardness he felt at the restaurant earlier. If he thought about it, he would walk briskly by and wait for a time when they were on common ground, just outside the building where they live, or in the elevator together. Instead, without stopping to wonder what she's doing with her back to the street, leaning over an open garbage bag, he walks up and says hello. She cries out, jumps back, dropping the container of food, and grabs a pipe.

"Oh my God, I'm sorry, I—Oh Christ!" Clarence backs away.

"Wait." She puts the pipe down and licks her fingers. "I've seen you before, haven't I? On the street, maybe—oh yeah! And you were at the San Marco today. I saw you watching me. It's the second time today you've caught me stealing food." She laughs; her eyes crinkle up; a lock of hair falls loose from her cap. Clarence laughs too, flattered that she expects him to take a little garbage-eating in stride, which he finds he can do. He introduces himself and shakes the small, licked-clean hand.

"I don't want you to get the wrong impression, that I'm going through a stranger's garbage—"

"Oh, no."

"It's for a show I'm doing, an installation."

"You're an artist?"

"I'm doing an exhibition of one person's garbage. It's like an archaeological dig, but instead of waiting thousands of years, I'm digging now while it's fresh."

"So this person—the owner of the garbage—is a friend of yours or something?"

"Oh, no, never. I've never seen him. I try to avoid meeting him because that would spoil it, you know. This will be a portrait of a person made out of what he throws away, what he discards, disregards, forgets about." She flicks her hands as if shaking off water. "Picasso you know would never get rid of old clothes. He believed that once he'd worn them they had a magic. And if you want to put a curse on someone in voodoo, you first have to get something of his—nail parings, pubic hairs. I chose this guy because he lives alone, he's in the neighborhood, and he's the only one in the building. It looks like they're getting ready to renovate."

As she talks, Lulu pulls on gloves and gets to work. She puts returnable cans and bottles into a separate bag, no doubt to redeem for money. A pair of worn running shoes delights her. Clarence doesn't know whether to believe her story about the installation or not, but he finds it inventive and amusing and Clarence puts a high value on being amused. He is so entertained that somehow twenty minutes slip by without his realizing. He's late for work and has to leave, he tells her, but they'll be seeing each other a lot, since they're living in the same place.

"We are?"

"My friend and I have an artist's loft for the summer. It's someone her grandfather—"

"You? Not—and the girl? The girl with you at the restaurant? That's not your friend who's living with you?"

"Yes, Edie. It's her grandfather who—"

"I didn't expect—she's so—grown-up. All grown-up. And I
was—oh, she saw me eating off his plate—"

"Look—it's not—Edie's cool. You don't have to worry."
Clarence finds himself holding Lulu by the shoulders as if she
might fly apart.

"She'll hate me! Does she hate me?"

"Edie?"

"Who? Edie! Does she hate me?"

"Of course not," Clarence says, "how could Edie hate you?
She doesn't know you. Edie doesn't hate anyone." He won't tell
Lulu that Edie said she was going to try to avoid Lulu, that Edie
was definitely put off by Lulu—because what's the sense of making Lulu feel bad? For some reason she cares what Edie thinks of
her. And Edie will like her, because Clarence does, even though
Lulu's a little dotty. Dotty. Clarence loves the word. He loves
dotty women. He wants to protect them.

He gives her a hug, tells her not to worry, and then runs—
because he's really seriously late this time. It's only as he arrives
at the restaurant, panting and wet from running in this heat,
does he realize that Lulu, of course, must be too broke even to
buy food, which is why she steals it out of garbage cans and off
other people's plates. He'll take her care packages from Maude's.
They won't mind at the restaurant. It's food they'd be throwing
out anyway.

LULU COLLAPSES ON THE CURB, HER FOREHEAD PRESSED
against her knees. She's sick. Not from eating the sesame noo-

dles, which were perfectly fresh and good. How could this happen, after everything had been coming together so beautifully? How could she blow it like this?

What did she say at lunch? She was vamping, giving Richard full value, exaggerating certain traits—he brings that out in her. And she continued the performance for the kids because she knew they were watching. When she held the plate right up to her mouth and shoveled in Richard's pasta, she caught, out of the corner of her eye, a frisson of disgust on that girl's face, and it made Lulu chuckle inside. It is her joy and her art to elicit frissons. She had no idea that the girl was Ray! All grown-up—a young woman—Edith—what a dumb name. Her name is Desert Ray, and she's beautiful, but now Ray will never know Lulu, never know her own mother. Because Lulu can't tell her, not now.

THE RAIN

THE HEAT—WITH TEMPERATURES BREAKING THROUGH TO the hundreds—lasts ten days. There are brownouts on the East Side. From a rooftop in Brighton Beach, a twelve-year-old trying out a new gun kills a mother of two on her way to the grocery store. On Upper Broadway in Manhattan, a band of teenage girls armed with razors randomly slash female pedestrians across the face and arms. In Queens, a Korean-owned produce store erupts in flames under suspicious circumstances. The mayor and the governor both appear on the evening news, announcing stepped-up police surveillance and urging citizens to stay calm.

The rain when it finally comes is more punishment than relief. It whips the city with water so warm it feels like blood on the skin. Litter floats in the streets and clogs the sewers, forming ankle-high puddles that people must leap or slog through.

Edith returns from the library, clutching the fruit of her labor wrapped in a plastic garbage bag. In the cubbyhole the interns share as an office (or playpen as it's called), the others are having lunch.

"You're getting everything wet," Peyton says.

"Well, it's raining."

"What are you working on anyway? Whose piece?"

"He didn't tell me. He just said go out and find stuff on heart disease."

"I don't know why he sent you and not someone in research." Peyton returns to her salad and book, pulling her skirt around her legs.

Edith herself doesn't understand why Henry gave her this assignment. He came in when she was the only one at her desk. He hadn't spoken to her since she arrived; she was Geraldine's protégée apparently, and Henry didn't feel any responsibility toward her. But on this particular morning he seemed in the mood to chat, and as there was no one else but Edith, he chatted with her. He really is so easy to talk to, once you get to know him. Edith got him laughing about life at Grimsby College. He said it reminded him of his high school in Missouri. As he left, he asked her to take on this research project and get back to him in two days.

"Maybe he chose you because your grandfather's a doctor," Ben offers. "And you help out at his clinic a lot."

"That must be it," Edith agrees, although how would Henry know that about her?

The area where Edith works is a warren of white cubicles without real walls, just partitions that can be moved depending on the need. Instead of halls there are passageways. She threads through them until she comes to the front of the building where there are real offices with doors and windows. These are not luxuriously furnished. In fact, they are shabby, with desks and chairs of the kind that Edith has seen in old black-and-white movies. No one on this row has a computer. They have classic Underwoods. There are books everywhere, flung onto shelves and piled on the floor. Martin's office is in the corner, flanked by Geraldine's and Henry's.

"Horrors! Don't bring that stuff in here!" Henry cries. His desk is covered with papers and books. "It's for Martin. Do you have money for a cab? Good. Get a receipt. . . . Yes, right away. . . . You don't know where he lives?" He scribbles the address and hands it to her. "Off you go."

As she is leaving Henry's office, Edith runs into Geraldine.

"Oh, Edith, what on earth—you're soaking wet. You didn't go out in this! Quick, into the ladies' room and put yourself under a hairdryer. With this insane air-conditioning—"

"I'm going out again. I have to take something over to Martin."

"Martin. No. Why?"

"Henry—"

Geraldine grabs her arm and drags her back into Henry's office. "Henry, there's a deluge out there. Take a look."

Henry glances at his cloudy window.

"We can send a messenger. We don't have to send Edith."

Henry sits back in his chair and looks at the two of them. Geraldine drops Edith's arm.

"Edith looks like a strong girl. A little rain won't hurt her. And she has to be there because Martin might have questions. He might have points he wants her to investigate more thoroughly.

He's going to be working with her on this project, Geraldine. I know that Edith is your discovery. You should be happy that I'm giving her this opportunity."

A blast of rain hits the window behind him. "I guess it's out of my hands," Geraldine says, as if the storm has had the final word.

THE STREET IS SOLID WITH TRAFFIC THAT MOVES ONLY IN convulsive spasms. Edith soon gives up on finding a cab and ducks into the subway. When she comes out at Ninety-sixth Street, the rain is blowing in horizontally under her umbrella. She has to struggle to hold it over her bag of papers and books. What must she look like, wet and disheveled, carrying a garbage bag? She tells herself it doesn't matter, that the point is to get the research materials to Martin. But of course it does matter. Even if she were looking her best, she'd still be nervous about meeting Martin. She's picked up on the mystique about him that pervades *Ubu*—conversations about what "he" wants, how "he" likes it done. Since Edith has been at the magazine, only two people, Geraldine and Henry, have had access to Martin. Now for some reason, Edith is going to be the third.

Edith turns off the avenue with its sterile high-rises, onto Martin's street where plane trees bend before the wind and low nineteenth-century town houses are graced by flower boxes and wrought-iron fences. She hesitates before opening the gate to Martin's house, and disturbing the peace of the dwelling. The grates on the lower windows, the sticker announcing that the house is protected by an alarm signify that the occupants will resist intruders. She checks the number twice to make certain it's right. Before she can put her finger to the bell, a clamor rises within, a howling booming protest—a dog, Edith realizes, not the wail of an outraged domicile. There's a placating female voice, footsteps, and the front door opens after much turning of latches. Only an iron grille separates Edith from the hell hound and its keeper. Edith wonders if she made a mistake and came to the wrong house.

She had been expecting that Martin's home and Martin's wife would carry on the same self-righteously shabby style of the office. Mrs. Weatherstone was supposed to be a little gray, a little plain, with a careful, critical, intelligent face. Instead Edith sees a vision of opulence: a long oriental runner on the floor, glimmers of polished silver and brass, old wood. Most of the light is gathered into the woman and radiates out, from the creamy skin, the tawny hair, the flash of jewels on her fingers.

Is this Mrs. Weatherstone, Martin's wife? She will neither affirm nor deny it. Henry did call, didn't he? The woman stares at Edith as if she were a fiend. Maybe Edith does look menacing —she is soaking wet. She explains once more, a little louder, enunciating carefully, who she is and why she's here.

Finally Mrs. Weatherstone—it must be she, although she still hasn't said a word—lets Edith into the hall. The dog whimpers, wags its whole body, and presses against Edith, who pats it, grateful for an excuse to bend her head and avoid Mrs. Weatherstone's scrutiny.

"She's a failure as a watchdog," Mrs. Weatherstone observes. "If anyone managed to break in, Freddy would just slobber all over him. Everyone's always been kind to her. She has no reason not to trust."

"I'm afraid I'm ruining your floor." Edith indicates the puddle at her feet.

"The rain is horrific. I've been watching it all morning in the garden. It's like a monsoon—not natural. Where does it come from—all this water? What does it mean?" Mrs. Weatherstone goes on about global warming, melting ice caps, changes in the jet stream. As Edith's eyes become accustomed to the light, she sees that Mrs. Weatherstone is not as young as she first appeared.

"The research Martin wanted—" Edith indicates the plastic bag still cradled in her arms.

"Oh, yes." Before Edith can object, Mrs. Weatherstone whisks the bag away and hurries off upstairs, leaving Edith, in wet clothes, unwilling to follow across the carpet. Besides, the dog is in the way.

Mrs. Weatherstone reappears momentarily. "I hate to send you out again in this but it's going to last all day and as you say, you're already wet."

"I'm supposed to—Henry said I should talk to Martin—to explain the research?"

"He's sleeping."

"Should I wait?"

"It could be hours—" Mrs. Weatherstone's voice rises in impatience.

A male voice, it must be Martin's, calls from upstairs.

"Wait here," Mrs. Weatherstone whispers, and goes back up.

Edith removes her shoes, pushes the dog aside, and follows. As Edith nears the top, Mrs. Weatherstone is starting down. She seems shocked to see Edith, affronted, but Edith stands her ground. The older woman's irrational behavior only strengthens Edith's resolve. She's helped her grandfather in situations where a patient, or the relative of a patient, has become unreasonable, even hysterical, and Edith has learned to counter with a steady calm. It's become an almost automatic response.

They are poised in wordless standoff when Martin calls: "Flo? What the hell's going on?"

Mrs. Weatherstone's lips twist into what could be a grimace or a smile. She stands aside for Edith to pass.

So this is Martin, Edith thinks, drawing near to the figure on the bed in a room made even darker than the storm outside would warrant, by heavy drapes drawn across the windows. *Martin.* His white hair, flattened in back from lying on the pillow, rises in a nimbus around his face, which is surprisingly young— not exactly handsome, but the eyes are intelligent. He isn't anything like what she expected, but he looks familiar somehow.

Martin puts on his glasses and studies her, as if the storm has brought him an odd new specimen to be examined and classified.

"Flo, she's wet. She'll catch cold sitting around in wet clothes. What's your name?"

"Edith Seagrace."

"Seagrace. What kind of name is that—English?"

"Maybe, or Native American. I'm not sure. It's my father's name, and he died when I was little. My mom's not much on history, or names."

"And Edith's an odd name for someone of your generation. They're all Jennifers and Sarahs now."

"It was my grandmother's."

"You're not an Edith at all. It's completely wrong. But you're used to it."

"I'm not, actually. I always thought I should have a romantic name—like Desdemona."

"Desdemona!" Martin laughs. "Yes, why not? Edith is much too utilitarian a name for a young woman who comes flying through the storm of the century to get to the bedside of someone she doesn't even know. Desdemona, why don't you go into my bathroom and blot yourself on whatever towels you find in there? There's a robe on the back of the door that you can wear while Florence dries your clothes."

"Oh, no, I'm fine——" Edith says, although her skirt is clinging to her legs, and she's keeping her wet blazer on because her thin blouse is transparent when wet. But Mrs. Weatherstone is showing her to the bathroom, where a worn flannel robe is hanging on the door. It smells faintly but comfortingly of someone else.

What an odd leap into intimacy Edith has made, from being a stranger at the door to wearing Martin's (it must be his) robe and sitting in his bedroom. Edith's shy about surrendering her clothes to Mrs. Weatherstone. "Just tell me where the dryer is. I can put these things in," she says.

Martin waves impatiently. "Let Florence do it. You'll get lost. Pull that chair up next to me." He seems to be sifting through the articles she copied, his eyes restlessly scanning the text, but when he begins questioning Edith on specific points, she understands that he's read the whole stack. He has Edith write down four specific areas where he wants more research; she'll have to get on the phone to the American Heart Association, the National Heart, Lung, and Blood Institute and get hold of the writer who seems to be the expert at the *Times*. "And go into the living room and get the phone—it's just plugged into a jack— and bring it here."

Martin's on the phone with his cardiologist when Mrs. Weatherstone comes back with Edith's clothes on hangers. They've been pressed, which makes Edith feel embarrassed, as if her privacy has been invaded. When she's in the bathroom changing, she fixes her hair with what must be Martin's brush.

Her face looks different; her eyebrows are more prominent or something.

"Let her go now, Martin, before the rain starts again," Mrs. Weatherstone is saying.

"You did well." Martin reaches for Edith's hand. His fingers are silky, like a woman's. "I'll see you in a few days, when you've finished."

"This is Thursday, Martin," Mrs. Weatherstone reminds him.

"If you have it on the weekend, I'll see you then," Martin says, as if it would be an honor for Edith and a concession on Martin's part.

CLARENCE, ON HIS WAY TO BREAKFAST AT TWENTY-PAST-two in the afternoon, is surprised when the outer door of the elevator opens and a cyclone of wind and water whirls in on him. At its center, like a water witch, her long hair streaming, is Lulu. He catches her in his arms and she looks up. "Oh, you wonderful boy! Where do you think you're going? You can't go out in this."

"Just around the corner for a cup of coffee."

"Oh, but you can't. You'll perish. No, seriously, I want to make breakfast for you. A friend came over yesterday and brought groceries—you won't believe the extravagance. I could have lived for the rest of the summer on what it cost. Designer food, ridiculous. But it doesn't matter. I can tell you're trying to say no, but if you do you'll hurt my feelings. You've been so—more than nice. Those little bags of food have saved my life, you've no idea. Now I want to do something for you. You have to let people give back when they can." She puts her key into the slot next to her floor, starting the elevator again. All the while she's crooning about how she has Colombian coffee and two kinds of jam. Clarence laughs at finding himself being shanghaied by a woman old enough to be his mother, although his mother must be a good ten years older than Lulu and would never wear a sopping wet dress that clung to her body and would never let her wet hair curl around her face.

Clarence is curious about seeing Lulu's loft. He hopes he won't find piles of garbage around.

The door opens onto a sweep of polished wood floor, immaculate walls hung with art (Clarence spots two Rauschenberg prints right off), recessed lighting, overstuffed chairs and sofas.

"It's a faux loft," Lulu says. "Most of the space is for sitting around talking about art, and the place where you *do* art is a little room in the back, but Molly—this is Molly's place—is a faux artist. She goes up to the Vineyard for the summer and she has a place in Miami Beach for the winter, so her loft is free a lot of the time. She likes me to stay. You know, a pipe could break and she wouldn't find out about it for two months, the way this place is run, or not run."

"And when she comes back, where will you go?"

Lulu shrugs. "Something will turn up. Look at me. I'm making a puddle on the floor. Hang on. I'm going to change. Don't leave. I'll be right out to cook your breakfast."

Clarence wanders the room, inspecting the art, half-hoping —because it could make a good story—that she'll reappear in a silk kimono, but she comes back in tights and a man's workshirt, the sleeves rolled, ready for business.

Breakfast is fresh-squeezed orange juice, French toast, Irish bacon ("If you knew what this cost a pound, you'd faint"), coffee with real cream. She sits opposite and takes such pleasure in watching Clarence eat that he overdoes it. (He tries to keep his

weight down; otherwise he looks beefy like the rest of the men in
his family.) The storm rages on the other side of the window
while Clarence eats and Lulu sips coffee. Lulu, who seemed so
eccentric and bizarre when Clarence caught her stealing food,
now reminds him of mothers of friends of his—attractive, confident, dispensers of meals and kindnesses.

Lulu takes him into the studio where she keeps her collection
of garbage. It's all clean and sorted. The few organic pieces—
leftover food, apple cores, eggshells—have been sealed in glass
jars and labeled. She's experimenting with different ways of displaying her finds—mounted on Plexiglas, suspended from wires.
A complete set of clothing is laid out on the floor: a worn, sweat-
stained Chicago Cubs hat; an oxford cloth dress shirt, buttoned,
with sleeves rolled up, a frayed T-shirt underneath; a pair of
college athletic shorts from USC with the elastic gone, an athletic
support visible underneath; mismatched socks and the running
shoes that Lulu had been so delighted to find the night Clarence
saw her at the garbage cans.

"So that's him," Clarence says.

"That's the husk of him," Lulu says. "I wish he'd throw out
some long pants so we could tell how tall he is. I mean, should I
put the sneakers here? Or down here?"

Lulu's project today is to make a collage of the subject's mail,
which is mostly appeals for donations or sweepstakes offers, all of
which he has thrown into the trash unopened. There are enve-
lopes from bills: electric, telephone, credit cards, bank statements.
There is a postcard of the Eiffel Tower, written in French.

Although Clarence is an art major at school, he often wonders if he's really an artist or only attracted to the field because it
provides a wormhole escape route from the suburban Philadelphia culture in which he was raised. But today with Lulu, he's

completely absorbed in the task. Hours go by and he doesn't notice. They work together as equals. The talk is mostly about art and artists, many of whom she knows personally.

They also talk about Edie. Lulu's worried that Edie doesn't like her; she passed right by on the street yesterday and didn't even smile, which doesn't sound like Edie. "Maybe she was thinking about something," Clarence says. "She's pretty into her job."

"Oh? What's she doing?" Lulu brushes a scrap of an electrical bill with rubber cement.

"She's interning at this magazine—*Ubu?*"

"Oh yeah. I know *Ubu,*" Lulu says, and dips her glue brush into her coffee mug.

Clarence removes the brush and puts it into the glue pot.

LULU HATES TO SEE CLARENCE GO. SHE OPENS THE WINdow. The rain has stopped at last. Damp air seeps in over the sill. Lulu stands eating a cold piece of French toast, watching cars negotiate the flooded street below. The swish of tires in the wet, punctuated by horn blasts makes a melancholy concert.

Her parents died on such a night, in a car that skidded into a truck. Lulu has thought about it so many times that it seems as if she were there in the car with them, but she wasn't. They'd left her alone (she was fifteen), and she'd sneaked out and gone riding around with some older friends in a VW van, smoking pot, drinking beer, being cool. The van was tippy going around corners. One of the headlights was busted. Lulu should have been killed. Instead it was her parents in their boring beige Dodge.

They left her before she could leave them. Their neat little tacky house in Sacramento, their careful saving ways weren't her way. To them she was a wild child, their failure because they hadn't succeeded in making her as fearful and quiet and gray as they themselves were. They were two orphans from the Depression. All they wanted was safety, security, a weekly paycheck.

Lulu eluded foster care and got the hell out of Sacramento. San Francisco was the place to be. She fell in with a group of musicians and writers who were stoned a lot of the time but smart. The craziest was a lawyer—Curly Larkin. He took her to New York and they stayed at the Chelsea Hotel for a couple of weeks. She wrote a story about some of the freaks living there and took it over to *Ubu*. Nadja hired her before she even read the story.

Nadja's gone. Lulu knows that much, but she hasn't kept up, doesn't know who's still there. Who saw Desert Ray and fell in love with her, gave her a chance? And how strange that Ray should be repeating Lulu's pattern. *Ubu* of all places. Lulu's read studies of identical twins separated at birth, reunited as adults, who turn out to be living almost identical lives—down to dressing alike, or giving children the same name. Is Ray a genetic copy of Lulu? Will she go on to repeat Lulu's life?

Lulu has to laugh at this notion, because her life has certainly not been the norm. From the little she's seen of Ray (too little; Lulu tries to detain Ray when they meet by chance, tries to start a conversation but Ray avoids her), it seems to Lulu that Ray is more grounded than Lulu was at her age. It's hard to judge, of course. You never know what's going on inside someone's head, but Ray seems to take it for granted that she has a rightful place in the scheme of things. This is an assumption that Lulu could never make. Lulu admires people like this. If she had thought about it, it would have been one of the qualities she would have wished for her daughter. The doctor, the doctor's plain, stumpy daughter, and her gangly husband, seem to have given this to

Ray. At least Lulu can take some comfort in seeing how Ray turned out, and can take some credit for finding her a good home.

Lulu would never have given Ray to an agency or strangers, but the doctor was persuasive. He held out his big hands for Lulu's baby, and Lulu surrendered her burden. Ray, who'd been crying, screaming all night, suddenly was calm. Lulu could see the rigid little body go soft in his hands, and the baby opened her eyes wide to take him in. He looked back calmly, as if he already understood this baby and was making plans for her. He made Lulu realize that she hadn't any plans at all for Desert Ray.

Lulu tried to take Ray back once. Lulu was at Parsons, but she had a job at a gallery which paid pretty well (she was involved with the owner), and she was living with friends in a loft on Greene Street. There was room for a kid; her friends said they'd help out. Lulu got so excited about the idea that somehow she thought she could just go back to Compton Falls and get her baby back. All she managed to do was terrify the little kid. Lulu's lucky she didn't end up in jail. "Basta!" She flicks her hands away from her, as if memories were things that came from outside, crawling across the floor.

BALD TIRES SPIN ON SLICK PAVEMENT. THE CAB SCREECHES around a corner, wobbling on its chassis. "I'm not in any hurry," Florence volunteers, but the driver, whose name is an odd collection of consonants and vowels, seems not to understand. Or maybe he's on a suicide mission. He jerks to a stop in front of a small brownstone surrounded by high-rises.

It's been years since Florence was on this block. Didn't it used to be entirely low buildings? Unless she's on the wrong street. But this is Geraldine's entrance; she remembers now, and there's Geraldine's name. Florence pushes the button and Geraldine's voice comes crackling over the intercom. The carpet on the stair is stained; there's a faint smell of natural gas. On the second floor, a fight is taking place behind closed doors. Florence hurries past. At least the stairs probably keep Geraldine in shape, Florence thinks, because Geraldine would never do anything as self-indulgent as join a health club.

The peephole is flicked open. Florence smiles into it foolishly. A few dead bolts are turned. Florence finds this excessive, as she just talked to Geraldine over the intercom, but maybe living alone all these years has fostered a kind of paranoia in Geraldine. There's a smell here that Florence had almost forgotten—you get it in cheap motels, waiting rooms of bus stations—of cigarette smoke permeating upholstery and even the paint on the walls. Florence remarks that Geraldine's place has hardly changed. Geraldine objects: She's had the sofa reupholstered; the curtains in the bedroom are new—well, maybe three years old. What Florence means is that it still looks like a first apartment, not permanent. There are plastic milk crates standing around filled with books and papers. It's really the handiest way of storing things, Geraldine says. Florence stops herself. Geraldine wouldn't have any wine in the house, would she? Geraldine produces a bottle of Dewars, the only alcohol she has, and pours them each some over ice.

They sit on the sofa, facing a long blank wall, no chairs or anything except for the ubiquitous crates. Harsh lighting and an unfortunate shade of paint on the walls makes Geraldine's skin look sallow.

"Why did you choose this color?" Florence asks.

"There's no window here, you know, so I thought if I painted yellow walls it would be like bringing in sunlight." Geraldine takes a healthy swig from her drink. "I don't use this room much. I'm mostly in the bedroom. Funny, isn't it? You think my apartment's small, but I have a whole room I never use."

"Oh Ger, you're so ascetic. You've gotten worse, you know. It's the Irish in you, the Irish monk."

"If I'm descended from a monk, then he wasn't all that ascetic."

"You know what I mean." Florence sips her drink. "Well, she made it. She got in to see Martin."

"I didn't send her. Henry did. I ne—"

"I just don't understand why you brought her into the magazine in the first place. That's the part that doesn't make sense. Of course she's going to try to finagle her way—"

"She's perfectly innocent, Florence. She has no idea."

Florence is aware of how close she's sitting to Geraldine, close enough to inhale the smoke from her cigarette. They both shift simultaneously to opposite ends of the sofa.

"What was it like, when they met? Did either of them feel anything, could you tell?" Geraldine can't disguise her eagerness. Florence doesn't believe that Geraldine is scheming against her consciously, but there is something unhealthy in Geraldine's involvement, as if she wants to be found out. Residual Catholic guilt. It never goes away.

"Why are you convinced that the girl is innocent?" Florence asks.

"I've had long talks with her, Flo. I know her really well, and she hasn't—"

"Ger, think about it. She comes to you—of all people—and wants a job at the magazine—of all places. Then she shows up at our house, in the rain, and pushes—*pushes* past me to get to Martin. She has a plan. Of course she has a plan."

"You think she knows."

"Ger, get real."

"FLORENCE, FLO, FLORENCE . . . HELP! GET HELP! Help! Quick! . . . Florence! For God's sake, Flo!" Martin tries to get the words past the gigantic thudding heart raging in his chest, flooding his body, drowning his cries. "Flo! Flo!" He can hardly hear himself. If only he hadn't asked Florence to take the phone out of his room he could call 911, get an ambulance. Paramedics. CPR. Florence doesn't know CPR. She should take a course. Save his life sometime. But how could she save his life when she won't wake up? "Flo!" It comes out strong and loud this time. The pounding has stopped.

Is it even beating? He's afraid to put his hand on it. He lies very still with his arms at his sides, watching shadows of leaves sift across furniture, walls. He closes his eyes and shadows settle like coins on his lids.

Upstairs Florence sleeps in the same room she's had since she was a girl. When Florence's parents died (her mother first, her father six months later) Martin moved down to the master bedroom but Florence preferred to stay put. She has two rooms: a study and a bedroom. She's a voracious sleeper. When they used to share a bed, Martin could get up three times in a night, and Florence would drift on oblivious. If they'd had a child, as she'd wished, Martin would have been the one to get up with it. Florence wouldn't have heard it crying. Poor little thing, wailing in the night.

Martin was dreaming about a baby. It seems extraordinary,

but there was one in his dream. He can't remember anything else, just the baby. What does that signify, a child in your dream? He'll have to ask Florence. Death maybe. A hollow sigh escapes his lips, rehearsal for a death rattle.

He's thinking about someone he knew years ago—she may have been in the dream. One of Nadja's finds. Someone Martin had a crush on for a week or two, and then she claimed she was having his child. Martin never believed her, not for a moment. She came back after he and Florence were married, tried to extort money, money he didn't have. That's when the magazine paid next to nothing; you took a vow of poverty when you joined the staff. Looking back now it seems cavalier, even cruel, how he turned the girl away. He panicked. The girl was in a position to ruin his life. She was a rootless wanderer, a hippie who believed in fucking everyone she wanted, not the sort of person you settle down with.

The colors of the night are shades of gray. The robe on the back of the door is gray, but in the light it's blue. It brought out the gold in Edith's eyes. They are unusual, much like his. It made him think—for the first time—that there might be a child walking around who carries his DNA. Some part of him to live on after he's gone. Is that why people have children?

Desirée. My God, how did he think of that? That was the preposterous name the girl said she had given the child. There was even a photograph that she tried to press on him but he wouldn't look. The heart jumps. *Don't think about it. It wasn't yours.*

One of the articles Edith brought today was about a defibrillator that can be implanted surgically to shock the heart back to normal rhythm. He'll call that doctor at Stanford tomorrow and get the lowdown. The satisfaction at having made a plan has a soporific effect. He falls back to sleep dreaming of machines that will keep watch over his heart, his errant heart.

FLORENCE DOES HEAR MARTIN CALLING FOR HELP. Florence is having a rare sleepless night. She had too much Scotch and too much talk too late in the evening. She's sweating, even though the air conditioner is turned up.

It's happened several times that Martin has thought he was having another attack and it turned out to be nothing, but Florence should go since she's awake anyway, to comfort him at least. The fact that she doesn't surprises her. This is how she recognizes that she is angry. Furious. He has a daughter, acquired through no effort or merit of his own, while on the floor above Florence's room are two empty chambers that she thought would hold their children. He robbed her of her own and let his illegitimate seed flourish.

Florence's better self flees her body while something hot and dark expands within her. If she let it loose, she could do amazing things: tear the house apart, strangle Martin in his bed; climb to the roof and wake the neighborhood with unearthly caterwauling. Instead she confines it, arms and legs aching with the effort, eyes glaring at the ceiling, ears harking to the rush of her indignant blood.

THE RAT

RAIN IS USUALLY BENEFICIAL TO THE CITY. IT WASHES urine from pavements, sweeps detritus from curbs, flushes particles from the atmosphere. But this rain, or monsoon as some are calling it, has had the opposite effect: It brought what was rotting under streets swirling to the surface and left it moldering in heaps. It tainted the air with a residue of something burnt and brown. People are saying that the catastrophic weather is both a punishment and a harbinger of worse to come. Edith and Clarence join in these conversations and express concern, but in their hearts they are thrilled. Heat and storm only heighten the adventure of being in the city. Because they have nothing but youth, they instinctively welcome change. Cracks in the old order—even the meteorological order—look like footholds and handholds to them.

Soot drifts in through the windows and settles on the table, the floor, the waiter shirt Clarence wore last night and left draped over a chair. Edith wishes he'd wake up so she could talk to him about Martin. She rattles dishes, sings as she dries her hair —to no avail. Clarence goes out to the clubs after work and doesn't get in much before dawn. He won't be up for hours, and she wants to get to the office early to finish her research for Martin. He's counting on her. It's not for an article; Martin wants the information for himself, but that makes it all the more urgent.

She hates it that she and Clarence are on different schedules; she resents it that he stays out so late. At school there was time to tell each other everything. He was the first and by far the best friend she made at Grimsby. He was there because three of his brothers had gone before him—all, like him, on football scholarships. Edith was there on what Clarence called a "smart person scholarship." Clarence was pledging the football players' fraternity. Edith was pledging "the pretty girls' sorority" (Clarence again). They went to parties together; in the eyes of Grimsby, they were the classic couple. Only the two of them knew it was a sham. Edith was the first straight person Clarence told about his homosexuality. He said he thought she'd understand because he'd noticed a look, a certain absence in her expression, as if she were only doing what was expected of her while she waited for her real life to begin. They developed a theory that their real lives were going on without them somewhere—New York City, probably, although sometimes Clarence thought Paris. It became a code between them: "not R. L.," they'd say, or "approaching R. L."

Now she needs to tell Clarence about Martin, how he belongs in her Real Life. She feels more like herself when she's with him—not at ease and comfortable as she does with Clarence, but more like her potential self. There is something about being with Martin that makes her mind work better. She sees now why everyone at the magazine is obsessed with him. And the Martin she knows is diminished, a sick man who takes pills to keep his heart in low gear. What must he have been before? Electrifying.

THE ELEVATOR STOPS ON THE FLOOR BENEATH. IT'S THAT crazy woman, Lulu, the one Clarence finds so interesting. She comes in dragging a garbage bag. "Oh, hi—Edie. I come across these cans and bottles in my work—I'm putting together a show —I don't know if Clarence told you. And, uh, I figure I might as well turn them in, recycle them, you know. And then I use the money for my morning cappuccino at the Dream Café. It's just one of those little rituals." She's wearing her hair loose today. It's entirely too much. Edith puts her hands up to her own hair, which suddenly seems excessive. Maybe she should be wearing it in a braid, at least for work. Long hair is a definite mistake on an older woman, makes her seem scattered, flighty, or is it that older women who keep their hair long tend to be that way in the first place? Edith thinks of Geraldine's smooth, chin-length hair with one elegant streak of silver, and decides that when she turns thirty she will cut her hair.

As if Lulu could read Edith's thoughts, she begins smoothing her hair, combing with her fingers. "Ooh, Rollerblades," she says. "I've been thinking about getting a pair. Are they as much fun as they look?"

"They're convenient. I use them for transportation," says Edith. The elevator stops.

Lulu rattles her bag. "I think I have enough for two. How about joining me?"

"Thanks. I'm in a hurry. I have to get to work."

Edith jumps the curb and skates off uptown, feeling guilty for not helping Lulu with her bag, and because she actually was going for a cappuccino before Lulu invited her. Clarence thinks Lulu's cool because she lives off other people, without a home of her own, without possessions. Edith finds it alarming. What if Lulu gets sick or has an accident? She has no cushion, no protection. Anyone who decides to be Lulu's friend is taking on a responsibility.

But it's more than that, Edith decides as she works her way uptown. Something about Lulu unsettles her. It's the way she looks at Edith, as if she wants something from her, something too big for Edith to give.

Edith switches on her Walkman. The tape is a mix Clarence made for her—all hard-driving city sounds. He uses it when he skates, says it gives him attitude. It does make her feel macho and tough, mean enough to withstand the men who, when she stops at streetlights, say things and make kissing sounds. Skates are just the thing for the city, because you notice too much when you walk, so many ruined people shaking their begging cups, or sifting through rubbish, or trying to sleep in shadowy doorways. The women especially. Edith can't help looking at them, fearing that she'll see a face on one that is so close to her own that she won't be able to deny the connection.

But that's Carolyn's vision of the fate of Lucille Arslanian-—not that she ever said it. She let it be known by innuendo, hinting that Grandpop saved Edith's life by taking her away from her mother. Edith, in defiance of Carolyn, has formed another picture, of someone in the arts perhaps, a designer, an artist, a dancer. Edith's mother, no longer nameless, shape-shifts in Edith's imagination, from homeless hag to established artist.

She could be in the city today, watching Edith as she skates by. She could be huddled in a doorway, or in the backseat of a taxi cab. She could be in that limousine. She could see Edith and cry out to the driver: "Stop this car!" and open the door, gather Edith into her arms. . . .

But the limo glides on. Edith, crossing Fourteenth Street, looks down to see a rat squashed under the grating, claws curled around metal, terrified eyes, as if it perished trying to escape from something below.

LULU WATCHES DESERT RAY SKATE UP THE STREET. SHE'S so much like Lulu! The way Ray has caught on to the downtown look—the way she got herself some Rollerblades. She's reinventing herself before Lulu's eyes. Lulu's always been that way too. It's a family talent, finding the way into the inner circle. Ray's good on skates, easy, strong. Lulu's always had confidence in her own body. Ray moves like a dancer, understands where her center of gravity is. Lulu wonders if she's ever studied dance, or thought about it as a career. There's so much Lulu wants to ask Ray, but their conversations never get beyond the perfunctory.

After Ray has skated out of view, Lulu takes her bag of empties and drags it up the street. She catches her reflection in a store window. Ordinarily it's a welcome sight; she likes the way she looks, but today her long hair flying out at the sides seems eccentric, even deranged. And the bag of empty bottles and cans hoisted on her shoulder—only the homeless, the down-and-out, are seen toting such bags. She's wearing a long skirt unbuttoned to mid-thigh, and the bare leg sticking out looks, not intentionally sexy, but like a mistake, as if she forgot to finish dressing.

Lulu looks again in the next window she passes, but the image stays the same. She can't get it to look like her, the way she likes to see herself, still young, innovative, a person who breaks the code on purpose, not because she doesn't know any better. This bottle-toting crone is someone else's vision of her—Ray's.

Lulu puts her bag down, pushes the hair from her eyes, and stares frankly at her reflection. She's not imagining it: The kid despises her, is maybe even afraid of her. Ray would die, she'd just die if she knew the truth—that Lulu is her mother. And yet Lulu can't get enough of Ray. She drinks her in. At the same time it's torture, because she can't help seeing herself reflected in Ray's eyes. When Molly calls again and pesters her, asking what it's like to be living near her daughter after all these years, Lulu will tell her that this is what hell must be like.

GERALDINE, WALKING SOUTH, SEES EDITH SKATING FROM the other direction. The headset and sunglasses, the long hair loose and flying, give an air of purpose and invulnerability. Geraldine's heart jumps at this vision of Edith, not the innocent child driven by an instinct that she doesn't recognize, but the avenging angel who knows everything, and who's going to force them all to acknowledge the truth.

"Edie!" That boy who works with her, one of the interns, catches Edith as she comes onto the sidewalk. Edith kisses him and then looks a little flustered. They're not at that stage—yet. In the excitement of skating, in the rush of blood through her body, she lost a certain reserve she usually has. He takes her hand. Geraldine hears him suggesting that they go for coffee, saying it's early, although it's not that early. Maybe they have five minutes, which is not really enough time.

Geraldine puts on a smile in case they see her, but they don't. As she watches them disappear around the corner—he with a guiding hand on her elbow—Geraldine keeps the smile until it turns into a grimace. What is it she's feeling that she won't let her face express? Longing—after their youth and her own lost opportunities? Jealousy—of him? Of her? Abruptly, she gives her head a shake, pivots on her heel, and strides through the revolving door so quickly that she nearly knocks down a messenger going the other way.

THE KEY

Friday morning Martin had Florence put the phone back in his room. "I could have died last night. I was calling but you were sleeping. I thought I was having another heart attack." "But you weren't," Florence said in a voice whose coldness surprised them both. Yesterday he didn't answer the phone, but today he picked up when Edith called to say she was coming by with more research material. Florence had been out in the garden and hadn't gotten to the telephone soon enough. She wanted to tell Edith it wasn't necessary to come on the weekend; she really should be reporting to Henry anyway, not directly to Martin. On Monday Florence plans to call Henry and ask him not to send the girl anymore.

The bell rings. Freddy goes into her mad-dog routine. Martin calls downstairs: "Flo, the door! Flo! Are you there?"

Yes, Florence is here but it's very hard to move through the hall and at the same time restrain the urge to hurl lamps and furniture. Control is difficult. Either you completely immobilize the body or you let it loose. Now that she has the door open, her hand freezes on the metal grille, unable to turn the latch. The heat and humidity, the wretched unnatural weather, have only served to heighten the blush on Edith's cheeks, to provide her with an excuse to wear a scanty top and skirt. She's bending down to remove her skates; she'll come in wearing only socks. Is that all right? she wants to know, giving Florence a look, which if Florence were as gullible as Geraldine, she might fall for.

"He's upstairs. I'm leaving." Florence opens the grille, admitting the girl while letting herself out. She actually closes the door in the girl's face. Now Florence is locked out of her own house. She waits for the girl to realize and open the door. But of course she doesn't, why should she? The girl has what she wants, Martin all to herself.

Florence puts her hand up to ring the bell, or maybe a knock would be more casual, but too much time has elapsed. The girl must be with Martin now. She'll have to come running downstairs and that will make Florence look silly, even unbalanced.

Why does she care what the girl thinks of her? It's Florence's house after all. She planted these shrubs, the creeping juniper, the privet, selected them because of their resistance to salt and drought, to the indignities of an urban environment. Florence is the one who had the security system installed after the night she surprised a man in the kitchen trying to make off with the family silver. And she paid out of her own earnings to have the entire house air-conditioned. She's the one who saw to the new flashing on the roof last year and the repairing of the stone facing where it was crumbling. Martin has no interest in, or talent for, home maintenance.

Florence remembers the day she moved into the house—not the boxes and crates, although there must have been such things —but a purple tricycle in the basement. She hadn't had one because of the war; metal wasn't wasted on toys; tricycles were precious and rare. She rode it around the basement feeling, if a three-year-old can have such feelings, privileged and blessed.

Her house, her house. The first time she brought Martin here to dinner she wanted him to see how it was done: cocktails in the living room upstairs, guests descending to a table set with silver and crystal reflecting and refracting the candlelight, and all this a mere setting for the talk, the luster of which outshone any material appointments, for the guests had been chosen and acquired with far more care and effort. Money buys silver. Power, prestige, experience, charm, and talent are needed to amass the human treasure.

Florence wanted to install Martin in her house and provide him with a table around which to gather his friends, with a guest room for the occasional illustrious foreign visitor. She wanted to enlarge what Nadja had created at the magazine and take it to the domestic level, to form a salon. Martin fulfilled her expectations. She can't fault him there. The harvest is already beginning: pages in celebrated memoirs recalling dinners here at which something clever or important was said. Always there is homage to Florence, her beauty, her grace, her talent for bringing people together.

Florence does care about what people think of her. This is why she can't bring herself to knock on her own door and give this girl the opportunity to report to the office that Martin's wife seems to be a little off, slightly unstable. "I'm losing it," Florence says aloud.

EDITH STANDS IN THE HALL WONDERING IF SHE SHOULD wait for Mrs. Weatherstone to realize that she left before she'd meant to, without her purse, possibly without keys. The dog whimpers and leans against Edith's leg. Maybe she should open the door just in case.

Martin is calling: "Flo! Flo, is that Edith?"

"It's me!" On her way Edith stops to look into the living room done in shades of apricot, cream, celadon, colors that would compliment Mrs. Weatherstone's hair and skin and set her off like a jewel. Edith can see her entertaining here evenings with the lights flatteringly low. What happened that made Martin's wife leave so abruptly? What could have dislodged the jewel from its setting?

The bedroom is dark and Martin is pale in the bed, but he looks better than he did last time. He's shaved, for one thing (she can smell cologne) and he's used a comb on his hair. It still holds marks from the teeth.

"Mrs. Weatherstone went out," Edith says.

"Oh? Where?"

"She didn't say."

"Just like that, without telling?"

"I think it might have been—spontaneous. She didn't have a purse with her. I'm not sure she had a key."

Martin dismisses her concern with a wave of the hand. "Florence isn't the kind to lock herself out. She's the essence of practicality. That's why writers and artists love her, because she isn't a dreamer like they are. She remembers their birthdays, their favorite foods, even their allergies. Actually I think she's got

it all on computer now, but still it takes a certain kind of personality even to think those things are important. She has an affinity
for material objects, never misplaces, never loses. Not the kind to
lock herself out."

Martin is so certain, that Edith thinks she must have been
mistaken. She tries to replace what she saw with a different version of Martin's wife.

"What did you bring me?" Martin asks.

"Would it be okay if I opened your drapes? It's really
dark—"

Martin puts a hand up to shade his eyes. Yes, she can open
the French doors if she wants. She exclaims over the trees, the
shaded deck, sensing how her delight pleases him. He used to
work on the deck in the morning, he tells her. If she likes, they
can sit out there. She could move the phone and the papers. No,
he doesn't need help. When Martin stands, Edith sees that he's a
much larger man than she thought, more robust. She was thinking of him as old, like her grandfather, but he's middle-aged, not
much older than Carolyn, who would probably find him attractive.

Martin phones his cardiologist with questions he's gathered
from the research. The doctor is sailing and can't be reached;
there's another number but only for emergencies. Edith suggests
they call her grandfather. He isn't a cardiologist or anything, just
a GP, but he's the only doctor in town and he's been practicing
for over forty years. He might be able to help.

"Edie, is that you? You sound different."

"It's me, Grandpop." What he means is that she's losing her
upstate way of talking, shedding those hick nasal a's. She and
Clarence have both been working on softening their regional ac-
cents. Since she came to the city, Edith's been making great pro-

gress. But she feels fake speaking this way to Grandpop, who somehow makes an upstate accent seem right, and honest.

Just hearing his voice sets off memories of the clinic, the medicinal smell, the throat clearings and subdued voices of the waiting patients, the sudden drama of the bleeding child brought in at the door. Grandpop, short and broad, moving at his own measured but efficient tempo, creating calm and order in the face of the emergency, unforeseen only in its details, because there are always emergencies at the clinic. The memories bring nostalgia. The clinic has already disappeared into time, as if Edith will never be able to take her place there again.

"We were wondering what happened to you," Grandpop re-proaches mildly, and Edith realizes that weeks have gone by since she called. She promises to call home tonight, or maybe tomorrow.

She passes the phone to Martin and leans over the deck rail. A gust of wind lifts her hair. Compton Falls, Grandpop and Carolyn, the clinic, fall behind the horizon as she admires the well-kept gardens enclosed in this block of brownstones. She wonders how many such secret valleys exist in the city, and if they're all as seemingly deserted as this one. She studies the plantings, the flagstone paths, the vine-covered arbors, already thinking of the words she will use to describe it for Clarence later. This is how they imagine Real Life, as going on in the same space, but hidden, unseen, because they haven't found the key, or the code, or the special glasses that allow them to see. She wishes she could get Clarence here to look at the garden and meet Martin.

A sleeping cat wakes and abruptly jumps from a fence. A small tree is shaking on the other side of the wall that surrounds Martin's garden. A foot reaches out tentatively—not a high-top sneaker such as an intruder might wear, but a dainty ballet slip-per—type flat. It's Mrs. Weatherstone, swinging herself onto the top of the wall, very gingerly, because there are rows of barbed wire that she must straddle. She crouches there, knees trembling, eight feet over the stone terrace. Edith looks at Martin talking on the phone. His heart. Don't alarm him.

The woman is mad of course, but silent and deliberate. No cry or gasp comes from her, even when she wavers and Edith closes her eyes—she's so certain that Mrs. Weatherstone's going to fall. What if Mrs. Weatherstone does lose her balance? Should Edith scoop her up quietly and call an ambulance, keep Martin oblivious and protected?

Florence lets herself down the side of the wall, hanging by her hands, her feet dangling. She drops into the flower bed. Fuck! She meant to clear the impatiens. Instead she landed smack in the middle. She scratches in the dirt, heaping soil back onto damaged roots. She'll have to buy new plants to replace what she destroyed.

The doors are locked. She'll break a pane with her shoe and hope the alarm isn't on. What a nuisance. She won't be able to replace the glass until Monday. Florence is just about to break the window when Edith opens the door.

Seeing the girl there, framed by the room, makes Florence feel violated, as if the girl appeared wearing one of Florence's own dresses. Edith inhabits the house with unconscious authority and indeed, she must think that as Martin's child she has more claim on the house than any living soul after Martin and Florence.

"I saw you from the deck upstairs. I thought you might have locked yourself out. Are you all right?"

Mrs. Weatherstone looks at Edith for so long that Edith

wonders if she should explain who she is in case Mrs. Weatherstone has forgotten. Finally Mrs. Weatherstone walks past without saying a word. On her way back to Martin, Edith sees the older woman sitting at the kitchen table, her head in her scratched and bleeding hands.

GERALDINE IS ON ONE OF HER WEEKEND WALKS, HER "REward," she would call it if anyone asked (although no one does) after working most of the day. Weekends Geraldine stays in her apartment, reading manuscripts that require quiet and concentration. She doesn't have Martin's quick brilliance, the kind of intelligence that can home in at once on where a writer has gone astray, what needs to be expanded, what condensed. But neither does Martin have her patience for detail. "I take care of the forest; Geraldine does the trees," Martin used to explain to writers coming into the magazine. He valued her mind for the way it complemented his. In recent years he seems to have forgotten that Geraldine provides this missing piece for him, or he's become so used to the way Geraldine fills in, that he thinks her mind is part of his.

Lately Geraldine has been entertaining a recurring fantasy: She is the one who is ill and Martin is visiting at her bedside. Ovarian cancer. She has fought nobly, but she is dying. Martin tells her that he never realized how much they all relied on her, what a vacuum she's left in the office, blah-blah-blah. Feeling sorry for oneself is something Geraldine's mother could never tolerate, but Mother is gone now and Geraldine is free to indulge. She walks on, head held high, while tears gather behind dark glasses.

Florence feels sorry for her. When she came over the other night, she was comparing Geraldine's ugly rooms to her own spacious house and was pitying Geraldine for having gotten the short end of the stick. Geraldine is Martin's alter ego and heir apparent, but her position can't compare in comfort and ease to that of Martin's wife.

Geraldine wonders if Florence remembers the conversation they had in Geraldine's apartment after the pregnant Lucille had skipped town. Florence brought over a bottle of wine and a pizza. They sat on Geraldine's sofa, the pizza box between them. Florence began by saying that Martin was a genius but like many great men, completely lacking in sense where women were concerned. Of course, she didn't believe Lucille's story, but she could see how it might have happened, how Martin could be seduced by a wily female, even tricked into fathering a child, or thinking he had.

It took a few glasses of wine for Florence to come to the point, not that Florence was drunk, or even tipsy. Alcohol animates her, warms her emotions and sharpens her wit. Geraldine remembers the quality of that night, how close she felt to Florence, like sisters—closer than sisters—as they laughed over poor Martin's ineptitude in matters of love. (Geraldine was fairly inept herself at that age, having had one angst-ridden affair that dragged on past college and was finally over, but Florence had had a whole string of romances; she wore them lightly.)

"Now tell me honestly," Florence said, leaning forward, as if there were crowds of people in Geraldine's tiny apartment who might be listening in, "do you have any romantic feelings toward Martin?"

Geraldine threw back her hair (long then) and laughed, like a pretty girl in a convertible who has dates lined up from here to next St. Swithen's Day. "Oh, God—Martin? No," she said, or words to that effect, when actually, yes, there was a little some-

thing going on between her and Martin, not dating or anything
—they were both so shy—but sometimes they stood nearer to
each other than was necessary, or their hands might brush; his
eyes, she thought, warmed when they looked at her. There was
something, but it was so delicate that it couldn't be named. It
needed time to blossom. Geraldine was certainly not going to
expose it to Florence at this early stage, like a teenager at a slum-
ber party confessing a crush.

"I didn't think so," Florence said. "In fact, I admire your
friendship with Martin. It seems so untouched by sexuality;
you're almost like two male friends. You respect each other's
minds. . . ." (Geraldine recalls a flattering digression here about
how Florence knew for a fact that Martin admired Geraldine's
abilities *enormously* and Geraldine's ears grew hot from the
praise.)

"I'm so glad. I thought you felt that way, but I wanted to be
sure, because if you'd said you were interested in Martin, I would
have backed right out of the picture. But it's silly, each of us
being so careful of the other one's feelings, while someone like
Lucille could come in and steal him from under our noses. He's
such a baby in that respect, so naive. I mean, obviously Martin is
not the sexiest man in the world, but he is—he has needs, after
all. I mean, someone's going to get him. It might as well be one
of us."

Looking back on it now Geraldine can almost laugh at her
poor young self. She swallowed the bait, let herself be reeled in,
and scarcely felt the stunning blow on the head. She was no
match for Florence, with her determination to not only get what
she wanted, but also be loved for it. Florence pulled it off so
skillfully that Geraldine never felt the slightest bit of resentment.
Now Geraldine sees that Florence must have noticed what was

going on between Martin and Geraldine, and decided to put Geraldine out of her misery, because Geraldine would have been no match for Florence.

Later, when Martin took over from Nadja and Florence left the magazine, Geraldine saw that she, not Florence, had gotten the best of the bargain. Geraldine and Martin became more intimate than ever in their working arrangement. Martin consulted her on all issues, great and small. He plumbed her mind and delighted in what he found there. He made her shine, while Florence seemed to lose her glow, at least until she began taking on lovers.

Still, it was Florence who engineered the arrangement and who forced Geraldine into it. Geraldine didn't mind Florence feeling sorry for her the other night. It wouldn't be so bad if Florence were to feel just a twinge of remorse for the way she snatched up Martin years ago. If Geraldine believed in such things anymore—which she doesn't—she would think that Edith's sudden appearance was a judgment on Florence. Maybe this suffering (and Geraldine has seen that Florence is suffering) will be good for Florence, in the end—a purgative for her soul.

Geraldine wanders on, thinking of what a charmed life Florence has led, how everything (pre-Edith) has seemed to work out perfectly for her. She completely loses track of where she is going, when she stops abruptly. Isn't this around where Edith said she was staying? One of these little streets west of Hudson, sharing an artist's loft with a friend. Yesterday, after Florence's nighttime visit when she made Geraldine feel like a gullible fool, Geraldine kept her distance from Edith. She's nervous that Edith will confront her, ask her outright about Martin. What would Geraldine say? She'd have to be truthful; she always is.

Geraldine scans the street, fearing—or hoping?—that she

will see Edith skating down the road, but there's only a woman rummaging through trash. Ordinarily Geraldine turns away before the sight so much as registers in her mind. This time something holds her eye. Perhaps the woman's clothes are of a style and quality one doesn't expect to see on a sifter of garbage, or maybe it's the woman's posture, not furtive, but open, balletic, inviting the onlooker to examine more closely. Whatever the reason, Geraldine's eyes linger long enough for a connection to be made with those eyes, looking straight at hers, seeing into her mind as if twenty years were only a day.

No. Surely not. Geraldine is wearing dark glasses, after all. Lucille may have thought she recognized her, but when Geraldine ducked her head and hurried on, Lucille would have figured she'd been mistaken. Geraldine has almost persuaded herself that Lucille didn't have time to realize who she was, when the laugh comes, pursuing Geraldine in the street, ringing off walls. Geraldine turns the corner, chased by peals of demonic mirth. She runs to the next corner, turns there and runs, then finally stops, hand at her throat, lungs aching.

She allows herself to lean against a brick wall, to catch her breath. The laugh was the laugh of a madwoman, but those eyes were lucid. *She knows everything,* Geraldine thinks, but isn't sure of what she means by everything.

SHAKE, RATTLE, AND ROLL

HENRY PAYS FOR THE CAB AND HOISTS HIS GYM BAG. There isn't much in it—a small towel and a T-shirt so he won't have to wear a sweaty one going home—but all the regulars carry such bags, and Henry is trying to look as if he belongs. He nods to a couple of homeboys passing on the stairs, taking two at a time not even breathing hard and keeping up their cretinous conversation, while Henry labors up three flights trying to save himself for the last one, which can be seen from inside on closed-circuit TV. He ducks his head so the camera won't pick up his face—fat, pale, and anxious. It's an unlikely time for him to be up and out in the morning, seven-thirty, and an unlikely place, a bodybuilder's gym, far uptown on the edge of Harlem.

Martin and the other senior staffers are still treating fitness like a yuppie fad, something to poke fun at, nothing anyone would admit to being interested in, although Henry suspects some of being secret joggers. *Ubu* has never run a piece on fitness (think of the advertising revenue they're passing over—for athletic shoes alone).

He's only slightly winded when he presents his card at the desk. "Hi, Louie." "How's it goin', Henry." He's been coming for only two weeks and already he's known at the desk. Henry squares his shoulders and looks around at the racks of iron plates for the dumbbells, the lifting benches bolted to the floor, the stainless-steel machines with pulleys and weights, reminiscent of medieval torture devices. Over by the windows Parker is on the StairMaster. He told Henry that when he's on it he is fueled by rushes of pure rage; he imagines himself tromping down a beast that keeps rising under his feet. Parker is responsible for introducing Henry to this alien environment. He talks obsessively about his "trainer," Steve, as if Parker were a fighter instead of a middle-aged literary agent. As a gift to Henry for his thirty-fifth birthday, Parker gave him a session with Steve. After that Henry's been coming on his own, five days a week. At seventy-five dollars a pop, Steve's an investment.

Thirty-five hit Henry with a force he hadn't anticipated. He'd thought he was impervious to birthdays. Thirty had been a breeze, an occasion for a party, nothing more. He was still young then for someone with his position, a boy wonder. Right before Henry's thirty-fifth, events piled up: two close friends died of AIDS; a former lover discovered he was HIV positive; Martin had a heart attack. Henry was suddenly aware of more space around him for expansion and also that time was limited. He could have forty years left, or four. But time was, even for him, finite.

Parker has been helping him through the transition. Parker talked Henry into letting Maya Freese handle his personal publicity. Henry didn't have to promise anything, just show up for a lunch with Maya and Parker. Maya won't expect payment; she knows salaries at the magazine are meager. Maya handles big names in entertainment, business, politics. It's worth it to her to have a friend at *Ubu,* especially since everyone else at the magazine treats publicists as if they were bearers of moral contagion. "Publicists are as necessary a part of the media as journalists," Henry said to Maya over lunch. Parker smiled. Henry is already getting more notice. His picture was in the Styles section of the *Times* last Sunday. Maya's a real pro. Of course, if Martin knew about Maya, he'd throw a fit. But there's no danger of word reaching Martin, who's virtually isolated himself.

Bruno and Henry talk about how Martin's lost interest. Bruno's an insomniac. He calls from Munich when it's three in the morning, his time. He likes having someone to talk to and Henry's happy to oblige.

Henry gets on the StairMaster next to Parker, and they nod curtly. Just last Saturday night, at the benefit in South Hampton, they hugged and kissed. Here they maintain the code of the gym, which is straight, veering toward homophobic. If Henry and Parker weren't under Steve's paid protection, they would not be made to feel as comfortable. Incidents might occur. There are other gyms where gays are welcome, but Parker won't go to them. Too many queers asking for favors, he says. Parker's a bit of a homophobe himself. He's been celibate for years, says that he figures the more people you know, the more unhealthy your life is. Parker's eyes are fixed on the screen of the StairMaster, but they catch Steve's entrance and follow him, turning away just in time so that Steve has to call out: "How's it going, Parker?"

Today Steve has a new exercise for Henry's ass. "I invented it in my sleep," he says. "You dreamed about my ass last night? I'm touched," Henry says. He gets down on a bench on all fours while Steve straps a leather cuff to his ankle.

"Are you sure this isn't going to make it even bigger?"

"Henry, you are going to have beautiful buns, believe me."

EDITH IS ON THE PHONE WITH HER GRANDFATHER. SHE went out Saturday night with Ben. He came over again on Sunday, so she forgot she'd promised to call.

"Edith, I've been thinking of your editor friend, Martin, and he reminds me of Billy Stout. . . . Oh, you remember him, darling. He had the car dealership out on Corey Road."

"Stout's Chevrolet?"

"That's the one. He had a heart attack, not too serious, same as your friend, but he wouldn't go back to work, wouldn't get out of bed. He was paralyzed—spiritually. He didn't leave the house for a year."

"What happened to him?"

"The business went all to hell, and his wife finally talked him into going back to work."

"And he was all right?"

"He died two, three weeks later."

"Of a heart attack?"

"Struck by lightning, on the golf course."

"Weird."

"Sometimes they get that way. Active men. They use the heart as an excuse to take a rest."

"I mean it was strange that he was struck by lightning."

"You remember that, don't you, darling? You must have been in grammar school."

"Oh, yeah. Somebody died on the golf course."

"That was Billy."

"But his heart was okay, before he was struck by lightning?"

"Evidently. By the way, have you met Lucille?"

"I've been real busy. I was going to look her name up in the phone book, but we don't have one in the loft, and I haven't gotten around to it."

There's silence on the other end.

"Grandpop?"

"You haven't just run in to her?"

"This is a big place, Grandpop. It isn't Compton Falls."

"But it's also a small world, smaller than you think. You know—uh—I don't want to be disloyal, but Carolyn may have given you a wrong impression. Lucille wasn't a monster. She was just a girl who had a baby too soon. I think you might find you have a lot in common. . . ."

With her other ear, Edith hears a voice on the radio talking about another day of record-breaking heat. Edith doesn't mind; she's getting used to it.

"It's a question of identity. Everyone faces it, but when you're adopted, the mystery is deeper—you see, darling?"

Through the scrim of the grime-coated window, she sees Clarence walking with a woman whose long loose hair and easy gait seem familiar, but not until they're crossing the street does Edith recognize the woman as the crazy lady downstairs. Edith had mistaken her for someone much younger.

LULU IS RETURNING FROM A VERY EARLY MEETING WITH her landlord, or gallery owner—well, the guy who owns the space where she intends to hold her show, she explains to Clarence. Josh Montero. He called the meeting early because he's a busy man, an art broker of sorts. He'll make the connection between the gallery that has the buyer but not the right piece and the dealer or collector who has the piece. Ancient art, mainly. He works from his home a lot and there's a certain amount of time he spends schmoozing with dealers and collectors. Plus he has a wife and baby.

The problem, as Montero put it to her last Friday afternoon when she went over to measure the space, was that he had a possible tenant for the gallery, and he didn't see how he could let her put in her installation as it would mean thousands of dollars in lost revenue for the month. He wouldn't give her the name of the potential tenant. He must have known that she could have checked it with her friends. He came closer. Didn't she believe him, didn't she trust him? he asked.

Lulu put the tape measure into the pocket of her skirt. She was neither alarmed nor surprised. When she made the arrangement with Montero, she suspected that she might have to pay in this manner. It isn't as if Montero is repulsive physically. He could lose a little around the middle, but he is a good ten years younger than she. She might even feel flattered that she still has something to offer in that department. He's crude, that's all. The mattress in the back. It was evident that he'd used it before. The whole thing could have been demeaning if she hadn't taken control, brought a clean cover from home, and insisted on taking her pleasure as well. By the time they'd finished he was quite sweet. He promised to deliver the art critic from *The Observer* to her opening. She said she had another friend working on it, but thanks just the same. She doesn't want her name linked with Montero. He's not her image.

. . .

CLARENCE, IN SPOTLESS WHITE JEANS (TOO TIGHT) AND aloha shirt, slicked-back hair still wet from the shower of whomever he stayed with last night, steps out of the elevator singing, picks Edith up, and swings her around. "I fell in love, deeply and truly."

"That seems to happen every weekend," Edith says. Clarence dances her a few turns around the floor, and they go into the Fred and Ginger routine that has made them somewhat famous back at Grimsby College. Clarence dips her and then she dips him back.

The new love of his life is a freelance photographer with a loft near the Seaport. He's only twenty-five, but he knows everyone. He's crazy for Clarence, but Clarence isn't going to let himself be too available, he says primly. Edith says that spending the night with someone isn't exactly playing hard to get. Clarence says that he might not be available tonight. He might be busy if this photographer calls, which he hopes he does. And how about Edie? That boy was kind of cute, her date on Saturday. Is it love? He's nice, Edith says, but she's not a romantic like Clarence, not ready to declare herself deeply and truly in love. And no, he did not spend the night. "It's a little soon for that," Edith says, spinning out from Clarence.

"It's always too soon for you, until it's too late," Clarence says.

Coming from anyone else, this remark would hurt, but Clarence and Edith have been over this ground many times, how Edith can never quite get to the point of having sex with a man, although she's had plenty of opportunities. It's Clarence's role to heckle and badger and urge her to "get it over with."

"You are not going to be young and beautiful forever," he says. "When I think of the examples of American manhood you've passed up, I could cry. You're frittering away your youth, holding on to your virginity as if it were a prize. These are the nineties, girlfriend. Nobody is a virgin anymore—not even twelve-year-olds are virgins anymore. And the way you dress—it's so butch. If I had your looks, I would flaunt it—wear slits up to my navel to show off my legs, get things cut down to here to show my cleavage."

"And you'd be raped before you got to the corner," Edith says. "People who dress like that do business down in the meat-packing neighborhood, and they're all transvestites."

"Only drag queens dress like real women anymore, and only queers appreciate romance. At least you should wear your hair loose again, instead of in that dorky pigtail. I mean you have the kind of hair—in Brazil they would come up to you on the street and cut it off your head. They do that there—hair snatching," Clarence says.

Edith goes to braid her hair at the bathroom sink, keeping the door open so they can talk.

"I hope that boy you were with wasn't a ghost date—someone you went out with just because it was Saturday night. We came here to start leading Real Life, remember?" Clarence calls after her.

Edith hasn't really considered whether Ben is "R. L." or "ghost." She'd like to talk to Clarence about it, but she hasn't time. She really wants to talk about Martin, but she needs a whole evening for that. There's so much she hasn't filled Clarence in on. Instead she says, "I saw you walking with garbage-lady. What was she doing out so early?"

Clarence takes his waiter shirt out of his gym bag and sniffs the armpits. "She was having a meeting with the guy who owns the gallery where she's going to do her thing."

"A meeting this early?"

"I suspect it was a sexual payoff," Clarence says.

Edith twists a holder into the end of her braid.

"You know, payment. Body barter. She doesn't have money."

"Gross."

"Maybe I'm wrong. They had that post-coitus look, you know. I met them as they were coming out. His hand was on her hip."

"She's such a—" Edith stops herself. She was going to use a word Carolyn might have employed, *slut*.

"You don't like her do you? You get very high and mighty. I've never seen you this way about anyone."

Edith considers for a moment. Clarence is right. She's thinking like Carolyn. She can feel her face turning into Carolyn's. She peers at her reflection, then slaps herself lightly on both cheeks.

"What's that about?"

"I don't know what it is, Clare. Something about Lulu makes me turn into my mother—into Carolyn! I get self-righteous or something. I guess I have a thing about women like that, who don't work, who pay with their friendship or even sex. It's so fake and it's so—I don't know. Women should have evolved away from that behavior. It isn't necessary."

Clarence puts his cheek next to hers so they are both looking in the mirror. "I know why she gets to you, you know what it is? She looks a little like you. Around the mouth. You're afraid you'll grow up to be Lulu."

Edith twists the tap on hard and squirts water into Clarence's face. He lunges for her and misses as she slips by.

"Coward! Come back and fight like a woman," he calls.

"I'm late for work. See you."

Clarence, wiping the water away, examining his features in the mirror, wondering how he appeared last night to Francis, tries on some expressions. Pleasant: too bland, reminiscent of his yearbook picture when he hid behind the mask of an innocuous smile. Alert and stern: too much like his dad. Delighted: too much like his mom, the social smile she pastes on her face when she goes out with Dad. Sexy: too dumb, like his next-oldest brother Andy. Clarence can't seem to get a face of his own, one that doesn't borrow something from his family. Maybe he wore an entirely different expression for Francis, one that never appears in photos or mirrors, one that eludes the self and can be observed only by strangers.

To GERALDINE'S AMAZEMENT, MARTIN IS NOT IN HIS BED this morning but on the deck, dressed, sitting in a lounge chair with the phone at his side. "Oh Martin!" Impulsively she takes his hand. "You look wonderful. You're feeling better—" He slips his hand out of hers, but her joy is undiminished. She's aware of a burden being lifted, as if she's been keeping some monster at bay and reinforcements are arriving. "Then you're coming back."

"I was never *not* coming back. I was waiting to get stronger—"

"Of course. But it's good to see you progressing." She pulls a chair over to sit beside him. "I can't do it alone, you know. It's too much—"

"Well, Henry—"

"Henry's the problem!" Geraldine says.

Martin flinches. Geraldine forces herself to sit back in her chair. She fumbles in her bag for cigarettes. "Martin, are you aware that Henry had lunch with Maya Freese? He was seen having lunch with Maya—"

"Henry likes to keep up, and Maya knows everyone." Martin waves the back of his hand in her direction, as if already fending off smoke from the cigarette she has yet to light.

"Martin, would *you* go to lunch with Maya Freese?"

Martin rolls his eyes.

"There's a reason for that, Martin! We keep ourselves aloof from publicists, from influence mongering. We're the only magazine that keeps itself pure from the taint of—"

"Geraldine, you spent too many years in Catholic girls' schools—"

Geraldine gets up to light her cigarette. She blows the smoke over the deck railing. Martin must never know how he can wound her. In the hospital when he comes to see her, as she lies dying of cancer . . . She takes a fierce drag and focuses on the garden, where Florence, on her knees, is scratching in the dirt. It never occurred to Geraldine that Florence does her own gardening, but there she is, in gardening gloves, wielding a trowel in the flower bed by the wall. Geraldine had wondered if Florence had begun coloring her hair, and now she sees that she has and is overdue for a touch-up. In fact, Florence looks almost disheveled, not herself at all.

"Edith is your discovery, isn't she?" Martin says.

Geraldine exhales slowly, using the cigarette as an excuse to keep her back to him. "She sent a letter, asking for an interview. It was addressed to me so I answered. Henry was put out. For some reason, he thinks hiring interns is his private—"

"But you knew first thing, didn't you?"

"Yes," Geraldine hears, as if her voice is coming from another place. *Yes, Martin, I brought your child back to you, the one you denied, the one you—*

"It shines forth. She's one of those extraordinary people. Not only physically, but intellectually. And yet she's modest, open."

"Well, Edith is certainly—"

"She said she'd like to do one of the front-of-the-book pieces. Nothing major. After all, she'll be going back to school in September."

"That's impossible!" She wheels around. Martin's glasses reflect the light, hiding his eyes. "You know interns never get assigned—it's not done," she says.

"It's not done." Martin mocks her in a prissy tone. Geraldine could hate him, she realizes. She sees how devotion could turn to loathing.

"If you're so set upon giving Edith an assignment, you do it. I'm not going to take this one on myself and have most of the junior staff up in arms. This is one time when you can do your own dirty work." Her voice cracks. She busies herself, stacking papers, organizing. Martin pretends he didn't hear her last remark. In her mind, she is already editing it, phrasing it in less emotional terms. She wishes she could retract it and give another version, but with the same—the exact same—content.

Seen in profile, he suddenly looks frail, not strong at all. What if he dies tonight, she thinks, with these last angry words on his mind. She moves toward him, as if she might—she doesn't know what—throw herself at his side and put her head in his lap, beg for understanding—after all these years he owes her that.

He turns toward her, light flashing off his glasses like a

shield, his mouth a tightened, narrow slit. She takes her papers and leaves, as if she just remembered something important she had to do elsewhere.

FLORENCE IS WAITING AT THE BOTTOM OF THE STAIRS. Does Geraldine have time for an iced coffee? Florence has fixed her hair and put on lipstick, but once they're in the kitchen Geraldine notices scratches on Florence's hands. "How did you do that?"

Florence shrugs. "Gardening." Geraldine can't imagine anything on Florence's well-kept terrace that would inflict such wounds. And didn't she see Florence wearing gardening gloves? She's gone quite gray at the roots, and she's getting little pucker lines around the lips. Geraldine can see what she will look like as an old woman—jittery and lonely, not what Geraldine would have predicted for Florence even a month ago.

"I saw Lucille," Geraldine says.

"In your office?" Sarcasm doesn't suit Florence; that's Martin's game.

"It was by chance. Sunday afternoon. I was walking around where Edith lives, I believe. I passed a homeless woman rummaging in a garbage can. For some reason, I turned to look at her and it was Lucille."

"Well," Florence says, as if a prison sentence has been handed down, unfortunate, but not entirely unexpected. "Did she recognize you?"

"Yes, it seems she did. At least, she laughed—"

"She didn't say anything, just laughed?"

"A maniacal laugh."

"What was her appearance? Unkempt? Layers of clothing despite the heat?"

"No, actually. That's what attracted my attention in the first place. Ordinarily I don't—"

"Of course."

"She was clean, at least, for someone rummaging in trash."

"Drunk? Had she been drinking?"

"Not, no—it was hard to tell. That laugh!"

"But she knew you, you said."

"Evidently."

"You spoke to her?"

"Not exactly. I was wearing dark glasses. I hoped she wouldn't recognize me—I—"

"Go on," Florence says.

"Well, that's it. I walked away, without making any sign of recognition, and Lucille began laughing. Just laughing. That sound!"

Florence looks at Geraldine, as if she's not sure she's getting the full story, as if some detail is missing, and she can't decide whether to probe further or let it go. Geraldine lights a cigarette, though she knows Florence will mind smoke in the house. Florence goes to the phone.

"Who are you calling?"

"Information."

There is no listing for Lucille Arslanian. Geraldine didn't figure there would be.

"She must be living with Edith," Florence says.

"Why would Edith let her own mother go through garbage cans—"

"I don't know. I don't know what her plan is." Florence rubs the scratches on her hands. "Obviously she has a plan—"

"That's crazy—" Geraldine says, then stops, because Florence really does look unhinged. She thinks of Lucille, and the way Geraldine herself reacted when she saw her, which wasn't exactly rational. Are they all cracking up?

PEYTON COMES IN LATE FROM HER LUNCH. "I'M EX-hausted." She flops into a chair, her long legs encroaching on Edith's space. Ben and Edith feign intense interest in their respective tasks.

"How did it go? Did you find anything?" Kylie asks.

Oh, Peyton's so bored with it all, but she manages to tell Kylie, in great detail, all the things "Mom" insisted on buying for her. At Princeton you have to dress sometimes, it's just required. Ben holds a pencil under his nose with his upper lip and waggles his brows. Edith giggles. Peyton leaves and doesn't come back for an hour.

THE FRONT OF THE MAGAZINE USUALLY HAS ONE SERIOUS editorial on an issue of national or international import. The rest of the pieces are lighter: an interview with a local eccentric, a visit to a quirky museum. These are unsigned. Thus major writers can dabble in a bit of froth; neophytes can see their work right up next to the big guns. The front of the book accords with the general democratic philosophy at the magazine.

Naturally the junior staffers have their eyes fixed on this entrée into the magazine. It is the prize they all covet—the copy editors, the fact-checkers, even secretaries and mail-sorters. The interns never get a crack at writing for the magazine. Their only hope is to make it to a paying position, and from there jockey for an assignment.

All of this is not chiseled in stone over the doorway. It is just something everyone knows. "Interns don't write," Ben said to Edith early on. It's not as if Edith didn't know the rules, but when she is with Martin she is aware of possibilities. She sees that paths can be blazed. And there is something about Martin that puts her at her ease. In the office everyone seems a little afraid of him, but maybe because Edith met him in his home and even wore his bathrobe, she feels comfortable around Martin. He treats her more like a friend of the family than some minion from the office, talking to her as if she were an equal, wanting her opinion. "Martin, do you think I might be able to write a front-of-the-book piece?" she asked as she was leaving on Saturday. He looked surprised, and then pleased. "Why not? I'll tell Geraldine to get you involved in something."

IT IS HENRY WHO FEELS THE GROUND SHAKE WHEN MARtin calls and asks him to give Edith an assignment—"just something for the front of the book," he says offhandedly. That Martin is phoning at all is a momentous occasion, a first since the heart attack. That the call should involve an intern, when Martin doesn't usually bother even to learn their names, is a seismic occurrence.

Edith passes in the hall. Henry invites her in. She stands in front of his desk. Take a seat, he says. She intrigues him, has so ever since he first saw her—or ever since he first saw Geraldine seeing her. It interested him that the girl had a power over Geraldine, one that she exercised unself-consciously, as if it were her right. This is why Henry sent the girl to Martin that rainy day. It interests Henry to put the pieces into play, even if he doesn't understand the pieces or the game. And it worked. There was a connection. In her mysterious way the girl seems to be able to influence Martin as well.

There's a sexuality to this girl—not blatant or studied—but

natural. If it were anyone but Martin, Henry would say he was putting the moves on her, but Martin is asexual. He's famous for it. Everyone knows that Florence had to go elsewhere for her satisfaction, and that was fine with Martin. Henry always assumed that Martin sublimated sexuality into work, which was why his mind could be so focused. Henry can't believe that Martin is chasing after some little skirt at this stage in life.

But he's obviously smitten, even if it's not in an overtly sexual way. And Florence is jealous; she asked Henry not to send Edith over to the house anymore. And Geraldine, too, didn't want Edith to go there. Disturbance attracts Henry. Martin, flanked by his two loyal women, Geraldine and Florence, has always been as stable, as inviolable, as a great stone Buddha. Now the earth is moving and the stone rocks.

"MARTIN ASKED ME. WHAT COULD I DO?" HENRY SAYS when Geraldine confronts him in his office. It's the end of the day, but his face glows, shiny and pink, like a schoolboy's in the morning. Geraldine knows he's mocking her but she hears herself going on.

"You could have refused, as I did. You could have backed me up and reminded Martin that the whole junior staff will be put out of joint by an intern—"

"I've already taken care of that. I'm giving everyone a crack at the front of the book. Everyone has an assignment—copy editors, interns, everyone." His voice is smooth, and he rolls a jade paperweight in his immaculate hands. He's toying with her, leading her on. Geraldine understands this, but she can't help crashing ahead.

"That's completely against the culture of the magazine,

which is noncompetitive, supportive, nurturing. It's going to turn this place into a pit of vipers. In a single gesture, you have shaken the magazine to the core," she says.

Henry turns his smile on her and opens his hands, rolling the jade onto his desk and setting it upright. It's a Buddha. Even in her anguish and rage, Geraldine notes that it is beautifully carved, expensive, and wonders how Henry came by it. He puts a finger on the Buddha's head and rocks it slowly side to side. She turns to go before he can lead her even further into self-parody. Already she senses that others are listening behind partitions, exchanging smiles over her histrionics.

"Shake, rattle, and roll," is what she thinks she hears Henry say to her back as she leaves.

THE SIGN

THIS IS A GOOD DAY. THE THOUGHT MOVES THROUGH Lulu's mind letter by letter like a bulletin in lights spelling out a message—a prophecy, Lulu wonders, or simply a statement of what exists at the present time? She did have luck this morning at the garbage cans. QB (she's decided to call her subject QB as in Questing Beast) must have brought a load out on his way to work. There were two Coke cans and three Perrier bottles, enough to put her over-the-top for her cappuccino. And his copy of the *Times,* which he often leaves elsewhere, perhaps at the office. QB does the crossword, and Lulu treasures these half-finished puzzles as footprints of his mind. He knows sports, Latin, French, current films, and TV. He's weak on popular culture before the seventies and current fiction. Surprisingly, he knows birds. Lulu cuts the puzzle out and adds it to her collection.

On the front page is a story about a man who disguises himself as a dog—Lulu has seen him. He's a homeless schizophrenic who's okay when he's on medicine, but sometimes he refuses or forgets to take it, and then he puts on the dog suit and goes around menacing people in the Soho-TriBeCa area. Every once in a while, the police haul him off to Creedmoor, but as soon as he has stabilized, he is released. A neighborhood association is arguing that he should be kept in the institution, but for legal reasons he can't and is being released today.

Lulu sips her cappuccino. She's sitting on the mattress in the back of Montero's space. Montero said she could work here. "You might as well, since I can't rent it until your show. Hey, we made a bargain and I'm good to my word. Ask anyone. They'll tell you." The offer was hardly altruistic on Montero's part. He likes having her here, indebted and convenient. Maybe he likes her. Yesterday he sent over cans of paint, a roller, brushes, and a ladder so she could do the walls.

When she hears the key in the door—Montero making an unscheduled visit—she isn't surprised. It often happens this way. Montero arrives, telling her he had to break an appointment or cut a meeting short to get to her. Today he's decided to be diffident. He strolls in, examines the paint, asks if she thinks she can do a good job, has she had experience with this sort of thing. She answers without looking up from the newspaper.

"You're wearing a suit," she says.

"Yeah, well, I have some meetings uptown—"

"And you just stopped in to look at the paint?"

"I want to make sure it's all right, if you know what I mean. The right kind of paint."

"It seems fine."

"Great, well—" He jingles the change in his pockets, paces in front of her while she slowly turns the pages of the newspaper.

"Oh, hell!" He tugs at his tie, yanks at his buttons, as if someone has dressed him in this finery against his will. He paws at her clothes, too. Hurry, hurry.

Gonads are without humor. It's the conscious mind reflecting on the antics of the body that makes sex funny. She would laugh at the cries, the gasps, the smack of sweat-slicked skin, the surprising perspectives she gets when her head winds up in odd places during frenzied gymnastics, but her thoughts are short-circuited by insistent messages from ordinarily mute body parts: follicles, epidermis, sweat glands, mucous membranes.

There are tears on his cheeks. She wipes them with the side of her hand and thinks she's done it before. What makes him weep, she wonders, but doubts if he could give an answer if asked. She strokes his back, hoping to keep him a minute or two longer. He's always the first to collect himself, often walking out the door while she's still dazed. Abruptly he looks at his watch and turns his back to get into his shorts. She lies spread-legged, in a mocking pose because she understands that he's blaming her for luring him here.

Surely he's fallen into such situations before, affairs that make no sense. The barter arrangement—sex for rent—was a ruse, a rationalization their minds agreed on in order to let their bodies have their way.

"I'm supposed to be uptown—" he says.

"Then go." She has one hand on her pubic bone, the other across her breasts. She closes her eyes and hears him grumbling. Her pelvis arches. He's beside her, wriggling out of clothes he just put on. A laugh rolls up from her belly and he joins in.

This time he is the one left dazed, still gathering his clothes and wondering how an hour went by, while she is tucking her hair into a cap, preparing to paint. As she mixes the paint, she decides that he in fact has not had experience with this kind of thing, does not understand the way it operates outside of time. He will try to make sense of it, give it a past and a future, not comprehending that it exists only in a sealed bubble of the present. He's trying to discover how it fits into his life, when it doesn't. Montero is a practical man: He has provided this bower for their trysts; he gave her the paint; he will try to contain, schedule, and control this thing, tame it and, eventually and inevitably, kill it.

Montero is fussing over his suit jacket, dusty from having fallen to the floor. He finishes her cold cappuccino as she pours paint into a roller pan. "I could have been out of here an hour ago. You tricked me."

"What if we'd been having lunch and you'd had to leave and I'd said, 'Go ahead, I think I'll stay for another cup of coffee.' It's the same thing."

Montero rubs his jacket with his shirt sleeve. "I don't know how I got messed up with you."

"It was your idea." Lulu has climbed the ladder. From this perspective, Montero looks like a rumpled, petulant boy.

He brushes off his trousers. "Another thing. This floor is ruining my clothes."

"It's your floor, Montero. Why don't you have it scraped and poly'ed. It would enhance the value."

Montero has his leather-bound appointment book open. "I'm busy all the rest of this week. How about Friday at five?"

"For the floor?"

He scowls.

"I'm always here. You know that."

When Montero leaves he locks the door as if the space with Lulu in it is his property. Would it upset him to know that there's a man who wants to marry her? She hasn't told Montero about Larry, but then she hasn't told Montero much of anything. Larry will be back in a week, wanting her to drop everything and run off to the Berkshires and look at houses. Her schedule could become crowded. Molly, giving advice over the phone, said Lulu should accommodate Larry, who's rich and adores her. "Men like Larry don't come along every day, not for women in our age group. You have to think of the future." But the show might be her big break. Opportunities like a one-woman show don't come along every day either, Lulu objected. Over the line there was the sound of words unspoken.

Lulu said Molly was always accusing her of not finishing projects, not carrying through on her impulses. Well, this was one thing she *was* going to finish. Then Molly said she couldn't even talk to Lulu if Lulu couldn't see that she was using the show to escape from other projects unfinished, namely Larry and Desert Ray.

Molly is disappointed that the mother-daughter reunion has not taken place. She can't understand why Lulu is not making herself known to Ray. "I behaved badly in front of her, before I knew who she was," Lulu said. "Behaved badly? What does that mean? Did she see you chewing out a cab driver? Dancing on a table? What could you have done that would be that bad?" Lulu said that she hadn't made the kind of impression on Ray that she would have liked, and that the girl had turned against her, decided she was a certain kind of person—it was hard to explain.

Of all Lulu's friends, Molly has known her the longest. She knows Lulu's history, the marriages, the affairs. They met at

Parsons and were in that first group show together. They both married older, wealthy men. Molly stayed married to hers. Lulu has been married three times. The first lasted eighteen months, the second three months, and the third six weeks. It has been a long time since she's had either a husband or a home.

Three abandoned husbands. One abandoned child. Molly contends that Lulu repeats a pattern—leaving loved ones before they can leave her the way her parents did. Lulu sometimes thinks that it is the reverse: She is so desperate to set down roots that she does it badly, chooses stony ground instead of fertile. It is possible that she and Molly are both right: She is desperate to establish a family and terrified that she will and that it will founder.

For the first three months after Desert Ray was born, Lulu didn't leave the commune, never went into town. She hid herself and the baby in a farmhouse without electricity and running water, "like a wild animal," the doctor said, scolding her for not coming in for inoculations for the baby, frightening her with stories of what could have happened.

It's as if the baby understood from birth that she and her mother were surviving on charm. Ray was a delight to hold; she'd go to anyone; she was quick to smile, slow to cry. And Lulu behaved impeccably. She was a friend to all, male and female; made no sexual liaisons, thus avoiding enemies. She cooked; she sang; Ray cooed and smiled. Madonna and child. The commune pets. They would be living there still if the summer had gone on forever.

But summer left around the first week in October. The harvest, which was supposed to keep them through the winter, was disappointing. Most of the commune went south like migrating birds. Lulu caught a cold and gave it to the baby. One night Ray woke screaming, burning hot. Lulu stayed up bathing Ray's limbs in cool water. In the morning she bundled her in blankets and hitched a ride to the clinic in town, where she met the doctor who wanted Ray for his own daughter.

Lulu is painting the wall. She is good at this. She is good at almost anything she puts her hand to. She probably could have found a way to keep the baby if it hadn't been so cold, if Ray hadn't been ill (it was only an ear infection, as it turned out), if the doctor hadn't been so determined.

Lulu tries to think of the path her life might have taken if she'd kept Ray, but, looking back at it now, the path seems as blocked as it did then, life's possibilities reduced. She makes a mark on the wall, a point of stasis, the point of going nowhere. Then she rolls two intersecting lines through. She stands back and looks at what she's made, a white X on a dingy wall. She chooses one line and extends it to the end of the wall. This is life with Larry in Massachusetts. How far it is from the nexus of choice. With her roller she makes other paths, long and short radiating from the center, a starburst of possibilities. Finally she obliterates the design with long smooth strokes until the wall is uniformly white. As she is doing this, it occurs to her that she and Montero may have found each other in order to undo the order they have created in their lives, as an excuse to throw out the plan and start from the beginning. She steps back and looks at the wall, blank, a surface waiting to be marked, engraved, incised, spattered, decorated. A beginning.

The sun, having cleared roofs of buildings across the street, penetrates the veil of dusty windows and licks the edges of her neat piles of garbage, the unconscious or considered castoffs of QB, whose portrait she hopes to discover in the pattern of his refuse.

What did QB mean to her and why was she seeking him? Clarence asked Lulu. Nothing, she said. The Questing Beast was only an excuse for the quest. Clarence said something must be driving her, that there were risks involved in sifting through someone's garbage. There had to be a strong motivating force. Risk was part of it, Lulu answered, as well as the breaking of a social taboo by invading garbage cans. And part of it was the urge to reorder that which has become disordered, reversing entropy by an act of will. QB was randomly chosen because the dumber the choice, the more open-ended the search, the more possibility there was for discovery.

Clarence had been satisfied with her answer, and Lulu had thought it was brilliant. Now, as she walks around her treasure piles, she wonders if she's really found anything or if she's only covered up, with all this activity, something she would not find.

MARTIN, WHO IS ACTUALLY SPORTING A SUNTAN NOW, AS if he's been vacationing in some seaside villa instead of convalescing at home, greets Geraldine from his chair on the deck. He rhapsodizes over the weather, the perfection of a summer day and so forth. It's the first Geraldine has noticed the weather, although she's been up for hours. She admits that it seems to be decent, rare in this summer of devastating heat punctuated by catastrophic rains. She's annoyed with Martin for not sharing in the general concern over the alarming change in weather patterns, for having missed so much, shut up in his air-conditioned bedroom. It might get hot later, she cautions.

She has just come from her hair colorist, but she won't tell Martin this. What everyone thinks is a fluke of nature, the dramatic silver streak, is actually a carefully maintained bit of artifice to which she devotes a couple of hours every five weeks and a scandalous amount of money. Her colorist, Basil Smith, a one-time painter, is a genius, but he's becoming too well known. The place was jammed with women from the publishing and art worlds, having their heads repaired for the Photographers' Ball. It's a charity event for photographers with AIDS. *Ubu* always gets a table. Geraldine assumed she'd go this year as always, but the date slipped her mind.

"Martin, did you know the Photographers' Ball is this weekend?"

"Geraldine, have you seen the paper?" Martin waves the *Times* at her.

"Something about the ball?"

"It's terrible. Read this."

It's an article about a homeless maniac. Geraldine says it's deplorable that a story like this, which should be in the B section, is featured on the front page. "It's that new regime over there. You used to be able to count on finding only major national and international—"

"Did you notice the neighborhood, Geraldine, the neighborhood in which the madman stalks his prey?"

Geraldine scans the piece once more.

"That's where Edith lives. A young girl like that walking home alone nights unprotected. She attracts attention. It's almost inevitable."

Geraldine has already thought about getting Edith away, far away, from that part of the city, because of Lucille. Geraldine really can't imagine, as Florence would have it, that Edith is actually living with Lucille. She doesn't believe that Edith even knows about the woman. If Edith were trying to keep a secret of that magnitude and complexity, it would spill out into all her dealings with Geraldine, and Geraldine hasn't detected a single false note in anything Edith says or does. However, Edith is bound to run into Lucille sooner or later. The homeless typically occupy small areas; they're homeless, but they have a sense of territory. It's possible that Lucille roams Edith's neighborhood daily. The shock of recognizing one's own mother sifting through trash—how could Edith survive it?

"I've been thinking of inviting Edith to move in with me for a while. I have a sofa."

"We have a whole floor—two rooms completely furnished. It's criminal to have vacant rooms while he's wandering those streets —I'd never forgive myself."

"I'm not sure Florence would go for it," Geraldine says. It's marvelous how stupid Martin can be, how completely blind he is when it comes to his own wife. He's made her into a posterboard cutout, the smiling image of the perfect hostess-wife, opaque and flat. He refuses to acknowledge her dimensions or her mutability.

"Florence loves having guests." Martin waves off Geraldine's objection. "And she'll feel free to get out more if she knows there's someone else in the house. It's a perfect symbiotic relationship."

Geraldine smiles at his choice of words, because Edith has not come into Martin's life to comfort him in his old age. Edith, however unwittingly, has come to expose them for what they did —all of them, Geraldine, Florence, and Martin. And Martin calls the relationship symbiotic! A majestic oak might feel the same if some young vine laid a tendril on its root. How long would it take the oak to catch on to the peril, to realize that the vine was covering its leaves, robbing it of sunlight until at last the oak was only a lifeless stick supporting the vigorous, still growing, still reaching vine. *Parasitic, not symbiotic, Martin. Look at your own wife, the scratches on her hands, the way she has of muttering out loud. It's already beginning.*

"Did you know the Photographers' Ball is this weekend, Martin? Has *Ubu* taken a table? I wasn't notified."

"I left all that up to Henry. It's his crowd, his thing."

"But I should be there, too, to represent the magazine—"

"You always hate it—"

"That's not the point. If Henry's there and I'm not, it sends a message—"

"Well, you don't have to get whiny about it—"

"I'm not whining—"

"If it means that much to you, simply tell Henry. He's got a whole goddamned table."

Geraldine asks if she can smoke. "Sit downwind," he says, and then regrets being unkind to Geraldine, his oldest and most loyal friend, more loyal than Florence, certainly, or Henry. Until recently his relations with Geraldine were pure, uncomplicated. Working with her, their two minds seamlessly meshing, has at times brought them near to ecstasy. Yes! It's no exaggeration. They understand each other's mental processes. Intimately. In a way, it's more intimate than sex.

It's that ridiculous affair Geraldine had that changed things between them. It threw Geraldine off-center, made her want things from Martin that she'd never wanted before. When Geraldine is needy, she brings out a cruel side of him because he can't stand to see her weak. It frightens him. What will she want? What will she ask? Will she pull him down with her? She looks like a buzzard, hunched over the deck rail, dragging on her cigarette. If only she wouldn't get so upset about that ball. Martin knew as soon as he told Henry he could fill the table any damn way he pleased, that Martin had made a mistake, that he should have at least checked with Geraldine first, but Henry was so insistent and pushy that Martin took the line of least resistance. He hoped Geraldine wouldn't mind, or wouldn't notice. He knows she never enjoys herself there.

His arteries are constricting; his poor heart labors. You'd think Geraldine would spare him, in his condition. The plan to move Edith in, which appeared so simple before he mentioned it to Geraldine, seems fraught with difficulties. What will Flo really say? She's been unpredictable lately. If Martin didn't know Florence better, he'd say she was jealous of Edith, but Florence is not a jealous woman. Martin has had flirtations, infatuations, in the past and Florence has taken them with good humor. And, of course, Florence has had actual love affairs. A couple of times Martin feared he was going to lose her, but she always came back (emotionally; she never physically separated from him). Each time Martin behaved himself. She can hardly justify feeling jealous if Martin takes an interest in a young woman, a fatherly interest.

His chest tightens. He knows she'll object. If he mentions it, she'll be angry. This is what Geraldine meant. He watches her puffing away; her sharp shoulder blades stick out like stunted featherless wings underneath her summer jersey. What happened to her? She was an attractive woman, intelligent, curious. Her bitterness is tearing his heart. He can feel it making minute tears in the muscle of his heart.

HENRY IS STANDING OUTSIDE THE DOORWAY OF THE PLAY-pen, watching unobserved. Ben is juggling grapes with his mouth, spitting them into the air and catching them. They drop and bounce across his desk. Edith is turning rosy with laughter. Courting behavior. It gives Henry a pang, a Proustian recall of lunch in the cafeteria at high school when he would watch such scenes of the Alpha couple flirting with each other, and he would catch himself envying the girl and wonder what was wrong with him.

Not that he's lusting after Ben, a lovely boy. Henry's known him since he was a little fellow whose ears stuck out too much and made his mama, Miriam, worry; the head grew up to the ears, and he's a handsome young man. Smart, but not pretentious like a lot of them.

Henry has come here for diversion. He and Geraldine had a confrontation. She asked if he'd reserved a place for her at the Photographers' Ball, and he said the table was filled. When he'd actually saved a place for her. It was the way she asked, with the expectation that of course he hadn't, that made him say it. She's furious. There's no way he can back down.

Edith is laughing—her pink gums and perfect teeth, the flush on her creamy skin. No wonder Martin loves her (in his repressed way of course, in a way that makes him take the role of benefactor instead of what he'd really like, which is to play the part of lover). And Geraldine loves Edith, too, in much the same way. Ben loves Edith as well, and unlike Martin and Geraldine, probably has no confusion whatsoever as to *how* he loves her. But Henry is the only one who has a ticket to the prom. It's so funny! It's such a funny idea! Henry is going to laugh out loud. He has to walk away a few steps and take some deep yoga breaths, compose his face. That's better.

"Edith, could I see you for a minute please?" Ben looks up instantly, protectively. (Ah, young love! It's amazing that it still exists.) Edith drops her eyes and stands like a chastened school-girl. Henry leads her outside, to a private corner, and puts an arm around her shoulder.

EDITH CAN'T BELIEVE THAT CLARENCE WON'T GET OUT of bed and come to the phone. She knows he's there. It's only one in the afternoon. She pleads with him over the answering machine, but he doesn't respond. Clarence is the person she wants to tell. He'll be thrilled and will know just what she should wear. Ben said it was a mistake to go, that Peyton and Kylie will be envious and make her life miserable, for nothing, because the Photographers' Ball is full of social climbers and sycophants, everyone's old, she won't know anybody and wouldn't want to anyway.

Edith decides to call Carolyn. The conversation gets off to a bad start because Edith hasn't called in a while, so Edith has to apologize. Carolyn wants to talk about the weather; she heard it was terrible in the city this summer, and there's a homeless criminal being released into Edith's very own neighborhood, did she hear about that? It was on TV last night.

"There are so many crazy people around, one more isn't going to matter," Edith says.

"You know, it's the girls from out of town who always get killed; they're the ones you hear about. Because they don't know enough, they don't—"

"Mom, I'm calling because I have news. I got invited to this major party where all these famous people go."

"Who invited you?"

"This guy at the magazine who's really important."

"How old is he?"

"It's not like that. He's gay."

"He's a homosexual?"

Edith should have known it would be hopeless trying to explain to Carolyn what an honor it is to have Henry invite her to the Photographers' Ball. Whenever anything good happens to Edith—whether it's getting the lead in the senior play or a solo in the choral recital—Carolyn has objections. It's as if Carolyn feels it's her maternal duty. Edith wants to tell someone who will be happy for her. Ben's probably right. Everyone at the magazine is going to be envious. Except Geraldine—cool, sophisticated, so unlike Carolyn. Geraldine will be happy for her. Edith goes off in search of her mentor.

FLORENCE SEES A HANDSOME OLDER MAN STOPPED IN traffic, watching through the windshield of his white Mercedes as she strides uptown, and she remembers that she is an attractive woman. It's getting late; she really should take a cab, but it's still light, the temperature is balmy, and Florence is savoring the freedom of spending an entire day out of the house. She decides to prolong it by walking home. She's just been to see Basil, who was shocked at how she'd let her hair go. She explained about Martin, how she hadn't dared leave him home alone at first but now she was resuming her practice, seeing patients, and getting the housekeeper to stay with him. She has to. You can only neglect yourself for so long. She feels as if she is climbing out of a hole.

Her first day back at work was gratifying. A therapist she respects wanted her advice on a difficult case, and Florence had some good insights. She saw two patients, and she could tell they've been making progress.

Edith no longer seems like such a threat. Edith and Lucille. What can they do at this late date? Sue Martin for support? It's only money. They'll settle on something. Besides, Florence isn't absolutely certain that Lucille and Edith are plotting together. It seems unlikely that Edith would team up with Lucille if she really is the deranged garbage-sifter that Geraldine insists she saw on the street. Florence has to separate fact from conjecture. The girl turned up at *Ubu* looking for a job—a coincidence? Not likely, but perhaps something else led her to the magazine. It does not necessarily follow that Lucille sent her there, that they are cooking up some plot together.

People rarely act according to well-thought-out plans. They move according to whim, emotion; they react to events more than initiate them. It makes sense, in terms of evolution, that humans should be this way. Because circumstances change, minute by minute. It's more likely that what brought Edith into the city, to the magazine, and even to the bedside of her own father, was a series of events. Edith's progress could have been determined by a number of influences, everything from genetic predisposition to pure chance. But the human mind—Florence's own mind—wants to find the pattern, the plan. This need to find the plan, the connecting motivators, is what leads finally to paranoid delusions.

As a professional, Florence understands how even rational minds can go down blind alleys, rig up elaborate tales to explain simple occurrences. There is no such thing as a completely sane human being. The mind is not a monolith, but a turbulence of competing voices. Its balance is delicate, requiring constant corrections, adjustments from outside sources. Input. In her work she sees them—men and women—who've become deluded from living in isolation. Some are homeless (her *pro bono* work) and some are actually well-off, but they've all let social contacts wither. They've become entranced with the light show within their own skulls.

This is how it must have happened with Lucille. An original mind, artistic—Florence will grant her that in retrospect. The kind who lives on the margin of society, tenuous connections. Her background sketchy, with parents either not living or not in touch, so unlike Florence's own tight web of family and friends. A waif, a pretty waif. But in Lucille's case, looks could be a curse, encouraging her to go always to the next person—man or woman—who was fascinated by her. And then (Florence, examining handbags in a store window, sees her own reflection, the tiny lines around her mouth) age crept up, and the number of new people Lucille could captivate diminished. At a time of life when she should have accumulated a home, family, professional standing, she was left alone with her grand ideas spinning themselves into chambers of fantasia through which she wanders, mesmerized and lost.

CLARENCE IS HELPING LULU PAINT WALLS.

"Get out of here!" he says.

"It's true."

"You are such an unbelievable femme fatale. I'm going to take lessons from you."

"It's just something you're born with, Clare."

"So he's giving you the place rent free, and now the paint—"

"I bet he gets the floor done, too. I suggested it."

"When people walk in here on the night of the opening, they're going to take it all for granted—right? I mean, you see painted walls, shiny floors and you don't think, 'What went on to get all this together?' "

After a while Lulu says, "That's a good idea."

"What?"

"You know, to show more of the process. I was thinking that

before. The story is not just QB and his garbage. I could borrow a video camera. You could tape me doing my thing, going through trash, with my bags and gloves. Oh God, I didn't tell you this! When was it—Sunday—oh Clare, I wish we'd had a camera there. Someone I knew years ago—some uptight, very— oh, she saw me in the garbage can. She recognized me and she ran—"

"She ran? You're kidding!"

"No. She ran—you know, like—I don't know what she thought! Oh God, if we could have that on tape!" Lulu has to sit down on the step ladder, she's laughing so hard. Clarence laughs too, thinking about some woman tearing off up the street, her handbag flapping against her side, afraid of Lulu, of all people.

Lulu blots her face with her arm. Even though it's cooler outside than it has been—in the eighties instead of nineties or hundreds—it's sweltering in here. They climb down for a water break. Lulu takes a swig from a big bottle of Evian that Clarence brought over and passes it to him.

"And we could also rig up something—behind a screen maybe—a camera that I could start with a remote, that could record my transactions with Montero," she says.

"You're kidding, aren't you?"

"No, I'm not. I'm serious." Lulu stands back to admire her bit of wall.

"Well, I'm not going to stand behind a screen and—"

"Clarence, you're not listening. The remote." She clicks an imaginary remote at him.

"Oh Lulu, this is sick, it's twisted—"

"See? I'm shocking even you. I'm breaking taboos, bringing out in the open the garbage people don't want to see."

But is it art or is it pornography? This is the question they argue energetically, painting, having a wonderful time, until Lulu's landlord Lothario, a scary guy in a fabulous suit, comes in and Clarence has to go into an *echt* queen act to convince him that he has no designs on Lulu.

It's Clarence's night off and he's going home to change. Maybe he'll go out later to Industria and see if Francis is there. Francis hasn't called in a week, and Clarence won't let himself call Francis. Clarence is so immersed in thoughts of Francis that he nearly bumps into a burly character standing transfixed in the middle of the sidewalk, staring upward. A giant blimp, bathed in white light, is gliding across an indigo sky. Goodyear.

"That's lucky, seein' that." The big guy's voice is surprisingly subdued.

"It's the Goodyear blimp," Clarence says. "I've seen it on TV but never in person. I had no idea it was so large and—luminous."

"It's a sign that this is going to be a good year," the man says.

"It's Goodyear tires. An advertisement—"

"It's a sign." The guy's voice takes on an edge.

Clarence supposes anything is a sign if you want it to be. He casually takes his leave and continues down the street, thinking that quite possibly it is a sign and this will be a good year, for him and for the curbside mystic.

MIDSUMMER'S
NIGHT

FLORENCE HAS TWO TICKETS TO SHAKESPEARE IN THE
Park and Martin insists that she go—Martin who just a week ago
accused her of trying to kill him when she went to buy groceries
and Nora wasn't there to look after him. All her friends are out
of town. Even the ones who hadn't planned to spend the summer
away changed their minds when they saw what the city was
going to be like. So Florence called Geraldine, who seemed delighted to be asked. Florence said she had plenty of food in the
house and would take a picnic for the two of them—why not—it
would be fun, like old times.

But it isn't like old times because Geraldine acts brittle and
old, fussing at the crowds and the pushing. Florence doesn't
mind. It's exciting being in a mix of people. Everyone is coming

to see Shakespeare after all, so even if they're just kids and not white, many of them, if it's love of the Bard that is bringing them together . . . Geraldine thinks they've been bussed in by some public-spirited organization that decided they would benefit. They're not really here out of appreciation for . . . "Have some chicken," Florence says to change the subject. She opens the wine.

"I hope you didn't buy a new frock for the Photographers' Ball," Geraldine says.

"Oh, the Photographers' Ball. That's right. It's almost time for the Photographers' Ball." Florence is looking around, hoping to recognize someone who might come over for a glass of wine and relieve the tedium of Geraldine.

"Well, don't get your tiara out of the vault. Henry has given the whole table away to his cronies. Martin just turned the whole thing over to him, as if we didn't count, and when I asked Henry for a place, he said the table was filled and *then*—get this—he went right out and invited Edith to go with him. Edith came running to me, so excited. I don't know, Florence, I can't believe she's plotting and manipulating. She's so ingenuous, she was so certain I'd be pleased for her. But Henry—Henry's up to something. He knows, and he's plotting. He's got some scheme to use Edith to humiliate you and Martin—"

"That's ridiculous! What do you mean humiliate?" Florence finds Geraldine more and more irritating. Geraldine's hair falls forward, narrowing her face into something ferretlike. Her eyes glitter as she describes the embarrassing position both Martin and Florence will be in when Edith's parentage becomes known. Florence reminds Geraldine that Martin never knew about the pregnancy, and if Florence had a hand in planning an abortion, well, it was perfectly legal, and she wasn't even involved with

Martin at the time. It's not their fault if Lucille turned into a bag-woman. She was headed that way from the start.

Envy. That's what Florence is seeing on Geraldine's face. Florence has always felt that Geraldine envied her for marrying Martin, although Martin was never interested in Geraldine—he told Florence early on. And, of course, Geraldine has always had this rivalry with Henry. Florence did feel a little stab of jealousy —she'll admit it only to herself—when Geraldine said Edith was going to the ball with Henry, but she quickly put it behind her. Florence loathes those feelings—envy and jealousy. They tear at the insides, consume from within. She watches Geraldine stabbing out a cigarette on her plate of half-eaten food. Her problem is that she doesn't allow herself to take, and she resents others who do.

MARTIN HAS ASKED EDITH TO COME OVER AFTER WORK, and he has been in a state, worrying that she'll walk in while Florence is still here. When he hears Florence leave and lock the door behind her, a sense of well-being floods his soul, immediately followed by the realization that when Edith comes, Martin is going to have to descend the stairs to let her in, and, after her visit, he will have to climb those stairs again. He waits for his chest to tighten, for his heart to flutter in anticipatory anxiety, but nothing happens. His heart is light and happy. He changes out of his pajamas and robe into linen trousers and an open-necked shirt that a woman once told him made him look like a poet.

FLORENCE IS CARRIED ALONG BY THE SURGE OF FELLOW spectators heading for the park exit. Geraldine left at intermission; she hated the performance, the half-dressed boys and girls cavorting around the stage. "Gratuitous," she hissed, when Queen Titania removed her diaphanous fairy dress and bathed nude in the fountain. You'd think Geraldine, as a lesbian, would have enjoyed the scene of Titania being groomed by her hand-maidens. Florence found it very erotic. She loved the tumbling, the flame throwing, the bare-breasted nymphs on roller skates. She loved the whole mad insouciance. Poor Geraldine.

Florence in contrast is feeling aroused, loose, and free. She's recalling past lovers, past romances. "I've let myself get small," she says aloud, and realizes its truth. She's lost her larger self and has become a grasping, frantic, smaller being. Seeing Geraldine, narrow, stiff, and disapproving, freed Florence as much as seeing the Brazilian spectacle. Florence will take the side of youth, en-ergy, and sexuality any day. Let Geraldine pick at her wounds; Florence refuses to turn old and bitter.

When Florence gets to her house, she sees a light in the kitchen. There's been an accident, she thinks—a break-in, an-other heart attack, she doesn't know what. She rushes to open the door, which isn't completely locked, just the latch is turned, and she knows she locked up very thoroughly. She fumbles with her keys, drops them, finally gets the door open. "Martin—" and then she sees them at the kitchen table, with a bottle of wine of all things. The girl rising now, guilty, startled. Has she told him? Does he know?

The girl is gathering papers, saying she really should go, it's late.

"No, no, you can't at this hour!" Martin cries. "With that madman stalking your neighborhood. It isn't safe. We have room here. Tell her, Flo, tell her to stay."

Martin and Edith look at her with identical expressions. Florence, feeling her shoulders constrict, her lips purse, remembers Geraldine. She lets her shoulders drop and widen, her mouth soften. She is Titania. She is queen. They are asking her permission, but if she doesn't give it, they will continue. Look at them. Father and daughter. Florence can either be included or excluded, her choice.

"Of course she'll stay. Sit down, Edith. I want to hear how you worked this miracle of getting Martin downstairs. Martin, you look wonderful. Doesn't it feel good to be out of your room?"

Florence pours herself a glass from the bottle, which is two-thirds full. When she finishes regaling them with descriptions of the Brazilian performance, complete with mimicked reactions from Geraldine, the bottle is empty. Did Edith have another glass? Florence isn't sure. Florence doesn't feel drunk, just more lively, more like her old self.

"Flo, it's late. Shouldn't we put this child to bed?"

Edith's eyes do look a bit glazed. Has Florence gone on too long? She sends the girl up to bed and promises to look in on her as soon as she gets Martin settled.

THE TOP FLOOR OF MARTIN'S HOUSE HAS TWO ROOMS. In the front is a large study, book-lined, with a leather-topped desk, two leather armchairs, and a daybed in the corner. It's hot and stuffy, since the air conditioner hasn't been turned on up here, but Edith can see that in winter it would be a pleasant room with a fire in the fireplace. In the next room there's a commodious bed covered in Battenberg lace (Edith knows about this lace; she once wanted it for her bed but Carolyn said it was too expensive) and, on the ceiling, a hand-painted sky, blue with signs of the zodiac in gold. The French doors (Edith opens them) look out on the garden, and the breeze makes the lace curtains rise and fall.

She steps out on the balcony. The sounds of the city are muffled and blended here, like rushing water. She turns back to the room and makes a little jump of surprise. Mrs. Weatherstone, in a pleated white nightgown, is lounging on the bed.

Mrs. Weatherstone laughs. "I frightened you! I came to see if the bed was really made. Nora, who cleans for us, is supposed to keep these rooms dusted and ready for guests, but I hardly venture up here anymore, so she could have gotten lazy and let it go."

"No, everything's fine. It's such a beautiful room. Thank you for letting me stay—"

"I also thought you might need this." Mrs. Weatherstone hands her a new toothbrush and toothpaste, along with a white cotton gown with embroidery around the neck.

"Oh, this is too nice—"

"It's old. I never wear it anymore. Go ahead, try it on. I'd love to see how it looks on you. You can keep it if it fits."

Edith strokes the nightgown. It is beautiful, nicer than anything Edith's ever worn. But why is Mrs. Weatherstone suddenly so warm and generous? Edith thought she hated her. The woman's motives are mysterious. She doesn't seem drunk, although she did have several glasses of wine. She doesn't seem crazy right now, not as crazy as before. She's sitting on the bed, as if she and Edith are best friends, waiting for Edith to try on the nightgown. Edith takes it into the bathroom to change.

She stops to look at herself in the mirror. The gown becomes her. In fact, it looks as if it's hers, or could be hers if she were the daughter of rich New York parents, people like Peyton's parents must be. Edith undoes her braid and uses the hairbrush on the shelf. The light is so nice in this bathroom, not like the ugly fluorescent one at home. Carolyn loves fluorescent lights because they're cheap. When Edith complained that it turned her makeup blue, Carolyn said that it was ridiculous for Edith to wear makeup anyway.

"We call this the zodiac room," Mrs. Weatherstone says when Edith comes out, as if their conversation continued while Edith was changing. "I've always loved it. Mother had the ceiling painted in the forties. There was an Italian painter who'd been forced to flee Mussolini. His home was destroyed in the war, and he never went back. Mother sort of adopted him and got all her friends to give him work as well."

"I love stars on the ceiling," Edith says. "When I was little, my grandfather put some glow-in-the-dark ones on my ceiling, but they started coming unstuck and my mother made him take them all off." There's no place to sit but on the bed so she climbs up next to Mrs. Weatherstone, wondering as she does what Peyton and Kylie would make of this picture.

"It's strange seeing you in this room. We always had older guests, usually male writers," Mrs. Weatherstone says. "Originally, I'd thought of this as the girl's room. And the front one as the boy's room. As if I already had two children, existing somewhere in the future. Funny what the mind can do. And now you're here, in the girl's room. It suits you."

And then Mrs. Weatherstone kisses Edith on the forehead exactly as if she were her daughter. Edith watches her leave. What has caused this transformation? It can't be just the effect of the wine. Why didn't Martin and Florence have children, if they'd wanted them, had planned on them? Maybe Mrs. Weatherstone, like Carolyn, had terrible miscarriages and just gave up, decided not to adopt. Carolyn probably wouldn't have adopted Edith if Edith hadn't been practically dumped on the doorstep of Grandpop's clinic. Edith was very ill; her mother, the hippie, didn't have the knowledge or means to take care of her, and so she gave Edith to Grandpop, or at least that's the story Carolyn tells. Edith feels that Grandpop has a different version.

Edith settles into the sheets, enjoying the smooth feel against her skin, the slight scent of . . . lavender. Tonight, at the kitchen table, Martin didn't seem at all like a sick, old man. He could have been one of her friends. He established a music of conversation and made it easy for Edith to use words, so that she found herself expressing thoughts she hadn't known she possessed. He took her up to his level, one she'd never reached before, and when she looked down at how far they'd climbed she was amazed but unafraid.

She thinks Mrs. Weatherstone is the luckiest of women, to have been married all these years to Martin. As she falls asleep, she hears the liquid notes of a bird singing in the garden. In all the rest of the city there are only pigeons, but the Weatherstones have a bird that sings at night.

HOW EXTRAORDINARY I FEEL. MARTIN'S FACE IN THE bathroom mirror is smooth, a little flushed. The shadows under his eyes, the slackness of skin at the edge of his jaw, indications of morbidity that appeared on his face after the heart attack, are gone, miraculously erased. His hair, which Florence has been after him to have cut because it was so ragged, now flows smoothly back, the white mane of an artist, or a writer, not an editor. He climbed the stairs without even thinking—the stairs that he's been dreading as possibly fatal. He opens the French doors to get some real air into the room for once. He hears Florence's voice, her laughter from upstairs, and he smiles. She's with Edith; he knew she'd like her. Florence gets on with young people better than Martin does. They adore her. He drifts off to sleep hearing his wife's voice and the hum of other people's air conditioners.

He wakes in the night in a state of arousal. A figure in white sits on his bed. He thinks, *I am dreaming,* although he knows he is not. His hand is placed upon a breast, with the nipple erect and cool against his fingers. Lips, hair, hollows. It is familiar and yet strange. *It is you,* he thinks but doesn't say, won't risk breaking the spell and driving away this phantom, this figment of his imagination, this very real, warm visitor to his bed.

MARTIN, WHO NORMALLY WAKES SEVERAL TIMES IN THE night to make certain that his heart is beating, sleeps through until morning, completely forgetful of his condition. It's a shock to open his eyes and see daylight, to have let the night slip past. Did he die then? The ordinariness of the room reassures him that he is alive. But he's naked. He sees his pajamas in a heap on the floor.

Was it true, what he dreamed? It seemed both actual and phantasmagoric at the same time and, this morning, completely unlikely. He gets up, showers, dresses, and—yes—goes downstairs, thinking if he can catch Edith, see her, he will know.

Instead he finds Florence in the kitchen with Nora. They both start to see him.

"Did Edith leave?"

An hour ago, Florence says. Edith wouldn't stay for coffee. Her hair was still wet from the shower. It is ten-thirty, after all. He slept so late. Florence is going shopping. It's a perfect time, while the fall things are in, before most people are thinking of winter wardrobes.

"You look good," he tells her.

"Thank you." She smiles and he understands what he must

have known all along, that she was the night visitor, the seductress.

"I was just telling Nora to take a tray up to you at lunchtime. Would you rather eat down here?"

"No. No, I don't think I should be doing the stairs. I'll rest here and go back up, take them slowly."

Martin, sitting at the table, looks so frail that Florence is embarrassed to think of last night. It doesn't seem possible. What possessed them?

LUNCH

THE TEMPERATURE IS CLIMBING AGAIN—TRIPLE DIGITS for the weekend, they're saying. It's already hovering at ninety. Henry, sweating in the sun outside the office, surveys cabs panting steam from open hoods and tries to judge which of them might be able to make it to Sixty-first Street without boiling over, possibly bursting into flames. He almost wishes he'd let Maya meet him as she suggested, around the corner at the Gotham, allowed her to parade him past the agents, writers, and editors who congregate there. She was disappointed because, for Maya, being seen with Henry is like money in the bank. Henry realizes he owes her, but he couldn't give her that. This lunch will be about what he *can* do, what he's willing to do to repay services past and future.

He isn't aware that Geraldine is hanging back in the shadowy interior of the building, waiting until he has left before she will force herself out into the blinding heat to get a cab uptown to the Park Avenue Cafe.

"HAVE AN UNBORN CARROT," RYO YAMANAKA SAYS, AND hands Geraldine the bread basket overflowing with corn sticks, herb breads, and small peeled carrots with the tops still on. Ryo looks different. Perhaps it's because Geraldine has had time to acquire some emotional distance. Ryo no longer has the face of an intimate, but the mask of a business associate.

This is the first they've seen each other since the breakup, other than chance meetings at large gatherings, which were invariably awkward, with one determined to be civil and the other snubbing, and then each reversing her attitude at the next occasion. Finally Ryo called and said, "Look, this is silly. Let's have lunch and get things back to the level they were at before all that stuff happened." And Geraldine said fine, but not at the Gotham, where Ryo wanted. She chose this place, uptown and out of the way.

They order wine and pay careful attention to the recitation of specials. Ryo puts on a pince-nez to peruse the menu. Geraldine catches her peering at her with a mocking elfin expression.

"You have that mousy indoor look you get," says Ryo.

Geraldine resists the temptation to put the water glass to her cheek to cool a flush rising from her chest and neck. More than once she allowed Ryo to bathe her in the Japanese way, exploring her body with quick, inquisitive hands. She has lain helpless, feeling like an enormous Gulliver, while Ryo tied her to her bed with silken cords. Ryo twirls the top of a carrot between her teeth. Something's different about her chin.

"You're letting it get the best of you, Ger."

"It?"

"The aging process. You're giving up, letting yourself get out of touch. You'll become obsolete if you don't watch it." Ryo butters a square of corn bread and bites into it eagerly.

Ryo's avidity is what captivated Geraldine, her emphatic pursuit of pleasure, especially sexual, the extremes to which she would go to get it. Geraldine was brought up in the Celtic Catholic heritage of disdain for, verging on fear of, pleasure. To show enthusiasm for food was vulgar. To enjoy sex, to seek it out, was unthinkable. Before Ryo, Geraldine had always been a half-willing participant in sex. It was an abyss into which she would stumble by accident.

Ryo concentrated on Geraldine, explored areas of her body, loci of her mind, places Geraldine had been taught to shun and ignore—unclean parts, loathsome propensities. Ryo laid bare Geraldine's voracious capacity for pleasure. Even now Ryo could take Geraldine back to her place (it isn't far) and tie her to the bed, but she won't because she knows all about Geraldine; there is nothing left to discover.

Now that it is over, Geraldine can clearly see what she emphatically denied at the time: Ryo was using her. Ryo desperately wanted to write for *Ubu,* to break out of the fashion magazine ghetto and do some serious pieces on art. Geraldine believed in her and gave her the opportunity. And Ryo did very well. No one even hinted that Ryo's work was not up to *Ubu* standards. But there were warnings (digs from Henry, kind concern from Martin) that once Ryo had established herself at *Ubu* her ardor for Geraldine would cool.

Geraldine is grateful that Ryo has changed her perfume from the show-offy musk scent that after the affair would make Geraldine, catching a whiff of it on another woman, go weak with longing and loss. She is relieved that Ryo no longer wants to be her lover. Ryo doesn't even want to be her friend, not really.

What Ryo wants from Geraldine is an assignment. She wants to cover the first-night openings at the Soho galleries this fall— not merely critique the shows, but report on the texture of the event, how it's both small-town (everyone knows everyone) and big-city (make-or-break reputations on the line). It's a perfect *Ubu* piece. No other magazine would take it. And Ryo is the perfect one to do it—her dry sly wit, her insider's knowledge. She's turning her full attention to her plate now, as if the contract has already been signed.

Ryo knows a lot about Geraldine, but Geraldine has learned certain things about Ryo: She is terrified of her father, even though he's a tiny fragile man of eighty. She regularly calls him in Tokyo, reversing the charges, and speaks to him in a whiny little girl voice. Geraldine has overheard these conversations, and even though she doesn't understand Japanese, she knows that Ryo is pleading for money. The old man is rich but he sends her only small sums, and regularly threatens to cut her off entirely. Once, Geraldine had to pay Ryo's rent or she would have been thrown out on the street.

So little Ryo, greedy little Ryo, who is now ordering the most fattening dessert from the menu as Geraldine lights a cigarette, needs this assignment. What can Ryo give Geraldine in return, aside from an amusing piece for the magazine? Nothing. She has already taken everything.

"There's a time window. If we can't get it into November, there's no place for it. I'll have to look and see what's in there already."

"Get back to me today so I can work on it," Ryo says.

When they cheek kiss outside the restaurant, Geraldine sees the still-pink scar behind Ryo's ear—the surgeon's love-bite. Ryo has had something done. Geraldine isn't surprised that she has sent herself in for alterations. She can't bear the sight of anything worn or decayed—not even a wilting flower, or a chipped cup.

"Call me tonight," Ryo says and walks off with her chin tipped high, swaggering in her little black suit from that Japanese designer she charms into giving her clothes. *She's walking on the edge,* Geraldine thinks.

MAYA IS NOT AT ALL PUT-OUT OVER HAVING LUNCH up-town out of sight of anyone who could possibly matter, nor is she pouting at having been kept waiting (the cab *did* overheat and Henry had to find another). She wrinkles her cute retroussé nose, bunny-style, and says, "This place is fun." Henry takes her good mood for a bad sign. It means she's going to ask for something major.

First they discuss how well Henry's looking. Steve is Maya's trainer, too. They compare muscle-to-body fat ratios, the kind of diets Steve has them on. They speculate about Steve's social life. Henry would be perfectly happy to continue in this vein right through the meal, but the more Maya delays, the more he dreads what she is finally going to ask of him.

At last, over the native Maine blueberry tart, which they decide to share and not tell Steve about, Maya approaches the topic —Jeff Jerome. Isn't it time for an *Ubu* profile on him?

Henry agrees that Jeff Jerome is certainly a name, a possible subject for an *Ubu* profile. "But what's the story on him? Does he have a new project in the works? We can't just take a movie star—okay, a movie star *director/producer*—and profile him if there isn't any news."

"Families, Henry. He has a beautiful family—adorable Eurasian babies, plus there's a fourteen-year-old daughter from when he was married to Kate Townsend, who is luscious, in a wholesome way. And of course his wife—"

Henry deliberately takes too much on his fork so he can munch and consider Maya's ploy. She's good at playing young and cute, but Henry knows she's at least thirty and has a Harvard MBA. She must realize this is not an *Ubu* piece. It's the sort of puffery that *People* might run. "Have you considered *People?*"

She wrinkles her nose again. *"People*'s fine, it's a really good magazine for what it is, but the stock is cheap. We want something that's almost a work of art, get a really good photographer, make it a mood piece, Henry, you know—a hymn to the American family. No, really, Henry! That kind of attitude is what pervades *Ubu* and it hurts you with advertisers—you know—who get this idea of the typical *Ubu* reader as a sixty-year-old Luddite hermit living in a garret. Families buy Land Rovers, Henry. Anyway, it wouldn't have to be in the editorial section. Let fashion do it."

Fashion. That's a different story. Henry can sell anything to the fashion staff. "The kids are really pretty?" He licks his fingers to get the last crumbs of crust from the plate.

Maya's eyes widen. "They're beautiful."

"I'll talk it over with fashion. They'll most likely do it, you know, because, since I'm the only one from upstairs who treats them with respect, they think I walk on water."

If the table weren't so wide, Maya would probably lean over it and kiss him. "Henry, this is going to be a terrific story, and we'll do everything to make it easy for your people. You know,

I've gotta tell you, everyone's talking about how you've turned the magazine around since Martin's fallen out of the picture."

"Well, I'm trying to spark it up a little. Bruno's encouraging me. But I'm getting resistance from some of the more senior editors." Henry is too diplomatic to mention names, but Maya understands.

She rolls her eyes. "Geraldine is from another era. She's like mother superior at the magazine, and that's the last thing you need if you're going to appeal to a young demographic."

When Henry was a boy his mother used to warn him that talking about people in their absence was a sure way of making them materialize. In his mother's limited social circle in small-town Tennessee, this invariably happened. His mother's warning was imprinted on his mind, and it is a conviction that he can't quite shake. He looks over his shoulder, expecting to see Geraldine glaring at him. Later, when he is putting Maya into a cab on Park Avenue, Geraldine does pass in her own cab and note that Henry has again been lunching with Maya, but Henry does not see Geraldine.

MARTIN HAS SHUT THE WINDOWS AND PULLED THE drapes. It's supposed to be ninety degrees today and the heat could put a strain on his heart. He is eating lunch and thinking about sex. He always considered it overrated. The fleeting moments of physical pleasure didn't seem worth the arranging and plotting. He used to suspect that men who devoted a lot of time to sex were not fulfilled in other areas—namely work—and welcomed the emotional Sturm und Drang as a distraction. He's always been more turned on by minds than bodies, would rather hold a manuscript than a mistress in his arms.

He never claimed to be in love with Florence. He admired

her, enjoyed her company, liked her vision of him and what he could become. When he asked her to marry him, he enumerated the reasons why he thought they would be a good match. He consulted her parents. It was all very reasoned and rational.

Like many beautiful women, Florence needs to be admired, doted on, lusted after. Martin doesn't mind when another man admires his wife, especially if that man is someone whom Martin admires. Martin came to enjoy seeing desire kindling in the other man's eye, watching Florence toss her head, lick her lips, extend her spine, transforming herself into another kind of creature, more alert and feral.

At the same time, Martin would brace himself for the disturbances he knew were coming—missed appointments; phone calls in the middle of the night; unexplained absences (although never for longer than a week). It was upsetting, but exciting too, like having a tornado raging outside your window. And in the midst of it all there would be strange flashes of desire between Florence and Martin, with the lover—although never actually present—acting as catalyst between them.

They discovered this by accident. Her parents were still alive, living in the house with them. Florence was taking courses toward becoming a psychologist. Ed Baker was in from Chicago. Martin had known him when they both spent a year as Rhodes scholars. He asked his in-laws if he could put Baker up; they were pleased to have him. Florence had been going through a dowdy period, and the visit from Baker revitalized her. Florence took an interest in the play Baker was working on. She would discuss it with him endlessly. One night as usual they stayed up while Martin went to bed. Martin fell asleep but woke in the dark, with the certainty that Baker and Florence had become lovers. When he heard them on the stairs together, coming up at last, he could tell by the tone of their whispers that they had been intimate.

As Martin waited for her to come to bed, he thought that he was angry, that he might say something, but when she slipped in beside him, he reached for her. She was receptive. It was the best lovemaking they'd had since the marriage. (Admittedly it hadn't been great to start with and had fallen off to sporadic, not very inspired attempts.)

It would have broken the spell to talk about it, so they never did, but their best times together were when Florence had someone else as well. Martin would find himself, not imitating the other man exactly, but participating in his potency, his maleness, even in his carelessness. (After all, however devoted a lover claimed to be, he was fucking another man's wife, not his own, and could afford to be less conscientious, less mindful of his partner, less inhibited.) Having the spirit of the third person in bed with them relieved Martin of the awful responsibility of being Florence's only source of sexual fulfillment.

Martin doesn't think Florence has had anyone for the past several years. He assumed that stage of her life was over, that her hormones had changed. Their marriage had settled into a peaceful companionship, which Martin preferred. Then, suddenly, last night Florence seduced him. This time the catalyst was the girl. It's her youth, her ripe unconscious sexuality that aroused both Florence and Martin.

His groin stirs as he recalls the way Edith looked the first time she came in drenched from the rain and he had her put on his bathrobe. The robe parted to reveal a glimpse of thigh before she pulled it closed. Another time, when she opened the drapes, she gave him the opportunity to see the shape of her breast under her shirt. Image follows image: the back of her knee, the nape of her neck, the top of her bra when she leaned over to pick up a paper. He managed to fool himself into believing that his interest in her was fatherly, but he'd been collecting stolen glimpses and hoarding them in his memory like—dirty pictures?—no, holy icons.

What if he has fallen in love? Could love be happening to Martin, at this stage of his life, as he is renouncing the everyday pleasures of a stroll to the corner, of a medium-rare steak? Would he grasp at the most dangerous pleasure of all? Maybe he should phone his cardiologist, explain the situation and ask if falling in love could be a side effect from the drugs he's been taking. How would he word that question? The cardiologist already told him to "resume sexual relations," as if it were an activity on a par with going to the office and climbing stairs. Last night Martin was as potent as he's ever been, reckless, abandoned, and he woke naked and alive. What if his doctor is right? What if he does have years left? Years to live.

He seizes the bell, ringing for Nora to clear away his plate. He's conscious for the first time that the bell is in the shape of a woman. He enjoys the feel of the slender waist, the tiny brass bosom on his fingers. He turns it over and looks into the wrinkled face of the hag.

THEY TAKE A TABLE UNDER THE SKYLIGHT, NEXT TO A small pool into which metal frogs spit jets of water. Two elegantly dressed men, in their twenties maybe, sit on the other side talking intently—about what, Edith can't imagine. Are they straight? Gay? One of each? A trio of women at the booth opposite have similar features, obviously related, but are they a mother and two daughters, two sisters and a daughter? The Japanese man who draws the waiter over to the tiered display of iced cakes—is he a visiting businessman? Tourist? Edith studies the ceiling, painted in various shades of green to look like tiles. Are the squares stenciled, sprayed on, painted free-hand?

"Are you sure you won't have a glass of wine?" Mrs. Weatherstone asks. She's having one, and of course she'd like Edith to join her. Clarence would order a glass; he might suggest a bottle. Carolyn wouldn't approve at all. She would find Mrs. Weatherstone entirely too much, from the golden profusion of her hair to her shimmery apricot silk jersey. A glass of wine in the middle of the day?

"Sure, why not?" Edith says, and Mrs. Weatherstone beams. When Mrs. Weatherstone called, Peyton of all people was in the office and listened—Edith could almost see her ears growing pointed—while Edith carelessly said that she hadn't any plans, that lunch at Barney's would be fun. Peyton said she didn't know that Edith was on such intimate terms with Martin's wife, and Edith said she stayed over sometimes when she was working late with Martin.

Mrs. Weatherstone is skilled at drawing a person out. Edith remembers that Mrs. Weatherstone is a therapist, a professional at coaxing thoughts into words. The wine, the splashing of water in the fountain, the enclosing gray-green walls encourage intimate exchanges. Other diners, at other tables, are leaning in toward each other, murmuring confidences.

The conversation has turned to the subject of adoption, something Edith doesn't ordinarily discuss. Florence brought it up; she'd learned that Edith was adopted, although she didn't say how she'd learned. Edith mentioned it to Martin, who might have told Florence. It flatters her to think that Martin and Florence may have been discussing her in her absence, that she could be that important to Martin.

Edith is recounting a day she'd long ago put behind her, a bike trip with friends to an abandoned farmhouse outside Compton Falls. "It was called the hippies' house. Some kids had moved mattresses in and made it into a teen sin palace. The other girls wanted to check it out, and I was going to until I saw it, and then I wouldn't go in. Even when they did and I was left alone out front, I couldn't.

"The biggest girl, Jackie, came out and said I had to. She led me to the porch. She had hair under her arms and didn't use deodorant. She grabbed both my wrists and tried to drag me in. It was sunny and warm on the porch but it was damp in the house, and there seemed to be this cold breath coming from inside. And there was the smell of Jackie's sweat. I started screaming and gagging, and my friend Sara came out and told Jackie to stop, and then Sara said that I had been born in that house, and that's why I didn't want to go in."

Mrs. Weatherstone reaches across the table and lays a gem-sparkling hand on Edith's. Edith feels that Mrs. Weatherstone would like to take her in her arms to comfort her, retroactively, something that Carolyn did not do when Edith went running to the library where Carolyn was working. First Carolyn reprimanded her for making noise in the library (there were only two other people there). Then she had to know who Edith had been with, and hadn't Carolyn told her not to ride her bicycle on that dangerous road. Finally Carolyn said that it was true, the woman who had given birth to Edith was a hippie living with other hippies in what they called a commune.

Mrs. Weatherstone orders another glass of wine. She seems to agree with Carolyn, that only an irresponsible woman would give birth in a house without electricity or running water, without a doctor. And yet Edith's grandfather wants her to find this woman, Edith says. He gave Edith her name, just before she came to New York. "It's as if he feels guilty, not just toward the woman, but toward me too. I feel there's another way of telling the story, that maybe she wasn't such a bad person."

"Have you looked for her, since you've been here?"

"I haven't even tried to find her in the phone book. I should. I mean, she could be living next door to me. It's stupid, but all I do is look at other women on the street, stare into their faces and try to see if they look like me."

Again the gem-sparkling hand reaches over to hers. "Sometimes it's better not to know," Florence says.

As they are leaving the restaurant, Edith stops in front of a dress displayed in a glass case.

"That would look lovely on you."

"I need something to wear for this thing I'm going to."

"The Photographers' Ball."

"Yes."

"This dress would be perfect."

"Do you think it's expensive?"

"You never know till you ask."

THE MOMENT FLORENCE SAW EDITH IN THE DRESS, SHE knew she would buy it for her. When Edith told about that house, Florence nearly cried. Thank God the doctor had the presence of mind to take the child away from Lucille. Now that the blinders of envy are off, Florence sees clearly that Edith is as innocent as Geraldine first believed. Edith doesn't know Lucille.

Florence, unable to contain her delight at having bought the dress for Edith, kisses her on both cheeks when they part outside the store. They're making some minor alterations and delivering the dress to Florence's house. Edith is going to change for the ball at their place—it will be much more convenient. Edith is Martin's child, but several salespeople took Edith for Florence's daughter, and neither Edith nor Florence bothered to correct them.

IT'S RARE THAT ALL THE INTERNS ARE IN THE PLAYPEN AT the same time. Usually they're filling in at the receptionist desk, or in the mailroom faxing something for someone, or at the copying machine. Today, just Edith's luck, they are all at their desks when she comes creeping back from lunch at three-thirty with wine on her breath. "You're just eating now," she says, referring to Ben's burger, Kylie's meatball hero, Peyton's plastic container of greens.

"There was a big crisis in production. It's the one time we really could have used you," Peyton says.

"Sorry." Edith decides to ignore Peyton's remark, about it being the *one time* that Edith could have been useful, as if Edith's been sitting around doing her nails all summer.

"We're really only supposed to take an hour for lunch, you know. Or maybe you don't know, since you weren't brought in the regular way—I mean, Henry *handpicks* three interns a summer. The interview is really more of an orientation. But I guess you have a whole different arrangement, since you're like an extra that Geraldine brought in," Peyton continues.

"I think we've all stretched that rule at one time or another," Edith says. "That time you went shopping with your mom, it was pretty late when you got back—"

"Not that it's any of your business, but I specifically asked

Henry if I could take some personal time that day, and nothing important was going on. I made certain of that." She transfers a delicate leaf from her salad to her mouth.

"Well, Florence insisted on taking me to lunch at Barney's and when we were leaving, she saw this dress that would be perfect for me to wear to the ball, and so I had to try it on, and then she bought it for me. She wouldn't take no for an answer. It was kind of awkward, actually." Edith hears these words coming out of her mouth, and has the temporary satisfaction of seeing Peyton choke on her salad. She almost wishes Peyton would turn blue so Edith could do the Heimlich maneuver on her.

Kylie, talking through a mouthful of meatball hero, says, "What kind of dress?"

"Um, it's got lace and stuff."

Ben shoves the rest of his burger into his mouth, crumples the wrapper, and throws it into the trash as he leaves. Peyton phones her boyfriend. Kylie looks at Edith and chews.

"Mom? Did I interrupt? You sound like you're eating something."

"Just a tuna sandwich. We're getting the library ready for fall —school, you know—and I didn't have a chance to sit down. How are you?"

"Something wonderful happened. You know that thing I'm going to, that, like, charity ball—"

"With the homosexual?"

"Yes. Well, you know how I didn't have anything to wear? Mrs. Weatherstone, Florence, bought me this beautiful dress."

"What?"

"A dress. It's beautiful. It's—"

"Who?"

"You know, Mom, Mrs. Weatherstone—Martin's wife?"

"Why did Martin's wife buy you a dress?"

"She's really nice. And I guess she doesn't have any children of her own, so—"

"Edith, people don't just buy people things. You have to give her money for it."

"Mom, you don't understand. She would be very insulted."

"Edith, *you* don't understand. People do not give other people things, especially people who are practically strangers—"

"But she's not a stranger. She's really nice and we're very close. I slept over at their house last night."

"Edith, be careful. You have a way of charming people, of getting people to give you things—"

Edith slams down the phone just as Ben is coming in. How much did he hear? she wonders. She doesn't care. "That's my mom," she explains. "Every time someone is nice to me she thinks I conned them into it. She just can't stand it when anything good happens to me."

"Well, it is kind of strange." He sits at his desk, with his back to her.

Edith looks at Ben's calm shoulders, the blameless bit of neck above his collar. She isn't angry with him for saying this, as she was with Carolyn. In fact, it was a strange thing for Florence to do. "It was weird. She made me try on this dress. I couldn't say no. The salesgirl put me into the dressing room with it, and I looked at the tag and it was eight hundred dollars! I just stood there wishing I could disappear, and the salesgirl and Florence kept coming and wanting to know what the trouble was, did I need help. Finally they both barged in and zipped me up, and

Florence started fussing over the straps, how they should be just a little shorter. We got into this thing—the salespeople were treating us like mother and daughter. At first I thought Florence would correct them, but she didn't, and it seemed rude for me to butt in and say 'No, we're just friends.' And we aren't—you know—friends. I don't know what we are. The salesgirl assumed Florence would pay for it, and Florence just took out her credit card and did! And all I could do was say thank you and pretend to be excited and—because the people, the salespeople, were all around us; they were our audience. At that point, it would have been like slapping Florence in the face to turn her down in front of everyone. Maybe I should call the store and—like—cancel the order or something?"

"Now you're more like you," Ben says.

"What do you mean?"

"Don't you feel it? Sometimes you get more like someone else, like Peyton. Don't let it corrupt you. *Ubu,* Henry, the whole scene. Don't get involved in their politics. Stay pure."

"Pure!" Edith laughs, more embarrassed than amused. It would never occur to her to think of herself as pure, or of *Ubu* as corrupt. She phones Barney's right away and tries to cancel the purchase, but as she's doing it, passed from one disbelieving voice on the phone to another, she realizes she has no control over the matter. Florence bought the dress on her credit card and is having it sent to her home.

"At least I tried," Edith says when she hangs up.

"Call Florence and tell her you changed your mind about going to the ball with Henry. Tell Henry you can't go," Ben says.

"I can't do that!"

"Why not?"

"Well, it's like suicide, isn't it? I mean—Martin's wife, then Henry. What kind of a place would I have here if I insulted two of the top people. When they're only being nice to me."

"Hey, this isn't your career. It's an internship, a summer job, unpaid even. You're going to be a doctor, remember?"

"Well, I still can't just insult people who care about me."

Care about you, or do they want something? Ben asks, which is absurd, because what could important adult people need from Edith Seagrace? Edith wishes she'd never talked to Carolyn or Ben about the dress. She was just getting excited about it—it is a beautiful dress. And it made Florence so happy to buy it for her. She tries Clarence one last time. Clarence will love it that Florence bought her a dress. But Clarence isn't in.

CLARENCE AND LULU ARE HAVING LUNCH TOGETHER OUT-side at the Caffè San Marco, even though it's hot and no one else is at the outdoor tables. It's not so bad under the umbrella, they decided, and there's a breeze. Clarence is reminiscing about the time he and Edie eavesdropped on Lulu at this same restaurant. "I love it that you persuaded that guy to order the puttanesca, and just now you tried to talk me into ordering it. But you got the lobster ravioli, both times."

"I like the puttanesca, but a whole plate of it is too much. Is the primavera any good? I've never had it here."

Clarence laughs at how she reaches for his food. "You were hungry that day."

"I'm always hungry."

They are drinking white wine. Clarence ordered a bottle, just to see it cooling in a bucket by his table. Clarence is feeling wealthy. He made a lot of money at Maude's, and now he has a real job, thanks to Lulu, in the art department of an ad agency uptown.

"To a real job," Clarence toasts.

"To real life," Lulu responds.

"Speaking of real life, how are the videos coming of the— you know—"

"Oh, pretty good. Interesting. Would you like to see them?"

"No!" Clarence puts his hands up. Lulu laughs and steals more of his pasta. "Don't get insulted or anything," Clarence says, "but I think of you as more like a mother than—well, you know. I mean, you're a lot younger than my mother, but it's still possible that you could be my mother."

Lulu, her mouth full of primavera, nods.

"I wish you were, or I wish my mom could be like you. We were so close when I was a kid—I was the only one who liked helping her in the kitchen, who noticed what she was wearing. I was like a daughter to her, but she won't accept that the reason I was like a daughter was that I'm queer."

"So you've told her," Lulu says.

"Not exactly, but if she hasn't guessed by now—I mean, face it, I do not dress like the other men in the Hennessy family."

"You should tell her."

"I've put out plenty of signals. If she hasn't guessed by now, I figure it's because she doesn't want to know."

"You have to *tell* her, Clare. Otherwise, it's always between you, and you can't say anything real to each other. Maybe she thinks you don't want her to know, or don't want to talk about it, or—"

For some reason, Lulu is getting very upset over this conversation, even more upset than Clarence is, and that's pretty upset.

He hadn't realized before Lulu brought it up how much it bothers him that his mother and his whole family are so blind to what's been happening to him. How much more obvious can he get? Lulu's going on about the bonds between a mother and her child, really getting carried away, especially for someone who never had a child. Clarence refills their glasses, something the waiter should do, but as they are the only people eating outside, the waiter has probably forgotten them.

Lulu suddenly stops in the middle of her soliloquy. She puts her hand on his, which is still holding the bottle. "Don't turn around, don't look, but Wallace is coming, and he's in his dog suit."

Clarence does turn, to see a burly figure in a plush dog costume bearing down on their table.

"I'll grab the wine, you get the food," Lulu says. But she's blocked by Dog Man. Clarence, plates in hand, is confused about what he should do.

"Excuse me, would you let the lady by, please?"

Dog Man turns on Clarence and with one swipe of his arm, knocks him back against the other tables. Clarence, trying to keep from dropping the plates, fails to break his own fall and lands on the sidewalk. Dog Man lunges for Lulu, who swings at him with the wine bottle and breaks it against the back of a chair instead. A crowd of men—cooks, waiters, busboys—erupts from the restaurant onto the sidewalk. Dog Man lopes off down the street.

Lulu and Clarence are fine, just shaken, and would go home, but the manager has already had someone call the police and would appreciate it if they would stay so they could fill out a complaint. As a bribe the manager offers lunch and wine all over again, on the house. Lulu accepts with such alacrity that Clarence wonders if they won't suspect her of having lured Dog Man to the table. He did seem to know her. "I've had some run-ins with him over the garbage," Lulu explains. They eat and drink too much in the excitement of telling the whole story to the police officers ("toy cops" Lulu calls them because they are so little and look so young).

The toy cops leave. Lulu and Clarence linger over the second bottle of wine. Lulu leans forward, and in almost a whisper says, "Clare, I have a baby."

"You have a baby, Lulu? Where?"

Lulu laughs. "No, years ago. I *had* a baby. Wrong verb tense."

"What happened? Do you know where it is? The baby?" Clarence hopes it didn't die. He couldn't bear it.

"I gave her up, but I know where she is. I see her almost every day, but she doesn't know who I am, and I can't tell her because she doesn't like me."

"Everyone likes you!" Clarence says.

"Nope. She doesn't. She is repulsed by me."

Repulsed! Clarence thinks she must be joking, but then he sees her face.

"I think it might be because I scared her once, when she was little. I think she remembers that, sort of subconsciously, and it colors the way she sees me now."

"How could you have scared her?"

Lulu sips her wine. "I went to see her once. I sneaked back up there. I honestly don't know what was on my mind, what my —intentions were. I just found myself on a bus one morning. I was wearing—you would've laughed to see it—big bell-bottom pants, platform sandals, no jacket—"

"You mean seventies stuff?"

"I told you it was a while ago. Anyway, I forgot how cold it gets up there—"

"Up where?"

"Oh, upstate, this little town. So here I am, in my platform sandals, sneaking down their driveway, which is long, like a dirt road. It's cold and it's been raining. I slip and fall and when I get up, there's mud all over one side of me, but I go on because I'm going to find my baby. I creep around the house, trying to see in. The door opens and I run behind a woodpile. This tot comes out —sweater and overalls, bushy hair, little rubber boots, serious face. She walks over to the woodpile. Maybe someone has sent her out for a stick of wood. I don't know. And I'm calling, 'Ray, honey, It's Mommy. It's Mommy, honey!' My arms are wide. I'm ready to swoop her up and carry her away."

Lulu's mouth quivers. Clarence moves to her side of the table, squats beside her chair, and puts his arms around her. He holds her as it passes through her like a summer storm, shaking her frame, leaving his shirt wet where her face leaned against it. The busboy, the waiter, and the bartender think it has something to do with the attack of Dog Man. They want to come over, but Clarence waves them away. He pats her back, then rubs it, waiting for the storm to pass. Lulu leans back, blotting her face with her napkin, pushing her damp hair back from her cheeks.

After a while, she says, "You know who my baby is, don't you, Clarence?"

And Clarence realizes that he does know, and that Lulu is right: Her daughter does not like her.

THE KISS

THE TEMPERATURE WENT UP TO A HUNDRED AND THREE
today, with brownouts in some of the boroughs, but all's well in
the Weatherstone house, delightfully cool in the living room,
where Florence and Martin are having a glass of wine before
dinner. Edith is upstairs.

"Flo, why don't you help her?" Martin says, worried that
Henry will come for Edith before they get a chance to admire
her in the dress. (He still can't get over that Florence went and
bought Edith a dress.)

"I will, but there's something I want to discuss with you first,
about Edith," Florence says.

Martin straightens in his chair. He hopes Florence isn't going
to say something negative. She's been so nice about Edith, not

jealous anymore. She seems to have fallen in love with Edith as
well.

"I know about Edith," Florence says.

"You do?" Martin is confused. Is it that evident? His heart
quickens. Maybe Florence has noticed something in Edith.
Maybe they already look like lovers, to the perceptive outsider.
And Florence certainly is perceptive. She's a professional,
trained—

"Martin? Are you listening?"

"About Edith—"

"I have to admit I was angry at first, jealous."

"That's understandable."

"Do you think so?"

"You had every right—"

"Well, it wasn't my best side. I wasn't proud of my behavior."

"I think your behavior's remarkable."

"Really?"

"Incredibly generous."

Florence appears pleased with his compliment. She takes a
sip of wine. "Well, it just seemed to me—I mean, I'm the one
who always wanted a child. And why shouldn't I welcome a
child of yours into our home. Even if she's not mine. I mean, that
whole business with Lucille was—"

"Lucille?" Martin has definitely lost a part of this conversation, maybe even the topic sentence.

"Lucille's child," Florence persists, but Martin can't hear
what Florence is saying because his heart is filling his ears with
blood. He hears only blood, surging through his system. Florence
should not tell him anything that would upset him. He has to
stay calm.

Martin is staring at Florence as if she's speaking to him from behind a pane of soundproof glass. She becomes alarmed, is about to rush to his side, call an ambulance, she doesn't know what, when he stands, and she turns to see Edith on the stair.

"Martin? Are you all right?"

Martin seems so perfectly calm and fine, walking over to the stairs, chatting with Edith, that Florence feels foolish. She actually thought he was having another heart attack. She sips her wine, holds the glass to her lips, and contemplates Edith on the stair.

What luck that they saw the dress together! In the store, strangers stopped what they were doing when Edith came out of the dressing room to show Florence how it fit. The salesgirl complimented Florence on the beauty of her daughter, and said that they seemed to have a "nice relationship."

Florence goes to stand beside Martin and see Edith from his vantage point. How the house becomes this child. Florence can see her taking the house on, as Florence did, caring for it and for Martin and Florence, too, bringing new blood into it—a husband, grandchildren. Does Martin see this? Does he see his daughter?

There's the bell. The car is here. Wait! She has to get a picture. The camera's upstairs, wouldn't you know. She'll get it. Stay right there. Don't leave.

Florence runs upstairs, leaving Freddy barking at the door. Edith goes to quiet her. She is startled to discover Martin behind her, standing close. With the dog barking, she didn't hear him, and he moved so quickly. She smells wine on his breath. He's taken his glasses off; she sees broken capillaries in the whites of his eyes, and the whites clotted and yellow in places. One of his hands lies awkwardly on her shoulder. His face comes close. She jerks her head back.

"Up here!" Florence calls from the stair. The flash blinds for a second. Martin reaches for Edith. She opens the door to Henry, who captures her in his arms and holds her while he makes hurried, hearty talk with Martin and Florence. Edith can tell that Florence wants to kiss her goodbye, but she dares not leave Henry's protecting arms. What she does is wave, and manage a thank you, a goodbye. "We'll see you later," Florence says. "I'll wait up for you."

GERALDINE REFRESHES HER GLASS WITH MORE ICE AND just another finger of Scotch. The floor plan for the apartment is secured by magnets to the refrigerator. It's in the West Village, where she dreamed of living when she first came to the city—a dream she'd nearly forgotten. When the realtor took her in through the foyer, a sound came from Geraldine's throat. The realtor turned, thinking perhaps that something was wrong, but Geraldine smiled, to let her know she was all right. She had no words to put to the cry—the groan—the sigh. And why should she bother explaining to a realtor what it meant to discover that her rightful home had been waiting on this street, behind this door, all along. The life she had been meant to lead—vases filled with flowers, friends gathered at the table, music on the stereo, and the clink of glasses raised in toasts. It had all been waiting. Why had she denied herself?

It's a sublease, furnished, with an option to buy. Perfect. She'll get rid of her old furniture, the ugly sofa she never liked, the hideous milk crates. Geraldine is looking forward to living with someone again. What she misses from her affair with Ryo, more than sex, was the way they grew comfortable being around each other, like living in a school dorm or a family. It's a more natural way to be.

THE PHOTOGRAPHERS' BALL IS THE ONLY EVENT WORTH coming in from the Hamptons for, Ryo Yamanaka thinks, doing a quick scan of the room, while responding to air kisses and photo flashes. She's at her agent's table, although any number of groups would have been happy to include her, even *Ubu.* Henry Reed asked her. It's interesting how the configuration at that table has changed from a year ago when the Weatherstones held court. No Geraldine. Geraldine hasn't gotten back to Ryo about the article. The bitch is probably going to let it conveniently slip her mind, which is all right. Ryo's relations with Henry are good, and Geraldine is obviously on her way out.

Look at him on the dance floor, twirling his delectable little prom queen. He's a good dancer. He moves the girl along, displaying her like a trophy. Ryo is a good dancer too, although no one here will ask her to dance. She learned in high school, when her father was sent to the States. Her father, insulated in his Japanese company, and her mother, in the cocoon of her house, stayed Japanese, but little Ryo was catapulted straight into an American high school. She was so busy trying to fit in—perming her hair, learning all the dances—that she didn't figure out that she was different not only because she was Japanese, but also and especially because she was gay. It's been a long road from aspiring to be a typical American girl to accepting what she is, Jap dyke. Finally she takes herself seriously, and other people respect her. Still, she wouldn't mind if someone asked her to dance.

HENRY SEES RYO YAMANAKA LOOKING AT HIM AND IN-terprets her gaze as one of envy. She wants to be the one handling this supple young body. Henry puts his arm out and the girl swirls around him. They're attracting notice. He draws her toward him; she smiles. She's his good luck charm. She's his line to Martin, whom he still loves. It pains Henry to have to go after Martin's job. But Martin's head is on the block. Bruno would have replaced him by now if Henry hadn't been around to take over and keep Bruno happy. Playing the usurper is a frightening role. Henry wants Martin's job, but he also wants his love and approval, the way he always has. This is why he needs Edith. As long as he possesses her friendship, Martin can't hate him.

They're playing a tango. Do you tango? he asks. They move unhesitatingly into it. She allows the music to inhabit her body so that Henry can lead her effortlessly. Why do they love her so— Martin and Geraldine? Even Florence now, initially jealous, seems to dote on her. Of course, Edith is delightful, fresh, unspoiled, but it must be more than that. It's a mystery that's driving him crazy, because he feels that the answer is supremely simple, something he should be able to figure out on his own, but can't. He could ask Edith, but he doubts if she would be able to answer, or even to understand, his question. For some reason, she is a medium, a conduit for all the emotions those three have felt toward each other over the years, emotions they blocked, diverted, repressed. It's all flowing freely now toward this mysterious young creature, who accepts the torrent as unquestioningly as a stone, lying smooth in the bed of a river.

EDITH DANCES. WHEN HENRY INTRODUCES HER TO PEOple, she smiles. She shakes hands. But the feeling has come back, of being in someone else's life while her own goes on without her. Her face has fallen into the mask she used to wear at Grimsby. When she looked like this Clarence would accuse her of having an out-of-body experience, of having been abducted by aliens. But he isn't here, so no one can tell.

Why did he do it? She keeps playing the sequence over in her mind, hoping there was some mistake, that she can see it another way, but it keeps coming back stronger each time. Martin tried to kiss her. Something went wrong, and Edith can't figure out what. Just when she felt the most sure of herself and the path she was on, she encountered—what? A chasm. She thought she and Martin were walking a road together, one of friendship, of teacher and student, but Martin obviously thought something else. The look in his eyes!

Her real self, the one Martin was helping her discover, is fading, leaving her emptier than before. Instead of taking an interest in her as his protégée, he was secretly admiring her legs, thinking of kissing her lips, and she was maybe even half-knowingly letting him look at her and think about her. Is that the person he was finding in her? She hates that person! She would rather cut her out with a knife than let her live inside her body.

"Edith, you have goose bumps all over. Here, put my jacket over your shoulders," Henry says. "They really overdo the air-conditioning in these places."

"IT'S NO TROUBLE AT ALL. I WAS *PLANNING* TO STAY UP and let you in. . . . But I thought you'd *planned* on staying. . . . You—" Florence, propped up in bed, catches a glimpse of herself in the mirror, brows drawn, mouth pinched. She hears her voice, like a disappointed child, or worse, a querulous old woman. "Of course, if you feel that way. . . . I understand. I only wanted to hear how it went. How about lunch? Come tomorrow and have brunch with Martin. . . . Well, how about Wednesday? . . . Somewhere near the office?"

Florence hangs up. What made Edith change her mind? Perhaps it's just as she said, that she realized she was going to be very late and didn't want to inconvenience Martin and Florence. She couldn't know that Florence would gladly wait up the night for her. Florence goes to remove the makeup she had retouched, looking forward to a post-party tête-à-tête in the zodiac room. Florence feels a little foolish now, in her best nightgown, but it's nice to have someone to look good for. She'd almost lost the feeling of what it was like.

MARTIN HEARS THE PHONE RING ONCE AND PUTS IT OUT of his mind. He burrows back to a scrap that came up unbidden from the discard heap of memory. Nothing's ever lost, they say. It lies dormant, waiting for the proper key—a taste of madeleine, the feel of a girl's skin—to bring it back.

Lucille was her name. She was about Edith's age when she came to the magazine. Martin preferred Geraldine and Florence, girls with polish. They used to joke about Nadja's infatuation with the flower child from San Francisco. Then Lucille turned in some work, and Martin had to admit that it had something—a spark, a new twist. He wondered if she were a true original, or if she simply belonged to a group that hadn't been heard from as yet. She was a novelty.

She was frankly sexual. Martin took her out to dinner to get to know her better. He convinced himself that his motive was professional, although he managed to avoid letting Florence and Geraldine know. They shared a bottle of Chianti. (Whatever happened to those absurd and touching bottles in raffia that seemed to be everywhere at that time? One never sees them anymore.) It was a strong wine, like blood, and not as harsh as some of them.

What did they talk about? He can't remember, only that they laughed and he began to realize that she was beautiful in a way he hadn't noticed before, and wittier than he'd thought. He was also aware of an undercurrent to their conversation, something dangerous but enticing. He had the feeling, as he walked her back to her apartment in the vicinity of St. Mark's Place, that he was embarking on an adventure that could mark a turning point in his life.

How long did it last? A few weeks at most—always at her place, always clandestine—but while it was going on, Martin didn't recognize himself. He'd read about but never experienced how the body can take over the mind, how people of strong intellect can perform brainless acts. Sometimes he would rationalize by saying that it was good for once to experience the kind of loss of control that is so commonly found in literature, that this adventure would be enlightening when it was finally over and he could look back on it.

The night it ended the curtain was blowing in the window, hovering over them. There was a hot breeze, unusual for September, and sounds from the street. Their bodies stuck to each other. After a while, he raised himself on an elbow to see if she was sleeping, but her eyes were open, as if she were listening to something far away. Her face was smooth and symmetrical in repose.

"What are you thinking?"

"I wasn't thinking. I was experiencing."

Experiencing what? She claimed to be experiencing nothing less than the penetration of her ripe and ready ovum by his sperm. She even claimed to know the sex of this zygote. Female. She would name it Desirée.

He expressed disbelief and then outrage that she had not

been using protection. He left her bed and never returned. When she told him later that the doctor had confirmed her pregnancy, he decided that she had been knocked up by someone else and had duped him into having sex with her so she could name him as the father.

Now as he lies with his hands cupped over his heart, he wonders if a terrible injustice weren't committed on that night, if the shock of his experience with Lucille didn't permanently damage him in some way, inhibit his sexuality. Never again would the mind let the body have its way. And it didn't until the heart attack, when the body rose up in revolt. The revenge of the repressed, neglected heart.

Abruptly he gets out of bed, finds his glasses, and goes into the bathroom where his pills are on a shelf above the sink. He takes the bottle of Lopressor, empties it into the toilet, and flushes. His heart doesn't need tethering; it needs unleashing. It's criminal to subdue the heart, to keep it at under a hundred beats per minute, in limbo between life and death.

Martin throws the empty bottle in the wastebasket. Of course, he can always refill the prescription tomorrow, have Nora do it. But he doesn't think he will. He's pleased with himself for having made an impetuous gesture. His heart actually feels stronger and younger for it. He's bored with worrying. His new concern is, does Edith think he's too old?

EVIDENTLY THE TOY COPS WERE NOT ABLE TO APPREHEND Dog Man, for Wallace Hoag paid Lulu a visit at the gallery, watching her through the plate glass, barking to be let in. Lulu hid in the back behind the screen until he went away. She decided to spend the night on the mattress rather than risk meeting up with Hoag in the street on her way home. He seems to be singling her out, maybe because they both pursue the same line of work.

It was a red-letter day at the garbage cans. QB threw out a complete suit of thermal underwear. Lulu sewed the top to the bottom and mounted it on a wire that hangs from the ceiling to the floor. It floats in the corner of the room like a shed skin, twisting on currents of air. Clarence stopped over to admire the effect and the newly redone floor.

Larry came later and took her to dinner. He's completely mystified by what she's doing here. His idea of art is something you purchase to display in your house, preferably something that appreciates in value over time. But they've had this discussion before. He's impatient for Lulu to finish the project and begin looking at houses with him. Larry likes his comforts. He's a big man, heavier and older than Montero. He did not want to make love on the mattress. Lulu would have liked to get him on tape. She's been learning a lot from watching the videos, although she's becoming a bit of a ham. She'll have to rein in her tendency to overact.

Molly is due back on the fifteenth of September and Lulu has made no arrangements. At the beginning of summer, she assumed that Larry would be taking care of her by then. Now it seems less likely. As Clarence pointed out, if Larry comes to the show and sees the videotapes, or even hears about them, it's bound to affect their plans. True. There are plenty of friends who could take her in. She should be on the phone, finding out which of them might be needing her for a while.

Of course there is no phone here, and it would be too late to call anyone now, except for the friends in California. Lulu spends a good hour torturing herself by thinking of everyone she should be calling, and about how she hasn't kept up, hasn't kept her lifeline open. She's gotten lazy, thinking she had Larry to take care of her. It takes a lot of work to maintain friendships—at least the kind of friendships Lulu has, where she is the one willing to service the other in return for material benefits. A list of friends who might be able to help scrolls through her mind. *Call X. Write to Y. Call Z. to find W.*

It must be a hundred degrees in here, without a breath of air. She can feel her body fluids seeping into the mattress. Usually heat doesn't bother her. She doesn't let it. But tonight she is powerless to deny it. The heat is smothering her—a frail, aging woman lying on a pallet in a space she doesn't own, has no right to. She is paying for it with the only medium of exchange she has, her body.

Lulu stops herself. Because she can't afford despair. Because there is no one who could stop her if she began her downward slide. No one who understands and cares—which isn't true, she realizes. There's Clarence. Clarence knows everything about her. He caught her at her lowest—scavenging food from the garbage —and offered her his love, his protection. Of all her friends, Clarence is the one she treasures just for his own sake, and not for what he can provide. And yet he gives her more than anyone. As she thinks about Clarence, it seems to her that he is a saint. He saw her going through garbage and he gave her food. He watches over Desert Ray in her stead, because she can't, she's not allowed. Saint Clarence. She'd do anything for him.

In the night Lulu wakes at the sound of the door opening, and her first fear—irrationally—is of Dog Man. But the only one with a key is Montero. She reaches for the remote and then turns on a light so he can find her. How did he know she'd be here? She hadn't planned to stay the night. Did he get out of his bed, leave his wife, just on the off chance that she'd be here? How often does he do this?

"I worry about you. This isn't healthy, you know," she tells him, but Montero is in no mood to discuss health. Lulu has decided that Montero has too much energy. It has driven him into addictions—marijuana, cocaine, alcohol. He's "in recovery" from all of them. Lulu's just another drug. He uses her body to focus inner turbulence. She calms him. Lulu, on the other hand, gets charged up from Montero. His raging need excites her, like walking the beach in a hurricane. It's an energy-transference arrangement, the kind of thing that when she was younger she would have mistaken for love.

THE WIND

THE WIND THIS MORNING IS STRANGE FOR NEW YORK—
hot and dry, with an edge like a knife. It reminds Lulu of Spain,
when the Solano comes howling out of Africa; or Southern California, when the Santa Anas blow in from the desert. Dust devils
rise in her path and snatch at her clothes. In a half-empty parking lot there's a roiling kettle of litter, twenty feet high. White
plastic bags with handles, the kind Korean grocers give out,
hover at the top like bloated birds of carrion. Sheets of newspaper twist, dive, and then shoot skyward. Smaller scraps caught in
the funnel give texture and form. Footsteps coming up fast at her
heels make her whirl and jump. "Sorry." An early commuter
rushing by. A reminder that it's dangerous to leave the body
unguarded on the street while the mind lets itself get caught in

the movement of wind-blown litter in a parking lot. Stay alert. Keep an eye out. This is the kind of wind that chafes nerve endings, ignites tempers, provokes outbursts.

EDITH CAN SEE THE WIND ON THE STREET, BENDING trees, rolling a trash basket down the sidewalk, but very little comes in the open window, as the loft has poor ventilation. She's staying home from work this morning because she has an appointment to try the Age Machine at ten-thirty in the home of the artist/inventor, on Third Street and Avenue A. This is her assignment for the front-of-the-book piece. It was Ben's idea originally; the inventor is a friend of his. The machine is a computer that alters a person's face to show how it will look in twenty years. For some reason Henry took Ben's idea away from him and assigned it to Edith.

"C'mon, Clare!"

"Chill, girlfriend." Clarence emerges from the bathroom, wearing his favorite turquoise cowboy boots and pink denim shorts. "What's it like weatherwise?" He looks out the window. "I think we have a wind situation."

"But it's hot. I heard it on the radio." Edith tries to contain impatience.

Clarence is rummaging in the closet. "My aloha shirt. I thought it was here. Have you seen it?"

"Maybe it's in the wash."

"Oh, Edie, this is your dress, your eight-hundred-dollar dress, way in the back. I never got to see it." He holds it up to his shoulders. "Put it on, just for a minute, so I can see—"

"Give me that!" She rips it out of his hands and jams it back into the closet.

"My, my! We must be having major PMS here. You can go have coffee by yourself."

Edith looks out the window, where a plastic bag is floating by. Since the night of the ball her life seems to be coming unmoored. Ben is being distant. Peyton and Kylie openly snub her. Edith's afraid to talk to the Weatherstones. She keeps thinking of Martin in the hall by the door, his hand on her shoulder, his face —What was the intention? The motivation?

She knew from the beginning that he was looking at her, that he liked watching her, but he was old and ill, which made him harmless, she thought. In her mind she hears Carolyn's voice blaming her for accepting favors from Martin, the dress from Florence, implying that there would be a price to pay. Edith feels the shadow of the woman who gave birth in an unheated farmhouse. What was her crime, what brought her to that state? What if Edith is repeating her mistakes, following some genetically determined path to misery? What if Real Life, that insistent pull she feels toward another way of being is the tug of an inherited degeneracy?

This concept comes right out of the nineteenth century. People don't believe in the criminal mind, phrenology, biology as destiny. She knows this, but every time she banishes these fears, they seep back in another way. What she needs is a good long talk with Clarence, the kind they used to have at Grimsby, holed up in her room or his, drinking herb teas, burning their candles from the botanica they found in the Latino section of Rochester. Clarence has launched himself into his Real Life without a hitch, without a backward glance. He doesn't need the long talks anymore, or maybe he's having them with Lulu.

· · ·

LULU IS FIGHTING THE WIND TO GET TO THE ELEVATOR door when it flies open, revealing Clarence and Desert Ray, looking so young and fresh that Lulu has to laugh. They're just going out for coffee, Clarence says. Lulu invites herself along, her treat.

"If you don't mind the look—cowboy boots and short shorts," says Clarence.

"If I had your legs, Clare, I'd dress that way too," Lulu says.

"Edie thinks it's over-the-top."

Lulu looks at Ray, who doesn't return her glance. "Mmm, now that you mention it, Clare, I think Edie might have a point. I mean, you look like a kid who came from somewhere else and decided to dress gay because he was in New York, you know what I mean?" Ray doesn't acknowledge Lulu's remark. If anything, she seems to resent Lulu for taking her side.

"I spent a fortune on these boots. I can't just throw them away!"

"Well, maybe you just don't want to wear them with shorts. . . ."

Lulu tucks her arm through Clarence's, and Edith actually resents it, as if Lulu were stealing her boyfriend. The two of them have so much to talk about, as friends do who see each other daily—Clarence's new job that starts next week; what he should wear; what his boss is like; Lulu's boyfriend, back in town from his long trip; Montero, who's "madly in love, but madly. Honestly, Clare, it's like rabies. He should be shot and put out of his misery."

As they swirl into the Dream Café, Edith stops on the pavement. "Clare, I'm going to be late. I've gotta go."

"Oh c'mon, Edie. You have time."

"No, I don't."

Lulu, on the top step, looks down at Clarence and Ray. Are

they quarreling because of her? Did she do wrong, assuming they'd want her company? Lulu pulls her hair back, trying to make it neater. Her clothes are spotted and mussed. She should have changed and bathed. Maybe she smells of sex. She looks a wreck, like an old wreck. She's frightening Ray. She can see her eyes getting round and dark, just like the time Lulu surprised her by the woodpile. "Oh, hey, you two probably want to be alone. I should go. I think I need a bath more than a shot of caffeine."

Clarence leaps the steps to keep Lulu from leaving and when he turns around Edie has gone without apologizing to Lulu, who's distraught. Clarence fusses over Lulu, gets her a cappuccino, makes apologies, too many.

"Clare, it's no good, honey. She hates my guts," Lulu says.

AT FIRST EDITH, ANGRY WITH LULU FOR STEALING HER time with Clarence, and with Clarence for siding with Lulu, walks fast, but then she realizes she's going to be a half hour early for her appointment, and slows down. This is a sort of no-man's land between Soho and the East Village where Edith doesn't generally go. The streets are forlorn, with papers blowing like tumbleweed down barren gray alleys, and dingy figures crouching in doorways.

A tangled head of hair, the exact same shade as her own, with the face hidden in a rough blanket, arrests Edith's attention. An empty paper cup is set next to the form, in a bare and hopeless bid for help. Edith stops, half against her will. She has to see the face beneath the hair; she would never forgive herself if she walked by without looking—yet she wants to flee, to run until her legs give out. Again, she's angry with Clarence for not being here, distracting her so that she wouldn't notice this mess of hair.

Edith reaches into her backpack for change to put in the cup, making more noise than is necessary, in order to attract the person's attention, but the bundle doesn't move. Edith inches closer. The smell of excrement hits her in the face. She drops the coins and turns away, but the blanket falls and she sees it, one eye swollen shut, the other meeting hers in a knowing way. Edith can't force herself to stay and parse out the features, to match them against her own. She hurries on, her arms clutching the pack against her pounding heart.

EDITH SITS AT A CAFÉ, DRINKING A CAPPUCCINO AND waiting for Ben. He was a little gruff at first over the phone, but Edith knew he would leave work and come to her. It took some begging; she had to act frightened. Well, she is frightened, really, Edith tells herself. Her hand, holding a puff of milk foam on a spoon, is shaking. She felt she couldn't go on to the Age Machine without Ben by her side. In the end, he sounded pleased to be needed.

What she is afraid of is seeing her mother in the Age Machine, coming face-to-face with Lucille. Why is she afraid? Grandpop sent her to find this woman. He thought Edith was old enough, mature enough to accept her. He wouldn't have sent Edith searching for a derelict, a crack addict. Lucille could be a professional woman, with a husband, someone like Florence. She could be someone like Geraldine. Both Florence and Geraldine have been kind to Edith, interested in helping her, in the way a mother might be. Why wouldn't Lucille be like them?

EDITH WATCHES BEN GIVE A HUG TO THE INVENTOR OF the Age Machine, Anne Dillon, who is not pretty, but attractive in an offbeat way, with her hair shaved halfway up, her small round glasses, a delicate gold hoop through her nose. Ben says she's just a friend, older, in her thirties, but she looks young. Edith wonders if they've gone to bed with each other and is interested to discover that she minds. The apartment is light and neat, not much furniture, some futons rolled in a bedroom. The computer is mounted in a black console facing a black straight-backed chair. There's something penitential about it, or confessional. Edith asks questions and takes notes: Anne's education; how she came upon the idea; where and on whom she has tried the machine; what happened at those occasions (amusing or interesting anecdotes).

"You don't seem that eager to try it yourself," Anne says.

"It's pretty amazing. You should try it," Ben says.

"If she doesn't want to, she shouldn't," Anne tells Ben. "Some people get upset. That's why I don't make a printout, because people could get obsessed, especially really good-looking people."

Edith feels Anne is accusing her of being vain. "I'm not afraid of growing old. It's a natural process. I don't expect to look twenty-one for the rest of my life," she says.

"And some people are bummed because they look like their parents. The first time I tried it, I came out like my mom. So I went and got this haircut and my nose pierced. So now I look like my mom with a ring through her nose."

"Edie's adopted," Ben says.

"That's so cool. I never had anyone do this who was adopted. So you get a kind of ghost image of what your parents look like now. Or parent. Most people tend to favor one or the other. I've found that anyway, that most people say they look like their mother or father. Although some have said they look like a grandmother, or an uncle or something."

Edith sits in front of the screen. "Well, I don't know how anyone looks, so it will be just me, twenty years later."

She sees her face on the screen, moving as she talks. Anne turns some knobs, freezing Edith's face into an image. She moves a cursor so that Edith's eyes are in two white line circles. She moves other lines to frame the face.

"It takes a minute," Anne says.

Edith watches a map of lines extend up her face from the chin. Her lids droop over her eyes, her chin softens and broadens.

The face disturbs Edith, but not because it's her own, grown older. It seems to belong to someone else. If she allowed herself, she could find the name to match the image. The face looks back at her, daring her to find it, to say it. She's relieved when, after a minute or two, the features fade away.

IT'S AN UNUSUAL WIND, BROUGHT ON BY A FREAKISH ME-teorological occurrence: a cap of high pressure over the Midwest, where there was a month-long drought during which the heart of the country baked under a cloudless sky. Finally a shift in the jet stream punched a hole in the air mass and it came pouring east, as hot and dry as a desert wind. It scours the proud lime-stone facade of the building in which the *Ubu* offices are housed. It rattles the panes of the windows, furnishing a subliminal irri-tant to the already harsh tone of the conversation taking place at the Friday morning editorial meeting in Martin's office.

"I specifically did not send the contract to Ryo Yamanaka because I did not think—" Geraldine says.

"Ryo assumed you had forgotten and I—" Henry counters.

"You could have asked me, had the courtesy—"

"I didn't see any reason why the piece should be turned down—"

"That wasn't your decision to—"

"Well, I'm sorry, all right? It's a minor . . ."

Geraldine looks around the room. When Martin's here he sits, not behind his desk, but on it, engagingly and informally, like a popular professor Geraldine remembers from Wellesley. The women editors take the sofas, with maybe a younger one on the floor or the coffee table. The men lean against bookshelves or the backs of the sofas. Until today Martin's desk has been left empty, with neither Geraldine nor Henry presuming to take that place. This time, however, Geraldine came in to find Henry already sitting on Martin's desk, feigning interest in something an editor was showing him, managing to look as if the editor had stopped him and he had carelessly rested his haunches on the nearest available surface. Geraldine took her accustomed seat on the sofa, thinking the others would be as outraged as she. But they accepted Henry's position with equanimity.

The composition of the editorial meetings has changed over the past few years, with more young editors who align themselves with Henry. No one is going to come to Geraldine's aid over this Ryo Yamanaka matter. They are doodling on yellow pads, looking out the window, avoiding eye contact. They know her history with Ryo and assume Geraldine purposely left Ryo hanging, who then went to Henry as her only recourse.

"All right, Henry, let it pass. In the future, though, could you do me the courtesy—"

"Certainly, Geraldine." He's all smiles and charm. The meeting continues. Wind assaults the building. Geraldine, thinking about cigarettes (smoking at meetings went out with Nadja) almost misses the next bit of chicanery that Henry is trying to pull off.

You've got to be kidding, she tells Henry. Under what pretext should *Ubu* run an obvious puff piece on Jerome? Does he have new work coming out?

Families, Henry says, the importance of families, a photographic essay in the fashion section. The three fashion editors, a trio of anorexics who always dress in black and don't have one working brain between them, nod assent. This is one that Martin will have to okay personally, Geraldine says, knowing there's no way.

"He already has," Henry says.

"Has what?"

"Approved it."

"Who?"

"Martin. He loves it."

"Loves it?"

"He thinks it's great."

Geraldine can picture Martin waving Henry off, agreeing with him just to get him to leave. "Martin is a sick man, Henry. You're taking advantage."

"A minute ago you said we had to have Martin's approval. I say we have it, and now you're saying it doesn't mean anything. If Martin's opinion doesn't count with you anymore, maybe Bruno's does, and Bruno happens to love—"

"Bruno has no right! He isn't involved in editorial. He shouldn't be consulted." Geraldine's voice rises as the wind moans around the corners of the building. Her eyes scan the room, looking for sympathy, agreement, an ally, but there is no response. No one is willing to rescue her.

FLORENCE HAS ASKED GERALDINE TO MEET HER AT THE Frick, Florence's favorite art museum because it's small, intimate, a former private residence, and sometimes on a summer day, practically empty, you can feel you are a guest, not one of the masses, elbowed along from painting to painting. It's possible to stop and study a particular work.

In this small circular anteroom, a single piece is hung, an annunciation by Fra Filippo Lippi, framed in gilt columns, a kneeling Gabriel in one section, and in the other, the Virgin. The power of Gabriel's crimson cloak in sculptural folds behind him is answered by the red garment the Virgin wears beneath her celestial blue robes. Red for sensuality, blue for spirituality. Red for blood, the blood of Christ, the menstrual flow, the blood of childbirth.

Fra Filippo Lippi, the artist monk, abducted the beautiful nun, Lucrezia. He made love to her and dressed her to pose as the Virgin, perhaps this Virgin, whose exquisite features express resignation and humility before the will of God. What was on Lippi's mind as his fine brush strokes melted into the surface of his transcendent vision? Lust for his mistress? The purity of the Virgin? Or the way the light fell on the folds of her gown?

And what was Lucrezia thinking as she stood burdened with his child? Did she consider herself a victim of his lust, of her own? Was she sinner or saint? She looks more resigned than happy to be receiving Gabriel's message. It was a woman's fate to bear children, not something she chose. In those days, one did not decide, "I'll destroy this one and keep another that comes at a more convenient time." Would Lucrezia have gotten rid of this one if she could have? Would she have turned the angel Gabriel away at the door? Such a delicate complexion. She couldn't have been older than seventeen. . . .

GERALDINE FINDS IT INCOMPREHENSIBLE THAT FLORENCE would keep her waiting like this, when Geraldine has taken time away from the office and fought through the wind for a cab to make this absurdly inconvenient meeting. Finally the guard at the entrance thinks to tell Geraldine that her friend left word to meet her inside. It's typical somehow of Florence to place her trust in a museum guard. There she is now, hidden away in a little hall. "I was waiting for you at the entrance," Geraldine says.

"Oh, dear. I left instructions—"

"You can't expect those people to care—"

Florence sighs. She'd forgotten how disapproving and severe Geraldine has been lately. Florence thought she should discuss her plan with Geraldine first, as a courtesy, but perhaps it would be better to just go through with it. After all, Edith is no more Geraldine's than she is Florence's. She is Martin's child.

But Martin has been curiously unable to accept the annunciation. Florence tried a second time to discuss it with him, and again he eluded her. Sometimes Florence thinks he's known all along and is embarrassed to admit it. Sometimes she goes into a dark spiral and thinks both Martin and Edith have known all along and have hidden it from her. But more and more she suspects that Martin can't bear to learn the truth. What is it about fatherhood that terrifies him so? When Florence told him years ago that she was pregnant, he turned pale. "How did that happen?" he asked, as if it were her fault and he had had nothing to do with it.

They are passing through the Fragonard room, one that's always been a favorite of Florence's, a fragile eggshell rescued from prerevolutionary France. The models must have been no more than fifteen years old. They don't have bones, just sweet molded flesh.

Florence had this boneless look once, but of course she didn't value it at the time. She was too preoccupied with being smart, sophisticated, grown-up. And she had no idea that one day she wouldn't have it anymore. The flesh falls away from the bone. Nothing to be done about it, or not much.

She admires Edith's smooth limbs. She enjoys looking at her, as a mother might admire her child grown to womanhood. That day in the store, Florence felt radiant with pride when Edith came out of the dressing room and everyone turned to look. It's a gift to be able to enjoy Edith's youth, in a way Florence never could her own.

"Amazing. They had kitsch even then," Geraldine says, examining the wall text.

"Martin doesn't like Fragonard either," Florence says. She isn't ashamed to be the sentimentalist in their group of three. She's always carried the burden of the heart. Geraldine and Martin are all mind, cerebral. Florence needs the warmth of lovers, children, and pets. Geraldine, like Martin, is an ascetic, happier with ideas than flesh and blood.

This covered courtyard, this stone bench by a gently splashing fountain, is where Florence means to make her announcement to Geraldine. It's a calm, neutral refuge where they won't be interrupted. Unfortunately Geraldine thinks it's the perfect place to launch into her latest grievances against Henry. One of the least attractive things about Geraldine—Martin thinks so too —is that she has not been able to accommodate herself to Henry's rise at the magazine. She can't see that there is room—in fact, *need*—for two of them in the position directly under Martin. Geraldine doesn't understand that she and Henry complement each other.

Geraldine soon realizes that Florence is not really interested. She is furnishing the kind of patronizing comments a therapist might employ with a deluded patient. It is evident that Florence assumes Geraldine is jealous of Henry, instead of genuinely concerned for the magazine.

From her hospital bed, Geraldine can barely make out Florence's grief-stricken face. Florence's voice catches as she says she never realized how fiercely Geraldine was fighting for the honor of the magazine, how selflessly she was martyring herself. . . .

"She wants to stay on in the city and work at the magazine, and it seems silly, with two extra rooms in our house where she could live—it seems unfair not to tell her about Martin. I told Martin, but he didn't seem to understand. You know what he's been like since the heart attack. If Edith . . ."

It takes a while for Geraldine to understand what is being said. Florence, in her biscuit-colored two-piece dress, ingeniously cut to conceal that she has put on flesh from being just a little overindulgent (Why deny herself a glass of wine, a piece of cake, when so many have flattered and told her a few pounds in the right place never hurt?). Florence, who's always had the beautiful house, who appropriated Martin as one more good thing she had coming to her and then shamelessly took on lovers, flaunted them, now is appropriating Edith.

"No!"

Florence recoils, as if she'd been slapped.

Geraldine lowers her voice. "It doesn't make sense," she says. "It won't work. If we tell her about Martin, we'll have to tell her about Lucille."

Florence recovers quickly. She has already thought about the Lucille problem. She wants to find the woman, move her into a residence for the homeless. Florence is on the board of a charitable organization that runs a model shelter, the best in the city. If Lucille needs psychiatric or medical help, Florence can get it for her. There's no reason why Edith shouldn't know who her parents are. The child will not go mad from the knowledge. Life is not a gothic novel, after all.

So this is how some people wind up having everything and other people nothing, Geraldine thinks, as Florence outlines how she's going to take over not only Edith but Lucille as well. But Geraldine has learned some things since Florence talked her out of Martin. This time she won't go without a struggle.

"Florence, I've rented an apartment in the Village, with a room for Edith."

"Oh dear, Geraldine."

"What do you mean, 'Oh dear'?"

"Have you told Edith?"

"I was waiting until I'd signed the lease, but we've spoken, in general terms, about living together. It's really something, Florence, how our friendship has developed. There's a sympathetic link you don't often see when there's an age difference like we have. But she tells me everything, and I feel there's nothing I can't tell her. . . ." As Geraldine expounds upon the friendship, she goes beyond what is, into what will be. For instance, Geraldine has not actually confided much in Edith. That will come, in the comfort of sharing a home. Florence hears her out with conspicuous patience.

"That is remarkable, Geraldine, and I don't doubt that you are the best of friends, but when it comes to living together, Edith is going to want someone her own age, with similar interests—"

"Then why would she live with you?"

"That's different. We're her parents. The house, you see, will be hers. When she gets married, she can move her husband in. There will be room for her children."

Beneath Florence's voice the fountain murmurs. Florence

speaks with assurance, as if explaining a law of nature. This is how it happens. Winners win. Losers lose.

CLARENCE LEANS WAY OUT THE WINDOW, LOOKING UP and down the street. It's Clarence's night off and he purposely did not go out so that he could stay home and talk to Edie, and it's ten-thirty and she still isn't here. He's really getting worked up about this—actually angry, in a way he never has felt toward Edie before. At the same time, he knows it's not fair, because Edie didn't know he was going to stay home for her. He just decided at the last minute and assumed she would come straight from work, as if there were a telepathic connection between them. There used to be. Clarence really believes that when they were close, at school, one would somehow know when the other needed to talk and would just show up. It happened so regularly that they didn't discuss it, took it for granted.

Well, the lines are down. If only he *could* communicate with her psychically. He would put his head next to hers and beam her the message. It is ripping him apart to see the way she treats Lulu. When he sees Edie with Lulu, he can't believe it's the same Edie. She has to be told. She's going to find out sooner or later, and when she does, she'll hate herself for the way she treated Lulu. It's for her own good, as well as for Lulu's that Clarence is going to tell her.

But she has to be told in just the right way. That's why Clarence planned the little supper, the wine, the incense (a special healing scent he picked up from a new friend who's an aromatherapist). And now she's ruined it by staying out. Maybe the telepathic line is still in working order, and she's decided she doesn't want to hear what he has to tell her.

Clarence goes back to cleaning his closet. As soon as Lulu

said it this morning, Clarence knew it was true. He hadn't wanted to admit it. All the clothes he bought for the city are wrong. He might as well wear a sign on his back: "Just in from Upper Darby." No wonder Francis never called back. Lulu's promised to go shopping with him, help him get the right things. Lulu knows.

EDITH IS STARTLED FOR A MOMENT, SEEING CLARENCE AT home, when she'd assumed he'd be out. He's in the closet, holding a garbage bag.

"It's after midnight," he says accusingly.

"Am I missing something? Did we have a date?" Edith looks at the table set for two, at the candles and incense. Wine glasses. "Clare! You made dinner!"

Clarence stuffs his aloha shirt into the bag.

Edith looks in. Not only his aloha shirt, but his pink shorts and turquoise cowboy boots, his beloved pink and purple lifter's pants—all his favorite things—are in the bag.

"Boy, she really has an influence on you," Edith says.

"She?"

"Lulu. One word from Lulu and you throw out all your clothes."

"I don't know what you're bitching about. You were always rolling your eyes whenever I showed up in this stuff."

"Bitching! I'm not bitching! I'm just remarking that you seem to have elevated Lulu into some kind of authority—"

"She happens to be one cool lady. I don't know why you—"

"Clare, I don't want to talk about Lulu, okay? It's all right if she's your friend. I don't understand it—I might even be jealous, a little bit—but you have a right to make any friends you want. I just don't want to have to see her or talk to her if I can help it."

"But you have to talk to her," Clarence says. "Here, sit down, sit down. Have some wine." He leads her to the table.

"I already had wine, at dinner. If I drink now I'll have a headache in the morning. It's late, Clare. I have to be at work early tomorrow."

"You can take the day off. Call in sick. Say you have a headache. This is more important!" Clarence takes a bottle of white wine out of the ice bucket, where it has been cooling all night—the ice is practically all melted. What does he want to tell her? What could be so urgent? Edith realizes that she doesn't want to hear it. Clarence is setting the stage, lighting candles, burning incense, turning off lights, like the time he told her he was gay. But then it was fine, because she had guessed it long before, and she could reassure him and they could weep in each other's arms. This time is different. She feels he could wound her, that it won't be all right afterward.

She pushes back from the table. "Clare, don't. Please don't."

"You know what I'm going to tell you, don't you?" His features, lit from the candle, look sinister.

Edith flips on the light switch. "Clare, I can't. I can't talk about it," she says.

DOG MAN

"CLARE, ARE YOU COMING OR WHAT? . . . CLARE?"

"I can't remember how to dress like an ordinary male person. I've lost the ability."

"An ordinary male person does not use eyebrow pencil."

"Just a little, with brown shadow to fill in—"

"It looks weird."

"But if I don't, I look piggy-eyed."

"But you look more normal, for a guy."

"Wait a minute."

"I'm going to be late."

"Just a sec. I want you to check my tie, tell me which tie looks more hetero. Wait just a minute. I'll get them. You look fetching today. Mmm, love that perfume. Can I borrow it some-time? Not today, of course. Here. Which one?"

"They're both a little—"

"Fruity?" Clarence lets his hand dangle from his wrist.

"Don't you have any with, like, stripes?"

"I hate stripes. That's what my brothers wear."

"Yeah, well—"

"Here. This one's blue. Blue is for boys, and it brings out my eyes. I have to do *something* for my eyes."

"Fine. Wear the blue. Why do you have to look ordinary anyway? If this guy you're working for is a friend of Lulu's—" Edith stops herself. Neither she nor Clarence has said the L. word since the night they argued about Lulu and Edith went to bed without hearing what Clarence had to say. In the few times they've spoken since, they have been careful with each other, keeping their conversations deliberately "lite."

"Lulu's well connected. You're reading her wrong. She has a lot of important friends. You know, she's given shows too. She's been written up in the *Times*—"

She's always giving shows, Edith thinks. Lulu's whole life is a show. But she doesn't say this to Clarence. "Now I'm really late," Edith says.

"That's okay. Go on without me. I'll only hold you back."

"I hate to leave you like this."

"No, I'll be all right. I have to focus, that's all."

Edith has to use the window in the elevator to put on her lipstick, because Clarence wasn't able to give up the mirror for even a moment. The elevator stops. A chill sweeps up her back. As it did in the Age Machine, her face is changing, turning into something older and wilder. She touches her wayward hair, like a Medusa crown of snakes around her head, but feels the neat braid she made earlier. Instantly she realizes what has happened: The light coming in from outside has transformed the glass from mirror back to window, and there is another woman, just her height, standing directly outside. The two images mix, the second face like a palimpsest showing through her own. It's only Lulu.

"Edith, it's Martin."

"Oh, hi."

"How are you? We haven't seen you in ages."

"Fine."

"Weren't you going to send me the latest article from the AMA Journal on angiograms?"

"I have it right here."

"I knew you wouldn't let me down. Shall I tell Florence to expect you for lunch, then?"

"Uh, no, it's something I can fax, so I'll send it right now. That way you'll have it. Things are really busy here, with people taking off, going on vacation. I have to fill in."

"We'd really like to see you, Edith. We miss you."

"I haven't been able—Maybe tomorrow."

"What time?"

"I have to see, okay? I'll call you."

"Who was that?" Ben asks when she hangs up.

"Martin."

"Martin! You're really in tight with him. I didn't realize—"

"In tight? I'm not in tight. He's my employer. I'm doing work for him—"

"Yeah, but you sound—I thought you were talking to a friend, or maybe someone you were going out with."

Going out with? Edith feels like reminding Ben that she's been with him almost every night, even though they're not "going out," which means sleeping together. How could he think she was sleeping with someone else? And Martin of all people. What does her voice sound like when she talks to Martin? She wants to ask Ben this, but she's afraid he's already told her. She decides she has something urgent to do and runs out, nearly bumping into Ryo Yamanaka.

Instead of stepping aside, Ryo stands her ground. "Mind if I come in?" Edith is forced to give way, to go back into the office. She clears a chair of papers.

Ryo introduces herself to Ben and shakes his hand, ignores the chair Edith cleared for her, and perches on a corner of Edith's desk, letting her tiny feet dangle in a childish way that belies the expensive, fashionable high-heeled shoes she is wearing. "I'm here for a meeting with Henry, and I thought I'd stop by and see how the other half lives."

She has the slightly unreal look of a celebrity viewed up close. Her hair is blacker than black, and her lips a purplish red. Her smell—it must be perfume—is astringent and chemical, and her dress is of an iridescent pleated material that makes Edith want to touch it. Ryo is famous but Edith doesn't know why. Henry didn't fill her in after he introduced them on the night of the ball.

Ryo surveys the office. "Couldn't they have found something smaller for you, like a refrigerator box or something? But, hey, you're going to be great writers and writers have to suffer. This office and the pay that goes with it sort of makes up for your overprivileged childhoods. You think the magazine's being cheap, but it's really all for your benefit. Believe me, I know."

As Ryo talks, she addresses Ben too, but when she looks at Edith she lingers, as if she is reading something in her features, finding information. Edith remembers the way Geraldine examined her face the first time they met, and Florence too. And Henry. What are they looking for? What are they finding?

"I can't spend any more time jawing with the youth of America, however pleasant." Ryo lays a hand on Edith's head. "Let's do lunch sometime. Call me."

Edith waits until Ryo is safely out of earshot and then looks to Ben to share a laugh, because Ryo's visit was either funny or disturbing, but Ben is not amused.

"Everyone loves Edith," he says.

"Who is she, a writer?"

"She writes these art-type things for *Ubu*," Ben says. "And she was Geraldine's big love who broke her heart, so be careful."

"I'll keep it in mind. It's hard to picture—Geraldine and Ryo."

"Yeah, Ryo's so little—"

"But she's tough, and quick. Geraldine is—"

"Geraldine's tough," Ben says. "You know she's Martin's hatchet man."

"But Geraldine's innocent too. No, she *is*—" Edith gives up trying to explain Geraldine to Ben. No one seems to see the side of Geraldine that Edith does. Geraldine *is* innocent. She believes in doing what's right, in a way that Edith doesn't think Ryo, for instance, does.

GERALDINE, CATCHING RYO COMING OUT OF EDITH'S area like a snake slithering out of a bird's nest, wants to rush forward, beat the intruder about the head, sound the alarm. What was Ryo doing in there? The snake metaphor is not apt, because a snake must plunder nests in order to survive, but Ryo feeds for her own greedy pleasure. What does she know about Edith; what has she divined? Like certain species of poisonous snakes that can sense the proximity of warm bodies, she has bones in front of her skull that can perceive areas of vulnerability. She knows that Edith is a hot spot, a focus of emotion. She knows that she can get to Geraldine through Edith!

Suddenly weak and flushed, Geraldine makes her way back to her own office and closes the door. She is beginning to comprehend that Ryo hates her and perhaps even sought her out as a lover so that she could hate her more thoroughly. Ryo *meant* to inflict torture. Geraldine, who is constantly beset with guilt over injuries she has inadvertently caused, has been slow to come to this conclusion.

She switches on a little electric fan that she has hidden behind a framed photograph of her nephews, and cools her overheated face. As her skin chills, a clarity comes: She understands that she needed Ryo because she could only accept pleasure if it came conveniently packaged with its own punishment. This is not an admission that Geraldine enjoys making to herself, but once she has done it, she is soothed. Because it means that although Ryo is intrigued by Edith, and drawn to her, she will never be able to harm her. Ryo has nothing that Edith needs.

". . . AND SINCE I WAS IN THE NEIGHBORHOOD, I thought we could meet for lunch. The menu is supposed to be organized around Zen principles or something. Anyway, it's very good. Are you free?" Florence asks over the phone.

"Um, no, I'm sorry. They're keeping us really busy here, and I can't get out."

"It's been so long since I've seen you. Since the night of the ball, isn't it?"

"I guess—"

"Edith? Is anything wrong?"

(What can she say? I think your husband made a pass at me?)

"I've been busy, with people here going on vacation, and then I've been looking for apartments."

"You haven't signed a lease yet, have you?"

"No, it's—"

"Because that's part of what I want to speak with you about—"

"Oh, just a minute. Henry wants to talk to me—about my article? Can I call you back?"

"It's not that it isn't a competent piece of journalism. It would be fine in the Styles section of the Sunday *Times,* for instance. But at *Ubu,* the philosophy, the *Surrealiste* legacy, if you will, demands that we go beneath the surface, even in a small front-of-the-book piece. No, let me amend that—*especially* in a front-of-the-book piece, we look for the moment when another dimension is glimpsed through a crack in the facade of the everyday. You see what I mean?" Henry lets his face take on the kind of expression he imagines her favorite professor might use, stern, but indulgent.

"I thought the assignment—"

"The assignment is deliberately vague, Edith, to encourage the writer to discover how the other dimension enters in."

"So you wanted—"

"I want to see what it feels like to sit in front of this machine. I want to experience the sensation of looking in the mirror and seeing myself age twenty years. You talked to Ben, didn't you? About how he saw his own face transform into that of his father?"

"Maybe I'm not the person to write this. Maybe Ben should.

I don't, I didn't have that feeling because I'm adopted and my mother doesn't look anything like me."

"You mean your adopted mother," Henry corrects. She looks puzzled. "You don't look anything like your *adopted* mother," he says.

"No. I don't look a thing like her. She used to put us in mother-daughter dresses to go to church, and used to cut my hair like hers, but we're really not alike at all."

"But don't you see? It would be interesting for someone who doesn't know her mother or father to catch a glimpse, a hint of what that parent might look like now."

"I could try, but I don't think it will work. Ben knows what his father looks like, so if his father has certain lines or features that Ben sees in the face on the screen, Ben thinks the two faces are the same—because of what his mind fills in, see? But I don't have that face in my mind, so I can't invent the rest."

Henry rolls a pencil in his fingers. It interests him that this conversation has brought a flush to Edith's cheeks. He feels her resistance; he read it in her writing. She found something in the Age Machine that she won't talk about, possibly won't even think about. He is beginning to understand that Edith is perhaps even more of a mystery to herself than to Henry.

"Shock," he says, standing up and coming around to where she is sitting. "The shock of seeing lines creep onto your smooth and youthful face. That is a surrealist moment. Shock, when the mind loses its defenses and the naked truth stands revealed."

He puts a hand lightly on the top of her head and marvels at the thick springiness of hair, the overabundance compared to his own meager covering. For the first time, it occurs to him that someday someone younger—perhaps Edith herself—will be pressing in on him, wanting his place.

"Do me a favor, will you, and give it one more try—not today—over the weekend, when you've had time to mull. Of course, I could always give it back to Ben, but maybe it's too easy for him. Sometimes the interesting stuff comes from a writer who fights the idea first, who wrestles with it before finally surrendering."

"HE SPECIFICALLY USED THAT WORD, *SURRENDER?*" Geraldine signals the waiter for a second Scotch.

"I think so, yes."

"I know you're fond of Henry, and he has been good to you. He has an ease with young people that's very enviable—I envy it myself. But Henry—how shall I put this?—has an agenda, and it's furthering the career of Henry M. Reed. I'm not saying that's wrong, all the time, but sometimes he uses people, manipulates them for his personal gain."

"But how could this—"

"I'm not saying that in this case he stands to gain anything by forcing you to attack a topic you're not comfortable with. I'm only advising you to be careful, to think for yourself. If you feel something is wrong, don't do it. Are you ready to order? The pasta here is very nice."

Edith learned early on to steer away from personal topics with Geraldine, but this evening it is Geraldine who volunteers stories about her childhood, her sisters who are both married. She doesn't go as far as talking about Ryo Yamanaka, but she lets Edith know that she has had affairs that ended badly.

"When you're young, you think there are always going to be men calling you up, taking you out, wanting—whatever. And then one day you realize you are probably going to be alone for the rest of your life."

Never has Geraldine been so open. Of course, she has had two Scotches, but Edith has seen Geraldine have two drinks and still remain guarded, always in character as Edith's employer and mentor. It's a little unnerving to be allowed to see this new side of Geraldine, but flattering too.

Afterward they walk down the street to visit Geraldine's new apartment, the one she'll be moving into in September. The people she's subletting from have been very accommodating, letting her have the key (they are away on the West Coast) so she can take measurements. Through an iron gate, down a few steps—it reminds Edith of Martin's house, without the dog, of course.

"Wait. There's a light here somewhere. I don't want you tripping in the dark. Ah . . . What do you think? . . . Look, there's a garden. Come out and see the garden. You could have little dinners out here, see? And the kitchen! You know by now what most kitchens in New York are like, don't you? Of course, the size of the refrigerator is insane for two people. It was the snob appliance of the eighties. Come look at the bedrooms. Isn't this neat? One person can be perfectly private in her room and the other can be downstairs with friends, watching TV, whatever. The bedrooms are sweet aren't they? And look, private baths. And there's a powder room downstairs, of course.

"So, you haven't told me. What do you think?" Geraldine takes a handkerchief from her purse and blots her upper lip and forehead.

"It's so spacious. I didn't know they came like this. Everything I've seen is so tiny."

"I decided so what? I work hard. So I won't be able to leave a big inheritance to my nephews whom I see once in five years at best. Let me treat myself like somebody who matters for a change, like a person who deserves a nice place." Geraldine thrusts her hands in the pockets of her trousers, striking a defiant posture, as if Edith had criticized her for spending so much on rent, although Edith would never presume to do so. Anyway, she has no idea what Geraldine can afford. She must make a decent amount.

"If you're going to have a roommate, you'll only be paying half the rent," Edith says, to show her she's on Geraldine's side in this argument.

"The roommate I have in mind isn't at the point yet where she can manage that kind of rent, so I'll be paying the bulk of it."

"That's nice of you," Edith says.

"Isn't it? And you know how, when you do something nice for someone, you can't wait to tell them, like when you buy a present for someone, you're more excited for them to open it than they are?"

"Oh yeah. I'm like that too."

"You are? I knew you would be. Now let me tell you who my new roommate is because I can't wait any longer." Geraldine kisses Edith on the forehead.

Something heavy, a moth perhaps, bangs against a screen. From the kitchen comes the sound of the massive refrigerator springing to life.

Edith steps back from Geraldine. She watches Geraldine's smile congeal on her face. Geraldine can't mean Edith, can she? That Edith is to live with her? How could Edith live with Geraldine? What kind of person would she be if she lived with her?

Geraldine takes her by the arm. "Don't say anything," she begs. "Think it over."

"You can let me off here," Edith says, talking through the partition to the cab driver.

"Here?"

"I've decided to walk the rest of the way."

"It's kinda dark."

"Look, it's my neighborhood, okay? I walk it all the time."

"The lady who put you in the cab—is she your mother or something?"

"She's a friend. I'm twenty-one years old and I'd like to get out now, okay?"

"I can't force you to stay in my cab, but look, the meter's off. Why don't you let me take you home? I don't want to read about you getting stabbed."

"I promise you won't read about me in the paper."

After the cab leaves, Edith realizes that it is, indeed, a lonely several blocks she will be going. She usually walks down West Broadway and cuts over. If Geraldine hadn't insisted on putting her in a cab, Edith would be better off. She didn't want to refuse the taxi because she still felt embarrassed about the apartment. Does Geraldine think Edith is gay? No, Edith doesn't believe so. But why would Geraldine think that Edith would want to room with her? How could she think that Edith would be that kind of friend to her, one who could share an apartment? Doesn't she have friends her own age?

Edith's footsteps ring out on the deserted street. She's walking hard, frustrated with the way things are going, the messes she's been getting into. She feels like a coward for avoiding Florence and Martin, but what can she do? Confront Martin? Tell him she's not interested in him in that way? It's the right thing to do, the only thing, but she's afraid of hurting his feelings, of embarrassing both of them. She's hoping he'll come to that conclusion on his own, and that they can go back to being the way they were. But what way was that? Obviously Martin saw it differently than she did. And Geraldine too has a different impression of what she and Edith are to each other.

Suppose Carolyn is right, about people being nice to Edith, giving her things—that they're doing it for a reason, that they'll expect something in return, something Edith can't give. What about Henry, who's been so helpful, so interested in her plans to work at *Ubu?* What if he wants her, not because she shows promise, but for some personal reason of his own?

Before she went to dinner with Geraldine, Edith called home and talked to Grandpop and Carolyn. For once Carolyn wasn't bossy or suspicious. They were both so warm and happy to hear from her that Edith for a moment thought of just taking the bus back to Compton Falls. She hasn't told them about her plans to stay in the city and work at the magazine in the fall. She's waiting until everything's arranged and certain, because she already knows what they're going to say. Then there will be two more people in the world whom she loves and respects but can't help disappointing.

Edith is so preoccupied with these thoughts that she forgets to stay aware of her surroundings. Finally something warns her and she turns. One street lamp away is the man who wears a dog costume. The last time she saw him he was shambling along the sidewalk, but this time he is galloping in a weird sideways gait, coming right toward her, with his nose—the muzzle of the mask —pointed up, as if sniffing her out.

She knows this is the man who was written about in the papers, but it makes her think of Martin too, because he's always talking about Dog Man, always worrying that he'll come after Edith. It's as if Martin wished this lunatic on her, and Dog Man is acting out Martin's wishes, stalking her, sniffing out something in Edith that she doesn't know is there. It was wrong to run from Martin. She should have confronted him. By not saying anything, by eluding him, she has in fact encouraged him. It was her own guilt that made her mute.

Edith doesn't run. She can't outrun this creature and it might incite him even more to see her fleeing like prey. She faces him, trying to look as large and threatening as she can, schooling herself to remain calm, not to panic. She hadn't counted on his size, how easily he can overpower her. She is amazed to find herself on the sidewalk, gagging from the smell, grappling with a body she cannot read, cannot get a hold of. She marvels at how her arms and legs have lost their mass and strength, have turned into insect legs, so easily snapped. She finds she cannot breathe. She wonders if he has crushed her and if she is dying.

She should scream, but this idea comes too late. Her mouth is open, but as in a dream, no sound comes. She tries to bring air from deep in her body to make the scream and suddenly it is there, but not from her. The scream comes from outside like a natural force, like wind. Has she died and left her voice behind? It goes on and on, raising commotion—horns, shouts.

Slowly Edith comes to understand that Dog Man has left, although she still feels the impression of his arms, his hands, his legs, thick and hard under the foul matted costume. Gentler hands are holding her. Voices discuss whether it would be all right to move her.

"I'm okay," Edith says. She lets them sit her up, and she opens her eyes to see that, miraculously, she is whole, not bleeding, not broken.

"Do you think you can stand? The car's right here—"

Then Edith sees that the person who is supporting her, who is on her knees beside her, encircling her with her arms, is Lulu. She has men with her whom she directs to help Edith up, help her into the car—no—limousine. Inside it's cool, with the smell of leather.

"Oh Edie, Edie, honey! Are you all right? Larry, is she all right? She's shaking. Turn the air conditioner off. Give her your jacket. She might be going into shock. It's okay, Edie. We're taking you home."

"How about some brandy? There's brandy—"

"Wait till we get her home. She lives right above me. Thank God we decided to come back to my place. I don't want to think about what could have happened."

"We should call the police."

"Let's just get her upstairs. My God, my hand is shaking. I can't even get the key in—"

"I'll do it. Let me."

"I'm fine now. I can go home," Edith says. It's true. She can walk. Nothing even hurts. As it turns out, nothing really happened. It's what might have happened.

"No, I don't want you going home alone. Clarence must be out. I've been ringing his buzzer like crazy. You know him—he could be out all night. I don't want you staying alone."

"Really, I'm fine."

"I'm sure you are, if you say so, but humor us, darling, because we just saved you, and we can't let go of you just yet. We have to give you a cup of tea, call the police, marvel at how we came by in the nick of time."

Lulu with her hair up, in high heels, in this place where she's living, which Clarence said was nice but Edith hadn't believed him, Lulu who travels in a limousine with a handsome, slightly older man, Lulu who has just risked her own life to rescue Edith and wants her to have some tea—or would she rather have wine?—is transformed from the Lulu who eats off other people's plates and turns soda cans in for money. How can they be the same person?

Lulu's friend, Larry, is watching them, can't seem to get enough of the sight of them sitting side by side on the sofa. "You know, it's the damndest thing—you two kind of look alike."

Lulu regards Edith full in the face, then jumps up. "Larry, hasn't the kid had enough horror for one night?" she jokes.

"She should feel flattered—" Larry protests. Lulu laughs and playfully bites his ear. Edith sees this as an opening to excuse herself—it really is late, and she has to be at work in the morning. This time Lulu lets her go.

THERMAL INVERSION

CLARENCE AND EDITH ARE HAVING ICED LATTES AT THE
Dream Café before work. Clarence is looking very correct and
businesslike in his suit. He has his hair slicked back and he's
wearing glasses (just for show. His eyesight is perfect). He's been
treating Edith gently since the incident with Dog Man. They
don't talk about Lulu much, but they've had good conversations.

Now they are discussing Ben.

"Well, we've come close," Edith says.

"Does he know about you? Your history?" Clarence asks.

"History? I'm only twenty-one, Clare. I don't have a history.
There have been boyfriends who haven't worked out—"

"So he doesn't know."

"What am I supposed to say, 'Ben, I'm a virgin'?"

The waitress looks at her with eyes already rimmed with black, even though it's only eight in the morning. She was probably never a virgin. There aren't virgins in New York. Ben was fifteen the first time. He told Edith. His girlfriend went to her mother beforehand, and her mother put her on the pill. "I can't tell Ben," she whispers.

"Edie, you've got to tell him. He already knows something is wrong, and he'll think it's him. If he's sensitive—and you seem to think he is—he'll understand. It's the best way. Believe me."

Clarence is so good at this. He catches his reflection in the mirror. He cannot believe how he looks. Lulu is helping him with his attitude, showing him that he doesn't have to be so out there to be out. As soon as he decided to drop his flamer act, he went home and told Mom—quietly, soberly, at the kitchen table. She cried, of course, but then she laughed when he persuaded her to sit on his lap so he could comfort her because he really wanted to crawl into her lap, but he would have crushed her—she's gotten so little, and he's gotten so big.

It was Lulu and Edith who made him decide to do it. He couldn't bear to see those two separated, and then he realized what had been keeping him apart from his mom all these years, and he decided to put an end to it. Then together he and Mom told Dad, and his older brother Andy, who reacted like two blocks of concrete. Clarence called his other brothers, which was kind of an ordeal. Sean wants him to go on a church retreat with him and pray for God to lead him back to the path of righteousness. Sean lives in Atlanta, not that that explains it. No one, besides Mom, cried. It wasn't the biggest shock of their lives, just a confirmation of their fears. At least it's in the open, and none of them have to pretend anymore.

Now, if he could only help Edie. He's dying to tell her about

Lulu. Every time they talk, he comes close. This morning even, he thought—he had actually rehearsed a little statement in front of the mirror but he realizes it would be wrong. Because if Edie wanted to know, she would have figured it out by now. It's dangerous to tell a person something before she is ready to hear it; it's like waking a sleepwalker. Edie knew Clarence was gay, but she didn't say anything, just kept quiet until he decided to tell her. And he appreciated her delicacy and tact. He even made a note of it at the time, that it was a classy bit of behavior that he should try to emulate. So Clarence has to keep his big mouth shut. But it's so hard!

RYO YAMANAKA THINKS SHE SHOULD HAVE STAYED IN Bridgehampton with Lisa, where it was boring but at least the air was good. Instead she's tromping around Soho, scoping out her piece and probably doing irreparable damage to her lungs. The air is putrid, yellow. It burns her eyes. But Ryo must work sometime, even though her needs are few and her wants are simple. Basic expenses must be met.

She has a list of galleries to visit where the artists might let her observe the installation. It will be helpful to do this because on opening night there is so much socializing that she will be able to pay scant attention to the actual art. Of course, the first Saturday night openings of the season are all about seeing each other and getting oneself positioned for the year; art is only the necessary backdrop.

This particular gallery isn't officially one at all, more a vacant space, but beyond the dirty window and steel grating Ryo can see the regulation shiny wood floor, the freshly painted white walls. When she pounds on the door it is opened by a tall slender woman in overalls and a baseball cap. Lulu.

Ryo remembers her. She's been away for some years, hasn't she? Yes, traveling, Lulu answers. Lulu's distinctly a minor player, marginal, did a few interesting video installations in the early eighties. There was an earthwork that was promising. But Lulu jumps around too much, has never settled into one distinctive style. Lulu is not ordinarily someone who would be given her own show. She'd be lucky to get a few pieces in a group show of emerging young artists. And she isn't young by any means. There must be a trick, a reason why she has been given this gallery that isn't really a gallery.

What is this she's working on?—bits of litter suspended from wires with a motor that turns a drum so that the whole thing moves. It fills the center of the space and, properly lit, will throw shadows on the walls. There are articles of clothing displayed so they look like human skins or disembodied parts, an exhibit of organic garbage neatly sealed in Ball jars and placed on a shelf as if some deranged housewife had been canning table scraps.

Then Ryo sees the video. Brilliant, positively brilliant! Because this is the story that everyone coming to the show will be trying to suss out: How did she get her own show? It blatantly confirms the worst of the rumors that will be circulating along with the wine and cheese. It is a stroke of genius, and madness of course. Furthermore, Lulu is writing up a schedule that she intends to post somewhere near the screen, giving dates for the first assignation, the donation of the paint, the donation of the floor work.

The rawness, the cynicism, the truth of it will offend everyone, which is what art is all about.

· · ·

RYO IS IN A HIGH MOOD WHEN SHE LEAVES. SHE IS AT-
tracted to originals. There are so few of them, even—especially—
in the art world, where so much depends upon belonging to the
right gallery, pleasing the right critic. She's revising her story. It
will be about Lulu and only Lulu. Ryo will station herself here
and watch the reactions. She'll make this woman's career—well,
she'll make her into a sensation. She doubts that Lulu will be
able to sustain the notoriety. Where do you go from here?

Ryo catches her reflection in a shop window and gives a pert
shake of her head. Lulu doesn't understand, can't begin to comprehend what Ryo is about to do for her. When Ryo told her she
was writing a story for *Ubu,* Lulu advised her not to waste her
time, as that magazine never ran stories on Lulu, something
about Lulu having unwittingly gotten on the wrong side of Geraldine years ago when they both worked there.

Ryo laughs out loud in the street. She adores it when dispa-
rate parts of her life come together this way. A man in a plush
dog suit ambles up, and Ryo amazes herself by reaching into her
Matsuda bag and pulling out a dollar for him. She never gives to
panhandlers. The man yelps his appreciation and lopes off.

FLORENCE THOUGHT MARTIN SHOULD AT LEAST MOVE TO
the living room for this meeting, should certainly put on some
clothes. She said it was a mistake for Martin to receive the publisher in bed, in pajamas, still playing the part of a sick man
when he's been up and around, downstairs and all with no ill
effect. But Martin wants them to understand that he is not well.
He's affronted that Henry and Geraldine are bringing the White
Rabbit into his home, his sanctuary. (The publisher's name is
Leonard Dealy, but they all call him the White Rabbit behind his

back, because of his pink-rimmed eyes and his flustered manner.) Martin wants them to feel that they are invading, shattering the tranquility he needs in order to heal.

Geraldine, angry, comes first and sits in the chair by the bed. Henry is cheerful, full of the false heartiness people feel they have to assume when entering a sickroom. The White Rabbit hangs back. He at least has the sensitivity to feel awkward. Martin does nothing to ease their embarrassment, doesn't invite them to bring side chairs from the living room. Let them stand and be uncomfortable. Then Florence, ever the good hostess, appears with chairs. There's an opportunity for the men to bustle over and take them from her. There's the clumsy ceremonial asking after Martin's health, during which he succeeds in making the conversation even more strained than it has to be.

Henry cuts the White Rabbit off in the middle of his platitudes. Henry thinks Martin knows, he says that Bruno has invested heavily in East Germany, buying a chain of newspapers, two magazines. He has to, in order to safeguard his hegemony in Germany. Also it's a passion with him. But he's had to borrow heavily to do it, and the publications are not paying off right away. It could take years. It's a drain on Bruno's emotional and financial resources, and it's making him anxious about his other holdings. He can't afford to lose money on enterprises that should be showing profits. "If the magazine doesn't haul itself out of the red soon, Bruno is going to run out of patience," Henry finishes.

Martin sits up straighter against his pillows and takes a good look at Henry. He's changed, looks leaner, harder. Six months ago he never would have cut the Rabbit off like that. Henry's moving out, out from under Martin. Martin sinks back into his pillows, feeling tired suddenly. Of course Henry wants his job.

It's only natural. How long will it take for him to get it? Martin hopes the struggle isn't drawn out and painful. He wishes there were some way he could be anesthetized and awakened when it was over.

"Henry, stop making veiled threats and come out with it. What does 'run out of patience' mean in this case?" Geraldine asks.

"I don't know what that might look like. Maybe he'll try to sell the magazine, or it might mean new management."

"And new management means replacing Martin."

"It could mean all of us."

"All of us but the one who's been cozying up to Bruno, leading him on tours of the fashion department, proposing stories to him before they ever get aired with the staff." An ugly vein has appeared on Geraldine's forehead. She should watch her own blood pressure. She should learn not to let externals cross the boundary into the body where they can cause damage. Surreptitiously Martin puts a finger on his pulse. It is steady. So far he's been doing fine without Lopressor. He's learned how to regulate his heart, how to shield it from harmful outside influences.

"Martin, Leonard asked if he could come along this morning to talk about the numbers, the circulation, the advertising pages," Henry says.

The White Rabbit's nose has turned pink. So Henry controls him now. Interesting, Martin thinks as he listens to the figures for this year's circulation compared to circulation a year ago (bad), to this year's newsstand sales compared to sales a year ago (bad), to this year's ad pages compared to pages a year ago (bad).

"What do you think we should do?" Martin asks. He avoids looking at Geraldine.

The flush on the Rabbit's face expands and deepens. His

voice comes out high. "As publisher, it would be inappropriate for me to suggest editorial changes. I would, however, like to undertake a more aggressive ad campaign on both fronts: to readers and to the trade. Until now we've had a sort of noblesse oblige attitude—"

"Arrogant," Henry interrupts. "We've never had a circulation drive, we've never done telemarketing—"

"Telemarketing! It's beneath the dignity of the magazine. We never farmed ourselves out to those ridiculous companies with their come-on schemes because it's an insult to our readers. How can you think of tarnishing *Ubu* by associating it with one of—"

"See what I mean?" Henry interrupts Geraldine. "That's the kind of attitude we've had: 'If you really want to read *Ubu,* then we'll let you become a subscriber. If you're not going to read us cover to cover, then to hell with you; we don't want you anyway.' "

"And what's wrong with that attitude?" Geraldine angrily falls for his bait.

"Because we're losing money, Ger. We don't have the demographics," Henry says.

The White Rabbit shifts in his seat so he's turned slightly away from Geraldine. "Henry and I have been talking, and there's a whole market we haven't scratched. That's the fitness and exercise thing. Henry says fashion is willing to do a whole issue on fitness gear, how-to, health spas, et cetera. And we thought we could tie it into the rest of the book with a feature article on—"

"Martin! I can't believe you're letting this happen!" Geraldine jumps to her feet.

"What? Letting them state their views without interrupting

with groans and gnashing of teeth, as you've been doing?" Martin finds Geraldine more wearing than the other two.

"But it's against everything *Ubu* stands for. They are invading editorial with suggestions to please advertisers, consumer articles, paybacks." Geraldine is practically in tears. Why won't she just give up as he has done? Can't she tell when she is beaten?

EDITH FEELS SOMETHING LAND ON HER SHOULDER, a cheese curl. There are two in her out basket and one in her lap. "It isn't good for your eyes to stare at a flickering screen, especially if there isn't anything on it," Ben says. Peyton and Kylie have gone to lunch. Ben brought a sandwich back for Edith that she hasn't yet touched. "Look, if you can't do it, tell Henry you want something else. He'll give you another assignment."

"He told me to struggle with it. So I'm struggling."

Ever since Dog Man knocked her over in the street Edith's mind has not been working as well. Unlike the bruises and muscle soreness which are going away, the problem with her mind—or maybe her spirit—has been getting worse.

Her feelings for Lulu have changed. Before Lulu used to annoy her; now she frightens her. This makes no sense because Lulu saved her life, and ever since that night, can't do enough for her. She took her to the precinct house to file a complaint; she calls the detective assigned to the case daily to find out what progress is being made. She calls Edith all the time to make sure she's all right. But it's too much.

Edith finds herself waiting to make sure that Lulu's left the building before she will venture out. She avoids lingering outside in her own neighborhood because she might meet Lulu in the street or the stores. She fears Lulu almost as much as Dog Man.

Edith has given up skating to work and takes cabs even

though she can't afford them, just because a construction worker made a comment to her in the street and she lost her balance and fell over. She hasn't called Grandpop and Carolyn because she doesn't want them to know, and she's afraid she'll start crying if she hears their voices. She's afraid of Martin, afraid even to speak to him on the phone. And she has not been able even to begin the piece on the Age Machine.

Ben looks over her shoulder at the blank screen. "Call Anne and tell her you have to come back for another visit, that Henry wanted you to see something, something you weren't looking for at the time, and uh—I'll go with you. I'll call right now, want me to?"

Ben, standing close, smells good, clean. He is good and clean. He's been being nice again, ever since she asked him to go to the Age Machine with her.

"I don't think I want to go down there," she tells him. "It gave me a creepy feeling, but then maybe that's why I should. Maybe Henry's right."

"Hey, it's only a little piece for the front of the book. You're not supposed to have to rip your guts out, you know what I mean?"

"Maybe I'll just tell Henry I tried but I can't do it."

"There's nothing wrong with that. It happens all the time around here."

"I'm not being a coward?"

"Are you? What are you afraid of? Getting old?"

"No."

"Getting wrinkles, getting jowls like I'm going to have?" He pulls his skin down with his hands.

"Oh God, no. Luckily I'm not going to be that ugly."

"So what did you see? What scared you?"

"It was so familiar."

"Yeah, well, it was your face—"

"But it was as if I'd seen it before—in a dream, you know, or a nightmare."

BEN HAS ENTICED EDITH OUT TO THE PARK WITH HIM SO they can have their sandwiches under a tree. He claimed she was being hypnotized by the computer screen. They're talking about what happens in September. Ben's psyched to go back to Amherst. Edith still doesn't know if she's going back to Grimsby.

"It all depends if I can get a real job at the magazine, with salary."

"Oh yes, pay. That would be a novelty, wouldn't it, to earn money."

"It's a necessity for me. My mom is not going to send me money to stay in New York. I haven't even talked to her about this. I lose a scholarship, stuff like that."

"Then why do it? It's only a year, not even."

"I've always felt out of place at Grimsby, like I wasn't living my real life."

"Real life!" Ben laughs. "And this is real? Working at *Ubu* seems real to you?"

Edith has to think about this. Lately *Ubu* has become a strange world, one in which she has a severe communication problem. She thinks she's acting one way and people interpret it a whole different way. She feels there's a hidden language being spoken here that she lacks the brains, or talent, or information, to decipher. Her problems with Geraldine and Martin make her wonder about other people at *Ubu*. Will Henry suddenly come up with a proposal for marriage? The thought makes her smile, and Ben instinctively smiles back at her.

And what about Ben? So far they've been pretending to be just friends, but at times they've come close to being lovers. It can't go on this way. Edith knows from experience that eventually Ben will stop wanting to see her. Maybe Clarence is right. Maybe Edith does have a problem. But she wants to be sure first, that she really loves Ben, that he's part of her Real Life, a concept he doesn't seem to understand. Is Edith still free to make that decision about Ben, or was it made at some forgotten point in their history together? Did she send a signal without realizing it, one that she can't renounce without losing his friendship?

GERALDINE, TAKING HERSELF FOR THE WALK THAT MARtin prescribed, finds her eyes are burning; her lungs can't seem to get enough air. The city is poisoning itself in its own foul exhalations. Or is her body reacting to that nightmarish confrontation at Martin's? It was like seeing her rescue boat slip out of the harbor leaving her alone and defenseless on the dock. Martin didn't even put up a fight. He just wanted to get rid of all of them, her especially. He doesn't care anymore. He's given up.

Geraldine tries to swallow a thickening in her throat that's making it difficult to breathe. She walks toward the park, hoping the few beleaguered trees will help increase the oxygen in the air. Is that Edith sitting on a bench? Geraldine walks faster; energy returns. Then she sees the boy from the office and she stops. They look so right together that Geraldine can't bear to insinuate herself into their cozy twosome, to see the look of respectful forbearance on Edith's face at Geraldine's interruption. He flicks a crumb from Edith's cheek. She laughs at something he's said.

Geraldine recognizes courtship behavior. Nothing wrong with it, perfectly natural, but why does it make Geraldine feel so lonely and left out? The boy glances her way, and before he can make eye contact, she hurries away.

Geraldine and Edith have been shy with each other. Neither has mentioned Geraldine's offer. This unwanted glimpse of Edith with the boy brings home the sad truth that a generation separates Geraldine from Edith, that even if Geraldine tries to ignore the gulf between them, Edith won't.

New scenes push their way into Geraldine's idyllic imaginings of life with Edith in her new apartment: Edith going out on a date and not returning until the next day, or worse, Edith bringing a date home for the night, coming down to the kitchen around noon on Sunday, after Geraldine has already cleaned up, and cooking eggs for some sleepy-eyed boy. Or going out with him for breakfast like a guilty thief.

Dating, falling in love. Because Geraldine has put all that out of her mind she assumed Edith had as well. In fact, for many years Geraldine was quite active in that respect. She wasn't an obvious flirt, but she was attractive and she used it with good effect—used it without naming it. She expected men and women to like and admire her, want to be around her. This is not something that Geraldine has thought of until now. Seeing Edith with the boy reminded her of her own effect on others, her own physical attractiveness, and also made her realize abruptly—like noticing that a silk scarf wrapped around the neck in the morning before leaving the house has been missing for some time—that it has left her.

She trips over a crack in the sidewalk. The air makes her eyes water. She passes a woman wearing a surgical mask over her nose and mouth. Maybe there's an air-quality emergency today. Geraldine doesn't watch TV or listen to the radio in the morning. She relies on her morning *Times,* printed the night before.

"Do you have the *Post?*" she asks. The vendor nods toward the pile of newspapers. The picture on the cover catches her eye. Jeff Jerome. Wasn't she just yesterday staring at layout pages with his face plastered all over them: pictures of Jerome with his wife, with his kids, with his wife and kids and dogs. This picture is of Jeff Jerome with his lawyer. It seems he's been charged with raping one of his daughter's friends. Geraldine buys four copies.

WHEN CLARENCE STOPS BY THE GALLERY ON HIS WAY home from work, he sees three giant video screens filling the space.

"They're great, aren't they? Larry got them for me. I called him this morning, and a truck pulled up this afternoon." Lulu stands in the center of the room, hands in the pockets of her overalls.

"Larry seems like a nice guy." Clarence walks behind the screens to view the pieces that used to be the main part of the installation and are now swept to the edges like so much—garbage. He wonders how nice Larry's going to be when he sees what's playing on the big screens. Not to mention what Montero's going to do. He'll probably destroy the screens and then Lulu.

"You think so?" Lulu asks. "I mean, poor Montero is already wrecking his marriage. What does his wife think when he leaves the house at two in the morning? She's got to know. He's using me—this affair—to shred his life. He can't blame me; he started it."

Clarence looks over the long underwear, the remnant of soap

tenderly preserved in a jar, the postcard from Paris. Something had been coming together from these fragile bits, not a breathing human being, or even an accurate representation, but the evanescent imprint of one man. It was the concept that someone could collect the ephemera that another being sheds; could reconstruct an image from the tailings; it was the idea of imposing order on disorder, reversing the second law of thermodynamics, like running film backward so that the shards of a broken plate leap together into a seamless whole; it was the attempt that was interesting.

Now Lulu is saying that it's been "done before." Some critic told her, said that people had put garbage in jars before, hung up long underwear. It bothers him that this critic was able to get Lulu to abandon her work without a struggle. "But the idea of building an image of someone from his garbage was new," he says. "The idea of searching for someone, anyone, as a journey of self-discovery, that was yours, and you're giving it up."

"This is what I discovered." Lulu gestures to the screens.

"It just seems like a cheap move to me. It's degrading."

Lulu stands beside Clarence. Her assemblages look pathetic, weak. What did she see in them? What was she really looking for? What sustained her through those weeks of trash-raiding? "I just don't see it anymore, Clarence. I lost it."

Clarence turns on the litter mobile. He loves its jerky motion, not at all like the swirl of wind-blown litter it's supposed to simulate, but endearing in its failed attempt. "Maybe you did get close. You got so close that you were frightened and ran away," he says.

"I'm not running away. I'm using it to get here," Lulu says, meaning the screens, meaning the disaster about to ensue.

"Well, you're losing me on this. I just want you to know. And what about Edie?"

"Is she all right, Clare? I wish you wouldn't go out at night, and would get her to stay home with you. I feel so much better when I know the two of you are safe at home. That scared me so much. It's funny, you know—maternal instincts. I would have fought him to the death for her. I really would have."

"What I mean is, after this show, you're never going to be able to tell her."

Lulu takes a bandanna out of her pocket and mops her face. "It's no good, Clare. I scare her. I can tell. It's even worse since I saved her life. It's best for her if she never knows. And to tell you the truth it will be a relief not to be living in the same place with her, not to worry all the time about what she thinks of me, because it's never going to be good."

Clarence wipes his brow on the shoulder of his T-shirt. "It's hot as hell in here. C'mon. I'll treat you to dinner. We'll go someplace air-conditioned and talk about this." He takes her hand. It looks so much like Edie's that he marvels at how he never knew until Lulu told him.

"You're sweet." She kisses him. "But I have to work if I'm going to get this done for the opening."

Clarence turns to look at Lulu, in the middle of her screens, in the midst of her own destruction. He wonders how many times she has come to this moment, how many times she has deliberately dismantled what she has worked to build.

"HAD YOU ACTUALLY SEEN YOUR FACE BEFORE, YOUR AG-ing face, in a dream? Do you have scary dreams about getting old?" Ben asks. Edith is sharing a pizza with him.

"No, not about getting old. It's about someone else's face

taking over mine, so I'm not the same person." She recalls her features reflected in the elevator window, superimposed by Lulu's, and remembers how it frightened her. But she doesn't say this. She watches him tip a slice of pizza so the oil drips onto the plate. She watches his fingers, long and straight.

"Doesn't everyone have nightmares? Dreams that wake you in the night?" she says.

"Like falling? I have that dream sometimes. But I read that it happens when your muscles relax suddenly in sleep."

"Falling, yes, or—someone dragging you into a dark cold place, or a face coming at you—"

"The face of your nightmares," Ben prompts. The pizza slice is still suspended, forgotten, over the plate.

That's the old dream, the one that used to wake Edith, and Carolyn would have to come lie on her bed beside her until she fell back to sleep. It's an old dream she had put out of her mind, but she had it again last night.

"You look frightened."

"What?"

"The pupils in your eyes just got big."

"That means I'm scared?"

He nods.

"I've been a little shaky—" She tells him about Dog Man.

"I can't believe you didn't tell me! I can't believe—I knew you were acting—like—twitchy. You know, you look like a normal person, but inside you're strange."

"Don't get angry—"

"I'm not angry."

"You sound angry."

"I'm upset. He could have—"

"He didn't hurt me or anything, just knocked me down, but

the police haven't found him yet, and it makes me nervous to go home alone at night."

"No wonder it's the people from small towns in the Midwest who are always getting killed in New York! That guy's out there, and you're still going home alone, in the dark?"

"Well, I can't stop living just because—"

"Let me call my mom. She'll put you up in our place for a while."

"No, I can't. I have all my things—"

In the end, they compromise: Ben walks her home and promises to escort her every night until Dog Man is apprehended. He gives her a hug, that turns into a kiss. Edith felt completely safe walking home with Ben, but when she sees the elevator, she suddenly can't bear the thought of getting in alone, of looking at the little glass window. Would Ben mind riding up with her? He doesn't think she's crazy? Of course not, he says.

WHEN GERALDINE BOUGHT THE COPIES OF THE *POST*, SHE was planning to deposit one on Henry's desk, send one down to the White Rabbit, take one to Martin, and keep one for herself. Then she thought better of it. Bad news travels fast. Why should she be the messenger? She has finally realized that she has lost her armor, her protection. No longer can she afford to make impassioned, reckless forays for the sake of the magazine. She puts the *Post* in her drawer and keeps her own counsel all day at her desk. The staff goes home. She has a few sherries in Martin's office.

Martin and Florence have had their dinner by the time Geraldine gets there. She shows the *Post* to Florence, not Martin, who has already gone to bed. Florence finds an apple for her, a piece of cheese, and some wine.

"It's not so much that he's ill and not in the office, Florence. It's that he doesn't care. Henry knows it. That's why he dares to do these things. Obviously Jeff Jerome's publicist put him up to this puff piece as insurance. She knew the whole scandal would hit the news media. She probably thought the piece would run first. *Ubu* would have ended up looking—it's too disgusting."

"Do you think Henry knew?"

"Oh, no. He was duped. The stupid, vain little—"

"What will happen now?"

"Oh, we'll pull the piece, put in some backlog stuff. It's a mess, but not as bad as what might have been. I would have called a meeting on it today, but Henry's impossible to work with anymore. It's better for me if he discovers the news on his own. For once I'm putting my own interest before the magazine. It's about time." She needs a cigarette. "Let's go to the garden."

"Wait, I want you to look at something. I got the photos back from the night of the ball, when Edith wore the dress—"

"Oh, yes." Geraldine's heart speeds up, as if she were going to see pictures of a former lover. She hopes Edith didn't tell Florence about Geraldine and the apartment. She wouldn't do that, would she? There's a picture of Edith and Henry in front of the limo. It's too dark, doesn't do justice to Edith's features, bleached by the flash of the camera. The other picture, taken from above, in the hall of the house, is peculiar. Martin has his hand on her shoulder. He is looking at the side of her head, where her face would have been a moment before. He is leaning slightly forward. She is leaning back.

"What do you think?" Florence asks.

"What do you mean?" Geraldine does need that cigarette.

"It looks like he was trying to tell her something, or even to kiss her. Do you think that's possible?"

Geraldine puts the picture under the light. "If I didn't know the people, I guess I would think it was a picture of a man trying to kiss a girl who didn't want to be kissed."

"You know, she hasn't been back since that night. When I call her on the phone she makes excuses to get off. I think the poor thing's embarrassed. Well, I don't blame her," Florence says.

Now they won't get her either! It's a selfish, vengeful thought, but Geraldine can't help herself. Florence was so confident that everything was going to work out. Fat chance that Edith is going to want to call Martin Daddy after this. "Did you ask Martin?" Geraldine asks.

"No, I don't dare. He's funny lately. One minute he's up and about, dressed as if he's going to the office, and then—you saw him this morning—he's back in bed playing invalid. What if he is in love with her?"

Geraldine thinks she'll die of nicotine deprivation if she doesn't get a smoke soon. She takes out her Marlboros, and Florence finally leads her to the garden.

WHEN MARTIN HEARS GERALDINE ARRIVING AT THE front door, he jumps back into bed like a guilty child who's been playing sick. He holds his hand over his heart for several long minutes until it calms down. When it looks as if she isn't coming up after all, he tries Edith's number again only to get the answering machine for the third time. "Well, Edith," he assumes a jocular tone, "this is yet another message from your friend Martin. I guess you can tell that I want to speak to you, so I will trust you to call me as soon as you get in. It doesn't matter what time. I miss you. Call me, love." Love! Why did he say that? There should be a way you could call those machines and delete messages, revise them. He detests those machines, won't have one himself. He always ends up saying something clumsy. He gets up, showers and dresses before he remembers that Geraldine and Florence are downstairs. He slips out to the deck. He can hear their voices below in the garden. Closing his bedroom door behind him, he creeps downstairs and out the door.

The air is close. It's an effort to fill his lungs. It's an effort to make his way to the top of the street, and yet it's not his heart, but his legs that are heavy and unresponsive, pushing through air that resists each step. His heart is ardent, nimble, and light. It flies ahead, up the street to hail a cab. The legs stumble behind.

MARTIN'S THIRD CALL COMES WHILE EDITH AND BEN ARE at the table having iced tea. Edith sits, unwilling to pick up and talk to Martin, not wanting Ben to hear. "Call me, love." How could he? What had she ever done for Martin to think of her that way?

"Well, I won't stay. You probably want to speak with him in private." Ben pushes himself back from the table.

"He's crazy," Edith says.

"Crazy in love."

"No! I mean, I don't know why."

"That's what they've been saying, anyhow."

"Who?"

"You know, people in the office. They figured you had something going with one of them—Henry, or Geraldine, or—well, actually, no one even guessed Martin. But they figured something had to be up. First you get a writing assignment, and then it looks like you're going to get a position on staff, and you haven't even turned anything in yet. You can't even do your first piece."

"Did you think—?"

"To show you how dumb I am, I thought you kind of had a thing for me."

"Is that really how people see me? Like some bimbo? The office slut?"

"I didn't. It got to be a joke how I would defend you. Wait until this comes out. I'll be able to hear them laughing all the way up in Amherst."

Edith brings her hair over her shoulder and undoes the braid, as if it is the only thing she has to do, as if no one else is in the room. She sweeps the hair back over her shoulder and fans it out with her fingers. She begins to speak to him, to tell him about Martin, and then she goes on to tell him about what Clarence calls her problem. "Do you believe me?" she asks.

"I believe you," Ben says.

He wants to believe her, to defend her against all the others who've been telling lies. They are lies, aren't they? Has Edith been encouraging Martin? What are her intentions? Edith feels a decision coming on. Is it a decision she is making from her own free will, or is it one that has been forced upon her? She is only certain of its inevitability.

"What's this?" Montero asks. It's the first he's been in, all day. He's in a suit and looks hot and tired.

"Video screens."

He stands with his arms folded and legs apart, watching her. "I know what video screens are," he says. "I mean how'd you get them, why'd you put them up, what're you going to be showing on them?"

"I'm showing the process, of how the show came about, you know, what went into it."

"What went into it?"

"Uh-huh. A critic came to see the work and, based on her reaction, I decided to go this way."

"What kind of critic?" He takes his jacket off. There are wet circles under his arms.

"Ryo Yamanaka."

"Oh yeah, I heard of her. She isn't a real critic. She's more like an art writer."

"Whatever. Anyway, she was intrigued by the video idea, so I decided to enlarge on it, and make it the centerpiece of the installation. You know, so it becomes more about process than the product."

"Are you going to play the video for me?"

"It's not ready yet."

"But you showed it to Yama-caca."

"*Yamanaka.* Only a little. I don't want you to see it till it's done."

"As your landlord, I think I should see it."

"Is that in the contract?" She smiles teasingly, edging over to the mattress. She flicks on the camera and presents her better side to it. He sits beside her. "What contract? I could kick you out of here tonight, with all your video screens, and you wouldn't be able to do a thing about it."

"That's right. You could."

"You're dependent on me."

"Completely."

"I could screw up your whole show."

"Yes, you could." She moves so that both of their faces will be in the camera's view.

"So why won't you show me the video?"

"Artistic integrity."

"Is that so?" He leans into her, and she rises to her knees so the camera can see.

IT DIDN'T OCCUR TO MARTIN THAT JUST KNOWING Edith's street address was not going to help him much. Somehow he assumed she'd be living in a building with a doorman, who would be able to ring him up. An absurd assumption, he realizes as soon as the cab lets him off. He forgot that she was staying in an artist's loft. There isn't even a lobby to the building, a converted warehouse with the butter & eggs sign still visible above the ground floor. There's an intercom but Edith's name isn't on it. He steps back and looks up. Two floors lit, the rest dark. He rings both. No answer. He rings again, then again. Finally a man leans his head out a window. He says he will call the cops if Martin rings one more time.

Martin looks up at the remaining lit floor, the one that didn't answer. The logical step would be to phone and tell her he's downstairs. But what if she isn't home and he has to leave yet another message on the machine? He tries to remember every conversation he had with her. Did she mention what floor she lived on?

The air is cooler; there's a breeze off the river. Pulse steady. Legs moving better now. It feels good to be out walking, out of his house and his neighborhood. He's whistling a song between his teeth, a big song with a soaring melody, one of those numbers that swell in the refrain. Martin's music background is weak. He tries to hide this when he's in conversation with friends and colleagues who are on familiar terms with classical music. The song continues louder now while Martin wonders what it is, where it's from, hoping it's an aria from an opera that he's absorbed unwittingly into his impoverished mental music library. "Knowing I'm on the street where you live!" He belts this out, stops, looks around, then laughs out loud. He's in love. It's like being eighteen again, although at eighteen Martin was too cool to fall in love, too cool to sing corny songs outside some woman's apartment, too sophisticated for romance, too busy and self-important to give way. The heart, the heart. It had to break before it learned to love.

BEN WANTS TO GET UP WHEN HE HEARS THE BUZZER. Why don't you answer it? he asks. It happens all the time, she says (although it doesn't). It's just kids passing in the street. The sound distracts him, but it makes her more intent. The buzzer becomes a third voice in their lovemaking, encouraging them, increasing their ardor. The passion surprises them both. How did it erupt out of their gingerly conducted friendship? Ben may decide that it was there all along, waiting to be released. But Edith feels dishonest. She is imitating someone, someone seductive and practiced. She feels as if she's playing a part in a play, but not for Ben. For another. She sweeps Ben's chest with her hair, then brings her head up so her hair flies back, and she suddenly pictures Lulu. This is how Lulu would be. And who is watching this performance, but Martin. He's down there in the street, holding his head like Dog Man, sniffing her out, piercing the wall with his eyes.

A TAXI PASSES, ITS "FOR HIRE" LIGHT A BEACON IN THE dark. It occurs to Martin that this is the first available taxi he's seen on this deserted street. The cab slows so Martin can see the face of the driver, his thick dark hair, his white skin, a young immigrant from Russia, perhaps. This young man is Martin's last hope, his last chance to avert some menace. Time expands. The cab rolls closer, the driver and Martin now making eye contact and Martin thinks how fate is not a clear deep channel, but a restless, twisting rivulet deflected by any twig that falls in its path. In this stretched moment as the taxi approaches, Martin reasons that there is nothing to be gained from walking the street outside Edith's building when he doesn't know which floor she lives on, or if she is home or out.

He stands at the curb, expecting the car to stop, but it goes right by. Martin looks after it, annoyed at the driver for passing him, but then Martin did not actually give the signal for the cab to stop. He did not raise his arm, shout, "Taxi," indicate his wish by any of the usual signs. Perhaps Martin does not wish to be rescued, to be snatched out of the delirium of love and delivered back to the safety of home, bed, sleep, and getting up the next morning. He has chosen the other path, the one that leads to destination unknown.

It is then that he sees her coming down the street, dressed not in the clothes she wears for work, but adorably, like a gamine, a street urchin, in overalls and a baseball cap, with her hair pushed up into it. He knows her by her walk. His face flushes hot. His arm stretches out in anticipation. Her name is on his lips. But instead of drawing her in, his gestures repel. Her shoulder turns, her head ducks, and she swerves. He rushes across the street after her. She puts the key in the lock and turns to look at him. The light from the street lamp overhead accentuates the hollows in her cheeks, the cords in her neck. Can time behave as erratically as the heart? Can it rip someone from youth and hurl her into middle age? Have the weeks since he's seen her turned into years without his realizing it?

"Martin? It is Martin, isn't it? My God, you look terrible."

"I haven't been well." He leans against the side of the building. A feeling comes over him that he knows is not simply fatigue, or breathlessness, or nausea. He recognizes it for what it is.

FLOATING

Mornings from nine-thirty to eleven are when Geraldine visits, which can be an awkward time because that's when the doctors make their rounds, and nurses and aides barge in without warning. There must be a schedule, some sort of plan but it's hard to tell because the general incompetence of the hospital staff coupled with the unstable condition of the patients combine to create a routine of chaos. Geraldine never knows when someone is going to interrupt her conversation.

She has been waiting outside in the corridor for the Indian man in the lab coat to collect his daily blood samples. He leaves with his little rack of vials, sort of like the milkman of her childhood making his delivery in the morning, only he is leaving with full bottles, not empties, red not white—she stops herself. There's a risk in carrying on these long rambling monologues. It encourages free association. She hears herself saying surprising things. Florence advised her to read to Martin, read anything, just to keep his brain going. It's a technique called hyperstimulation. But Geraldine prefers to speak to Martin. She finds it therapeutic, if not for him then for her. Besides, she can't help herself.

"Your poor arms, Martin, are purple and swollen where they've pricked and jabbed you. Most of these people don't know their job. If you could see some of them—they're babies. They must be interns, learning on you." She pulls the chair up close so she can speak softly. "It's funny, I always imagined you visiting me in my hospital bed. I would be dying of cancer, my face ethereally pale, my cheekbones made prominent by the wasting disease. You once said I had good bones in my face, do you remember? Early on, early on, when I first came to the magazine. It was nice to think about you visiting me, Martin, with your face contorted in sorrow and guilt. I'm ashamed to confess that I found pleasure from those daydreams, a pleasure that was —I don't know, voluptuous. I guess it's my Catholic upbringing, overexposure at the time of puberty to all those statues of saints with their bleeding plaster wounds. But even as I warmed to my fantasies I knew that they did not correspond to reality. You would never blame yourself for my sufferings. You don't feel guilt, Martin. I do. For everything. And I blame myself. I even blame myself for the way you've mistreated me. Because I allowed it. I should have walked out. I had plenty of offers. People were not blind to what was happening. But I stayed to protect the magazine, to protect *you.*"

The green line on the screen that records the activity of Martin's heart plummets, wavers, then climbs back to the previous level. Geraldine stops and takes a few deep breaths in lieu of the cigarette she wishes she had. Her own voice echoes in her ears, strident, not appropriate here. Will a nurse notice the depression on the graph and come to see what is the matter? The nurses' station, supposedly manned at all times, is vacant.

"Don't worry, Martin. I'm not going to bore you again with horror stories about what's happening at the magazine. I know you couldn't care less that Henry is turning that piece on Jeff Jerome into a tell-all scandal story—*Ubu* dishing the dirt on a movie star. It's enough to make you sick. Of course, you are sick already." She giggles at her own little joke. "To tell the truth, Martin, I'm not interested either anymore. The magazine as you and I know it is dead. It's gone. I'm just drawing my paycheck and putting in my time until they tell me to leave."

She takes a tissue from Martin's bedside stand and dabs at her eyes, unashamed of weeping in front of him, knowing he can't tease her. "It's dead, Martin, and you let it die. The one accomplishment of your life. You turned your back and walked away, just as you walked away from your only child, from Florence, from me. You didn't want love, Martin. You took it and used it, but in the end, you found it a burden. You shook it off because your heart could not stand up to the weight of it. And then your child reappeared and you fell in love with her eyes, which were your own yellow-spotted eyes of youth. It was a mistake because a hollow heart cannot fill with love for the first time at your age. It shattered like—"

She stops. Her voice has degenerated, from elegiac—if verging on orotund—to daytime television. (Geraldine watches, but only when she is very ill and unable to work.) She has never before allowed herself to speak in complete paragraphs. She never took the space in time to develop her thoughts, always restricting herself to brief editorial comments, especially when conversing with Martin, who would invariably interrupt, if not with words then with a shrug, a roll of the eyes, a sigh. Even a suppressed sigh. She was so sensitive to his every gesture, so easily intimidated.

The light on the screen is making jagged chicken tracks, as if Martin wishes to respond and this record of his heartbeat is the only method left to him. It writes in exclamations then wobbles uncertainly. She looks at the nurses' station. They must be on coffee break. There's a grizzled stubble on his chin; no one has shaved him today. A clear plastic tube connects a vein in his arm to a clear plastic bag of nutrients, sucrose, and distilled water, and a smaller bag of drugs. Another clear plastic bag, hung by the side of the bed, collects urine. He makes no sound, and the only part of his body that moves are his eyes under closed lids. And yet she knows he comprehends because he accompanies her words with the beating of his heart. There is something between them and there always has been. But she doesn't know what to call it any longer.

LULU IS WEARING A DISGUISE. IT IS NOT AS EXTREME AS that of her nemesis, Dog Man, who has been taken back to Creedmoor after he nearly killed a girl by pushing her into moving traffic on a street full of people. The disguise is a good linen suit, heels and hose, tasteful jewelry, something Geraldine or Florence might wear. Her wild and errant hair has been cut in a conventional chin-length bob and blown dry, to tame the curl. Dark glasses are not out of place indoors for women of her age, who often veil and shield themselves in this manner, as if they've endured too many assaults to survive one more. The disguise passes the test; Geraldine walks by without giving her a glance. Florence won't be in until one today; Desert Ray told Lulu that.

Lulu simply approaches the reception desk and gives Martin's room number. Florence has left instructions to admit all visitors, one at a time. She's encouraging visitors, although she hasn't specifically encouraged Lulu.

Even Ray doesn't know. Lulu didn't tell her because Lulu herself wasn't sure why she was coming to see Martin, if she means to absolve or blame, to wound or soothe. She doesn't know what she feels toward Martin. That night on the street was so sudden that Lulu felt nothing, except alarm that she might have a dying man on her hands, and mystification, that a person she had nearly forgotten could be so unexpectedly connected to her.

Ray says that they can't really tell if he will recover. The CAT scan showed he'd had a stroke as well as a heart attack, and no one knows for sure if his brain is functioning. He doesn't look good, all hooked up like this. Lulu walks around him as if she is viewing a complicated sculpture, and then she notices that his eyes, under closed lids, are following her. She pulls up the chair so she can sit near his head.

"It's Lucille, remember?" She takes his inert hand (soft as a baby's) in hers and the light on the screen does a little dance. "You're still alive in there, Martin! Your brain is working. People weren't sure. That's good, I guess. You were very proud of that part of yourself. It's a legendary brain, so nimble and quick, and stocked with information. Although maybe it's a burden as well. Such an opinionated organ, always wanting to be in control. The brain can't always be in charge, Martin. During love, for instance, it gets in the way. Love is a mindless activity. It frightened you, didn't it?"

She runs her fingers along the inside of his palm, amusing herself by seeing how the screen responds. She catches her own reflection in the screen and for a moment doesn't know who it is. "You wouldn't recognize me, Martin. I'm in disguise, dressed up to look like someone who might be married to you. That was my plan, remember? I tried to entrap you, but you were too sly for me. I thought that because you were ambitious, you would be a good father for my child. I couldn't quite persuade myself that I loved you, but I enjoyed our times in bed, your fumbling enthusiasm, as if you were Adam and God had just left you with Eve. The look in your eyes when you saw me naked, Martin—I felt like a goddess. I thought I wouldn't mind living with that kind of astonished admiration. Plus, I was desperate."

Martin's eyes are darting back and forth under his lids. She lays her fingertips on them. "See, don't laugh, but you were right, I was already pregnant, or thought I was. You have to remember that I was very young, and broke, and they didn't have those handy little pregnancy kits you could buy at the drugstore. There'd been symptoms. I'd been having an off-and-on thing with Tommy G., not the kind of person who could support a wife and baby. So I tried to snare you.

"Now Ray is convinced that you're her father, and I'm not going to tell her this whole story. She's got some very high standards, you know, that I can't live up to as is, but there's no sense in making it even harder for her to love me, because she is determined to love me. She's a good kid, Martin. I guess you know.

"But what if you are, Martin? I mean, now that I look at you, it's possible. You do kind of look alike. I mean, wouldn't that be the screwiest thing you ever heard?"

When the nurse rushes in, Lulu thinks at first that something is wrong with Martin, but then she realizes that she is the cause. Laughter, apparently, is considered out of place in the intensive-care ward.

FLORENCE HEARS A DOOR SLAM SHUT AND THINKS *IT'S over*. Her eyes fly to the screen recording the progress of his heart. Her ears pick up the hiss of oxygenated breath. The book she was reading is on the floor. That's what she heard, the book hitting the floor, not a door, metaphorical or otherwise.

He hasn't died. She sees that now and is ashamed for having dozed off, for having had a glass of wine with lunch before she came, a habit she's been getting into as it helps ease the transition between seeing clients in the morning and keeping vigil with Martin in the afternoon. She picks up the book, poems by Elizabeth Barrett Browning, something she found in the bookcase at home; it belonged to Mother. Florence thought it would be appropriate to read aloud to Martin, but now she thinks something with a plot, something easy to follow like an Agatha Christie, might be more what Martin needs to keep his brain functioning. It might be too easy for him to let the poetry fade into babble.

She could ask him of course, ask him to squeeze her hand if he wants to continue with the poems. Geraldine has been talking to him, demanding that he give her a sign if he can hear her, which would be funny if it weren't so sad, because Martin wouldn't respond to Geraldine even if he could. He would play possum until she went away. Would he respond to Florence, if she asked, if he could? She's afraid to try. She reads another. As she reads, she finds she doesn't have to follow it on the page. It's one she memorized years ago as a teenager when she had a crush on Elizabeth Barrett and Robert Browning. Theirs was her dream of a marriage—two poets in a book-lined study. They probably influenced her choice of a literary man as a husband. She was still a romantic even when she married.

At first she minded that Martin was decidedly not romantic. He was too ironic, too original for the usual displays, like saying "I love you," or giving her perfume or flowers. But as the marriage progressed, she appreciated his clear-sighted affection for her, the way he could accommodate her lovers without flying into jealous rages. He is a rational, civilized man. Florence took it on trust that Martin loved her in the only way he could. That's why she finds it hard to imagine him wandering the street outside Edith's house, like a lovesick adolescent.

When Florence saw the two of them—mother and daughter—in the emergency room, she reverted to her first impression of Edith. She imagined a plot between the two women, figured they had lured Martin downtown. It's a credit to her, to her professional training, to her largesse of spirit, that she was able to see through her own paranoia and realize that the truth was just dawning on Edith. It's a comfort to know that Edith did not betray Florence. It is Martin who once again has let Florence down. He gave another woman the child that should have been hers. And he gave another woman the love he should have felt for Florence.

She snatches up his hand. "Martin, Martin! Move a finger, just a finger, if you love me."

She meant to say "if you hear me." *How embarrassing,* she thinks, although no one is here to have caught her words. She stands, feeling foolish, holding her husband's hand, then places it, heavy and limp, back on the bed.

THEY HAVE PUT HIS BODY IN A BOX, SO NARROW THAT HE can't move, but of an airy material that won't cause chafing. Martin doesn't mind; it's for his own good. They have taken over the task of watching his heart, finally, so that he doesn't have to. The strain was getting to be too much. He needed a rest. Martin is resting. It's the first good rest he's had since that hot, unwholesome day when he took the dog for a walk and could hardly make his way home. Now he's back where they can keep an eye on his heart, take care that it doesn't explode, or implode. There's only so much a heart can take.

Another man, a person with a less active, less intricate mind, would rebel against the restriction of movement. But Martin has rediscovered a marvelous faculty that he had as a child. He'd forgotten he used to do this until the ability returned just when he needed it most. He leaves his body and passes through the wall—not to the other side—but just inside. He can hear what's going on in the room, can even listen to it intently if he wants, but they can't get to him. He is protected. He can wander throughout the house, rising effortlessly to the attic, descending to the basement, while the voices of his parents rage on (his father's mostly; his mother's is usually either inaudible or mute). He knows he's in the hospital—he's figured that out—but he's also back home. There's a tunnel through time that allows him to watch his parents, and everything that goes on in the house. Details are clear and precise, but tiny, as if seen through the wrong end of a telescope. This is the reverse of the way he used to see, when his parents were gigantic and the details blurry and indistinct. With pitiless acuity, the telescope examines marks on his mother's upper arm, a bruised portion of throat, three black hairs sprouting from the red knuckle of his father's hand. Sounds that used to make his stomach contract are now merely noises that he can listen to and identify, with all the dispassion of someone taking an auditory test: a car rolling over a cinder driveway and coming to a stop; a door being opened then shut with greater than necessary force; the tread of a heavy man upon a stair.

At the present time, and for his benefit and safety, his body has been placed under restriction. Hospital personnel arrive periodically to handle, poke, wash, turn, and discuss it. He heard someone say (a grave little female voice—nurse? doctor?) "Be aware that he could be hearing and understanding everything we're saying, but he is incapable of responding." He had to laugh. He's not incapable, just not in the mood. In fact, he did laugh but no one noticed.

Everyone is so intent on talking to him that no one hears what he is saying. They talk right over him—jabbering like monkeys—and then suddenly realize they haven't heard anything from him, so they demand that he give them a sign. Why do they need so much from him? Desirée is the only one who doesn't want anything, who will sit and listen.

The events that led him here are not in his mind. He has searched and searched, but recalls only a feeling of anticipation. Going to meet Desirée, going to see her. What derailed him from his purpose? He would like her to explain for him, separate plans that were made from events that ensued. There are lapses. Certain areas, categories of thought, are unclear. Her name, for instance. He feels that Desirée is not the name she told him, although it is her true name. How did he discover it? He knew from the first time she came into his room, soaking wet, forcing her way past Florence. He'd been expecting her, not in his conscious mind, but in his entrails, waiting for her to find him. He knows this for fact, yet at the same time, he realizes that he is not thinking rationally. But when he tries to sort it out logically, he becomes hopelessly twisted in thoughts without words, or words without thoughts. It makes him tired.

All he wants is to go away, the two of them. Bahamas? Virgin Islands? They can live comfortably on his retirement funds, devoting themselves to love, exploring its delights together. On this small island where nobody knows them, what will it matter? It's not as if she grew up under his roof, not as if he held her on his knee, bathed her and fed her strained apricots from a tiny spoon. They met as adults, freely consenting. Taboo is strong. Has to be, to counter attraction. Primitive, a tribal ruling. Had to do with regulating the distribution of property. But irrelevant in this case. Doesn't apply.

He senses when it's time for Desirée's visit and he crawls close to the wall so he can hear her come in. Florence ceases her noise and goes outside. He hears their voices blending conspiratorially and has to restrain himself from sitting up and telling Florence to let the girl alone for chrissake. Finally he hears Florence's high heels tapping down the corridor and then he emerges. Desirée understands why he doesn't speak out loud or even open his eyes. He can't risk being discovered. As soon as his heart has been fixed, they will go away together. They spend their time imagining what it will be like.

He smiles as he hears her walking around the bed, making certain everything has been done properly. She calms him; the rhythm of his heart smooths to match her own. They rest, already knowing how the sea will sound from bed in their new home, how the sun will kiss their bodies in the morning. The muscle of his heart will grow as strong and vigorous as her own.

Desirée takes his hand. (Someone came to visit him—was it

today? He thinks so. Her hand felt so much like Desirée's that he thought it was she, but then she started talking, babbling nonsense, and he fled back through the tunnel of time.) This is the true Desirée, the one whose spirit floated above him on that sultry night, like a white curtain fluttering in the breeze, waiting for the moment when she would become incarnate, the one who eventually sought him out and who longs for their reunion—in spirit and in flesh. The impulse to open his eyes is fierce, but he resists. She understands. She is waiting for his heart to mend so they can begin.

Florence's footsteps sound in the hall—coming back so soon! They have only seconds left. He wants to tell Desirée just one thing. She comes over and puts her ear close to his mouth.

So MANY PEOPLE ARE AFRAID OF HOSPITALS, AFRAID OF being with the unwell. Henry, for instance, is terrified and has avoided visiting. He hasn't even called Florence, as if she might be carrying the contagion and he could contract it over the phone. Instead Henry relies on Edith, pulls her into his office, closes the door, and asks her for details. Edith thinks Henry really loves Martin, that he will be sad if Martin dies. She's offered to take Henry to see Martin, to go in first and make certain he's all right, and to stand outside the door in case something happens, but when Henry heard that Martin had tubes in him, that did it. He said he couldn't stand seeing tubes going into people's veins.

Far from being disturbed, Edith is comforted by hospitals. When she enters Martin's room, she always looks for something to do, if it's only to adjust the blue oxygen tube at his nostrils or check his IV. Then she settles into the plastic armchair. The smells of Band-Aids and gauze, the rattle of carts in the hallway, the squeak of rubber soles on the highly polished floor, even the commanding voices of nurses and the feeble protests of patients comfort her. After all, she spent more time as a child in her grandfather's clinic than in the playground. It's a world she knows, and one in which she's been trained to be useful.

If she concentrates, she can hear the traffic on the street— horns and sirens—but inside Martin's room there is only the breathing. Aside from taking in oxygen, Martin makes no sound, no motion. He can rest now because he no longer has to keep track of his heartbeat. The monitor records it by his bedside for all to see, the ragged struggles of a rended heart.

She doesn't talk to Martin, the way Geraldine and Florence do, even though Florence has asked her to. Edith is afraid that if she speaks, he'll answer, even though he won't talk to anyone else. She feels that he senses when she comes into the room, that he's trying to send a message.

Edith is happy to give this time to Martin so Florence can have a break. Florence is wonderful, spending hours reading to Martin, talking to him, stroking his hand. Tears come to Edith's eyes when she sees Florence at Martin's bedside, how much she loves him.

Edith had to be the one to call Florence. She couldn't leave it to anyone else. She had to explain how her neighbor had found Martin on the street outside her door, how Edith heard scream- ing, then Lulu on the intercom saying come quick—no call 911 —get an ambulance. Edith thought it was the maniac in the dog suit, that he had attacked Martin. She and Ben (she, pulling on clothes, screaming at him to hurry, as if it were his fault) rushed down to find Lulu kneeling over Martin's body on the sidewalk. Edith picked up Martin's wrist and felt for his pulse, at the same time, bending close to his face to catch any breath.

When she felt the stillness of Martin's body, she became still as well, inside herself. It was as if she had entered into her grandfather's mind, his hands, or as if he had entered her body and was instructing its motions. Because she'd seen him do this, bring a person back to life—twice. And he'd had her practice on him and on her friends (he once gave a course in CPR to her Girl Scout troop). Edith took Martin's head in her hands and lifted it back, freeing his windpipe. Then she put her lips to his and blew into his mouth, once, twice. The chest rose and fell, rose and fell. She pushed his ribs with her hands and kneaded his heart back to life, over and over. Her hands left damp spots on his shirt. At last his eyes fluttered open. Ah ah ahhh, he said, and when she put her ear to his heart, she heard him sigh, "Desirée." Or did she hear wrong?

His eyes are scanning behind closed lids, reading, she thinks, remembering how he used to go through the pages she gave him. He often spends their entire time together moving his eyes this way, as if he has a large volume he must finish in a very short time. Her grandfather told her that eye movement could be a sign the brain is working. But her grandfather, speaking long distance, didn't give much hope.

Grandpop has been cool about Martin, objective. He finds it interesting—the coincidence and all—but he is not moved to pity that Martin might never know. There's something old-fashioned in Grandpop's attitude, that Martin should have taken responsibility at the time, that he doesn't deserve to know. Edith thinks there might also be a little jealousy. On the other hand, Grandpop is delighted that she found Lucille, as he calls her. He takes credit for their reunion. He wanted to speak to Lulu on the phone. Edith could tell that he was squeezing compliments out of Lulu: hadn't Edith grown up to be a fine whatever—and on and on. Lulu was kind, gracious even. She didn't accuse or blame. She did, however, keep a tight hold of Edith's hand throughout the conversation, as if the doctor might once again contrive to steal her away.

When did Edith know? When Florence came to the emergency room and recognized Lulu, called her Lucille? When Florence asked, "What did you two do to him? What did you say to him?" (Ben was standing right there, and had been with them all the night, but Florence discounted him. All that mattered were Lulu and Edith—"you two.") Or did Edith know when she met Lulu's eyes the first time she saw her, at the Caffè San Marco?

As soon as Edith recognized Lulu as her mother, she no longer feared Lulu, or despised her. Last night she and Clarence had a long talk about it. It was the kind of talk they used to have up at Grimsby, but this time they were sitting outside at the Caffè San Marco, where they love Clarence. (He knows everyone's name; the owner sent him over a free bottle of Clarence's favorite wine—Orvieto something.) "You were afraid of giving in to it," Clarence said. "Giving in to sex and to being a woman. Because if you were Lulu's daughter, then you would have to be like her, and look what happened to Lulu. I know, because it was the same with me. I was afraid of giving in to being queer." He divided the rest of the wine between them. "Sex is messy. You fall in love, you get hurt, or you hurt someone else. It's like, we should have evolved into something less stupid, but we haven't." Or at least that's what Edith thinks she remembers Clarence said. At the time it seemed profound and true, but now she isn't sure it makes sense.

Lulu has her own theory about why Edith was afraid. Apparently, Lulu went to Compton Falls once when Edith was very small, and tried to take her back. Edith became hysterical. Carolyn was going to call the police, but luckily called Grandpop instead, who came over and explained to Lulu that she could be arrested for kidnapping. Lulu feels that Edith retains a subconscious memory of that event. "I've seen you looking at me the same way, with those same scared eyes," Lulu said, making Edith feel deeply ashamed at the way she'd treated Lulu. No wonder Clarence kept trying to sit her down and tell her. Clarence is so nice.

Edith takes Martin's hand in hers. It's colorless, almost transparent, and smooth, unmarred by calluses, nicks, and scratches— the hand of a mandarin (the nails are clean and slightly longer than they should be) or a paralytic. The long blunt fingers are not like her own, which are tapered, more like Lulu's. But the square shape of his thumbnail corresponds with hers, matching like a talisman in a fairy tale. And her eyes, Florence says, are like his when he was young. It's odd that she never considered that there would have had to have been a father as well. It was enough to imagine a mother, to try to form an image from all the contradicting rumors, impressions, intuitions. Of her father there had been no news, no clue. That he should turn out to be Martin!

The restless movement of his eyes. Is he thinking? Is he taking in data from the outside world, or is he viewing an inner screen, passively receiving messages from dendrites dying one by one like lights going out on a Christmas tree? Does he remember Lulu at all? Has he entertained the idea that Edith could be his daughter?

The way Edith was drawn to him from the beginning, the way she went past Florence, right into Martin's room, as if an outside power were moving her. He must have felt it too. It was a connection so strong that it confused them. She sees that now. If Martin recovers, he will be told and he will understand how to feel toward Edith. Florence will explain.

Edith tries to think of Martin getting better, acting like a father, which will be similar to how Grandpop is. What gets in the way is how Martin was with her that night. She can't transmute that gesture into a fatherly kiss. And what she did with Ben while Martin kept vigil from the street, the way she felt, was not the way a daughter feels. If Martin would die before he regains consciousness, then these memories could be buried with him. Maybe she could transform him over time into father.

But she doesn't know anything about his childhood, or how he came to *Ubu,* or how he fell in love with Florence. If he dies now, his long and complicated history will be lost to her. And her Real Life, or the life she thought he would guide her to, will also be lost, if it ever existed. She turns his hand over in hers. This is her legacy, a few memories and the shape of her thumbnail. If he dies, she'll never be able to think of him as a father; he'll always be a stranger.

She hears a groan—not from those dry parted lips, can't be. Traffic in the street, she tells herself. The cords of Martin's neck stand out as if he's trying to lift his head, as if he read her thoughts and wants to protest. But that's impossible. It must be a trick of light. Edith glances at the monitor, then toward the nurses' station. Is anyone paying attention? His lips contort—an involuntary rictus, or is he trying to say something? She bends closer. She can see the shape of his skull, how flesh is already deserting bone. She puts her ear to his mouth and receives a rush of air. The smell makes her gag.

Martin feels her lips on his and waits to melt into delirium, but a buzzer assaults his ears. Her soft lips turn rough. There's a mob around his bed, white coats, green coats, pummeling his chest. Martin is looking at them from the wrong angle, from above, while his own body lies far beneath, almost hidden from sight. He sees what the matter is, why they are so agitated. They want him to come down from the ceiling and get back into his body. But he doesn't want to. Don't they have machines that can take over, just for a while? They continue to badger him. If they would just bring Desirée back, it would provide an incentive. As it is, it hardly seems worthwhile.

"CALL THE CODE." DID EDITH ACTUALLY HEAR IT, OR did she provide the term for what the medical team is thinking? Her arm is around Florence, bracing her for what the cardiologist is coming to say. The doctor's forehead is beaded with sweat and his white coat is mussed, as if he's been bested in a scuffle. He's slightly shorter than Edith, and stocky. In the wide-legged way he stands, Edith can see a sailor trying to keep his balance on a heaving sea. Edith tightens her hold on Florence.

MARTIN MUST HAVE FALLEN ASLEEP. THE ROOM IS PROfoundly still. He remembers a commotion—white coats and green coats. They're gone, decided to give him some peace. Geraldine was right; they are an incompetent group. The light. There's more light, but where is it coming from? Maybe from a window that Martin didn't see before. A sweet smell expands within him, and he sees Desirée, at last. But Florence is with her. Florence is weeping and Desirée supports her. There's something about this scene that is familiar, timeless.

Their shoulders are bent, and he can't see their faces. If he could, he would reassure them that he is only resting. He's quite content here on the ceiling; it's a trick he's perfected, one that he long aspired to. *Desirée, Desirée, don't look down, I'm up here. Raise your sweet face. If I could see your eyes. Oh, dear child, I can't bear the sound of grieving.* He tries to swim down to her but he's too light. Lines of communication have disintegrated. He's come untethered.

MIGRATING

For weeks the city was wrapped in a gritty mist punctuated by short blasts of rain and onslaughts of sun that made pavements steam and fashionable women suffocate under the damp weight of new fall clothes. It was said resentfully that by mid-September summer was supposed to be over. Global warming was darkly invoked, the demise of the planet predicted. Then a cold, dry wind out of Manitoba, bringing on its tail a host of migrating falcons, accipiters, warblers, and vireos, banished the choking smog. The natural order appears restored; weather is no longer a topic of conversation; the hottest summer of the century fades in the collective memory.

.   .   .

LULU SUGGESTED THEY MEET NEAR THE SEA LIONS AT THE Central Park Zoo. Wouldn't she rather meet downtown? Desert Ray asked; wasn't Lulu working on getting her show ready for tonight? Oh no, Lulu said, the show was ready and had been for days. She wanted to do some shopping, and the zoo would be convenient.

When Lulu sees Ray walking toward her in the park, she has to wave and call her name, otherwise she'd walk right by. "Edie! Edie! Here I am!" (Ray has asked Lulu to call her Edith, which she does, but she'll always think of her as Desert Ray.) Lulu's still a little shy with Ray, seeing as how she's only been her mother officially for a month now, but Ray comes right up and gives her a hug and a kiss. Lulu tries not to hang on too long. After all, there will be plenty more hugs, although Lulu still finds it hard to believe.

"It's part of my trousseau," Lulu says when Ray compliments her outfit. "I never thought rich would suit me, but it does." She checks her hair to make sure it's smooth, and it is. Larry's not sure he likes it; he says he prefers the wild Lulu, but Lulu can tell that Ray approves.

"So you and Larry are really getting married?" Ray asks.

"We haven't set a date or anything, but I've moved into his place here in the city, and I guess we'll get around to it, after the house is finished," Lulu says.

"I like Larry," Ray says. "He seems kind of old—I mean, older than you, but he takes care of you. I would be worried, you know, if you were still living in other people's houses, like when Clarence and I first met you. It will be nice, to live with someone you love."

Lulu doesn't say anything, since she isn't certain she does love Larry, at least not in the way Ray means, the way people do when they're young and getting married seems romantic. But Ray is right: Larry does take care of Lulu, and being taken care of is something Lulu is coming to appreciate.

They choose a bench in the sun. Lulu takes Ray's hand, and Ray allows it to rest in hers. Passersby take a second look at the two of them, and decide that, yes, they are mother and daughter, a striking pair, could almost be taken for sisters, the mother so young-looking, and the daughter so self-possessed.

"How's school?" Lulu asks.

"Hard. And I miss Clarence. But I study more with him not there, so I guess it's good." Ray lifts her hair back from her face in a gesture Lulu recognizes as her own. Lulu's glad that Ray seems to have abandoned that braid she wore all summer. It made her look like a French schoolgirl, or a very young judge.

Desert Ray is going to be a doctor. It's about the one thing Lulu never imagined herself doing, which was probably one of the deciding factors. It makes sense that Ray would want to be a doctor, because in the battle over Ray, it was the doctor who won, not Lulu. Who should Ray choose to emulate, to pattern her life after, the hapless, frantic mother who had entered the clinic, wondering how she could possibly pay the doctor for examining her feverish baby, or the doctor who reached out his big hands and calmly took the baby from her?

Well, at least Ray isn't going into *Ubu*. Lulu imagines that the atmosphere there is as poisonous as ever. "I think it's good you didn't go to work at the magazine," Lulu says.

Ray nods. "They wanted me to. Florence and Henry, anyway. They said Martin would have wished it for me. But I don't think that's what Martin wanted."

Lulu guesses that it's settled in everyone's mind that Ray is Martin's child. It's strange how no one would even entertain the possibility when Ray was born, but now it suits everyone that this should be so. Lulu searches her daughter's face. The eyes are like Martin's, but aren't her lips more like—"Do you play an instrument? Are you musical?" Lulu asks.

Ray shrugs. "I sang in the chorus in high school."

If Ray had become a rock 'n' roll groupie, would that have meant that Tommy G. was the father? To the doctor, Lulu had exaggerated her role and importance in the magazine, had hinted that Ray's father was a rising star there. The doctor must have felt a responsibility toward reconnecting Ray with her parents. He encouraged Ray to come to the city and look for a job at *Ubu*.

How strange that those girls—Geraldine and Florence— were involved with Ray all the time, and Lulu didn't know. They've fallen in love with Lulu's baby, when, at one time, all they could think of was how to get rid of her. No, it's Martin's baby they love. They loved Martin, those girls, but they were too prissy, or cool, or slow, to do anything about it. It was kind of fun when Lulu told them she was carrying his baby—to see their faces! But it was mean. Lulu's a much nicer person now. She was rough, out of control, in those days. Now Lulu has mellowed. It's fine if Geraldine and Florence want to love Ray.

Lulu spies a Sabrett wagon. "Ooh, hot dogs! When I was pregnant with you, I used to get these enormous cravings for hot dogs off a cart—you know, with sauerkraut and onions? And of course I was living in this commune, eating brown rice and squash. There wasn't a decent hot dog within fifty miles. Want one? How about it? My treat!"

"Um, no thanks. I'm not hungry."

Lulu really wants a hot dog, but she's afraid she'll gross Ray out, and she might spill something on her clothes. Hot dogs are awfully messy. She wants to ask Ray if she's glad she found her.

What stops her is Ray's self-sufficiency. Lulu still marvels at how Ray has this talent for not needing anyone, when Lulu needs everyone. She needs all the help she can get just to get through the day. She thinks it all has to do with timing. She's read that there are such things as learning windows—the optimum, sometimes the only, moment in a child's development when it can learn a skill, or a way of thinking, or even a way of feeling. Ray was orphaned—or abandoned—early in life, and somehow she programmed herself not to need love. She accepts it, but she doesn't need it. Lulu, on the other hand, was orphaned at the wrong stage in life, and she has been forever yearning after love. She needs it from everyone she meets, otherwise she begins to disappear. This is why Lulu needs Ray, but Ray doesn't need her.

This is why Lulu will not ask the question that is on her mind. Instead she asks: "Were you ever in this zoo? C'mon, I'll take you. The penguins pop out of the water like little toys. I always meant to take you—I mean, I realize you're a little old for zoos but indulge me. I'm harmless."

"I love zoos," Ray says, and gives her hand a squeeze.

"I CAME OVER EARLY—I SAW THE LIGHTS ON—TO SEE IF I could help," Montero says.

Lulu hadn't counted on this. She has been carefully avoiding Montero, dragging Larry (without telling him why) to chaperone her whenever she's been in the gallery. Her body, slow to pick up on certain decisions that her mind has been making, is pouring out hormones. Her heart is going crazy, trying to deliver more blood to all those areas that have learned to respond to the sight, sound, smell, or touch of Montero. "You look good," Lulu says. "Rested."

"Yeah, well, life isn't so crazy anymore, since you went and got engaged, if that's really what you are. Where did that guy come from anyway?"

"He'd been around, but he was away."

"You never told me."

"You never asked. There's a lot I never told you."

"I guess this guy's rich. You look nice."

"Thanks."

"Is he good—you know—"

"Why, Montero, you've become so delicate since we last saw one another. He's perfectly adequate."

"But not like—"

"Well, with us, there was a lot of fuel. The exploitive nature of the whole enterprise furnished conflicting emotions, hate, fear, revenge, scorn, all those good things."

"It looks like you've studied this."

"We can't really control our actions, Montero. We do what we have to do, but we should at least try to understand, even though what we come up with as explanations usually aren't close to the truth."

"It's funny, having this talk with you. We never talked."

"I guess we wouldn't be talking now if the mattress were still in the back, and if people weren't going to arrive at any moment." She looks toward the door as if they might be coming now.

He puts his hand on the nape of her neck. "I've done it in closets before, standing up. It's not bad."

One last time, oh, one last time. She owes it to herself, doesn't she, at least to her body, because, face it, making love with Larry is not the same as with Montero. She kept the videos. She watched them all and then couldn't bring herself to destroy them, even though it's dangerous to have them around. She can't help herself from imagining, as if watching the video, what it would be like behind the partition, tearing at each other's clothes as the first of the guests crossed the threshold. The only thing that stops her is Ray's face—not as she is now, but Ray at two, when Lulu went back to try to get her—Ray's eyes big and frightened, her mouth a little O.

Lulu forces herself to turn away and walk toward the door. "You're just a romantic fool, Montero. But this was a business deal, and after tonight I won't have to compensate you any more."

"Bring your wife and baby to the opening," she tells him as he walks by her in a sulk. "I'd love to see your baby."

"EDITH, COME TELL ME WHICH LOOKS BEST." FLORENCE IS standing in her underwear in Martin's room. "I feel I should wear the black, because it's downtown, but I really like the green better."

"Then wear the green," Edith says. She's staying with Florence for the weekend, and Lulu said she should bring Florence to the show. Edith feels close to Florence, as if she, not Martin, were her parent. Florence knew all along. Edith wishes Florence had told Martin from the beginning.

"Florence, why didn't you tell Martin that I was his daughter right away?"

Florence pulls the green dress over her head. "I thought he knew—and well, I was jealous, suspicious. You remember what I was like."

"When I saw you climbing into the garden over the wall, I thought you'd lost your mind."

Florence shakes out her hair. "I did, for a while. You created quite a disturbance, Edith, without meaning to, of course."

This is the first Edith's been in Martin's room since he died.

Florence cleaned out his things right after the funeral, repainted, rearranged furniture. "I'm not one of those widows who keeps setting her dead husband's place at the table," she told Edith. Edith thought Florence was right to get on with her life, and Martin's room is the nicest one—it has the deck and everything. Edith told Geraldine she thought that Florence's attitude was healthy. Geraldine had hinted that Florence wasn't taking the time to grieve properly.

Edith, looking around Martin's room for something that will remind her of him, feels she herself never grieved properly. Right after Martin's death, classes began, and she had to go up to Grimsby to register.

The morning after Martin died, Edith woke knowing she'd go back to school—even though Henry called and offered her a position at the magazine, mentioning Martin's "legacy." But Martin's legacy, what he gave her, was the realization of what it means to bring back life. When she found him on the sidewalk, without a pulse, only minutes away from death, and she was able to breathe into his lungs and see his chest rise in response, something fell into place for her.

In the hospital when Martin's heart stopped again, Edith was confident that she could bring him back a second time. Someone pushed her roughly out of the way. A nurse told her, more gently, to wait outside. Edith went—she had no choice—but she knows she could have saved him. Martin wanted *her* to bring him back. He wouldn't do it for anyone else. Absurdly, it hurt her pride that they pushed her out of that room. She felt entitled to be there, as if she had already completed her studies.

When Edith went back to Compton Falls to get her things, Carolyn came barreling out of the house to give her a hug then stopped, unsure of her impulse, of the appropriateness of what she'd been about to do. "That dress looks like you bought it at the Salvation Army," she said. Edith felt the familiar defensive bristle that always greeted these comments of Carolyn's, but this time she saw through it, understood that Carolyn was trying to restrain both herself and Edith before they did something dangerous, like break into tears, or fall into each other's arms.

"I got it in a flea market on the street for ten dollars. On rainy days it kind of has a smell," Edith said, then she put her bag down and hugged her mother. Over Carolyn's shoulder, Edith saw Grandpop watching from the porch.

He's pleased with himself now that Edith's come back. While Carolyn was watching *Masterpiece Theatre* on television, Grandpop persuaded Edith to walk him around the block for his "constitutional," although Edith had never known him to take the daily walk that he prescribes religiously for his older patients. They bundled up in heavy sweaters. It was much colder there than in the city.

"She's been a wreck all summer," he said, "and I kept telling her you'd come back."

"How did you know? I didn't even know until yesterday," Edith said.

"Hah! I didn't know a damn thing. That's what I told *her!* How the hell did I know what you were going to do? But you had to go, Edith. You were too docile, going along with our decisions for you—sure, sometimes you'd talk back a little—but you always got good grades in school, you helped out in the clinic. What I missed was the sense that it was coming from in here." He thumped his chest with his big hands. "If you're going to get through med school, it has to come from you. You can't fake it. So when you came up with the idea of going to New York for the summer, I convinced Carolyn that it was a good

decision because you had made it on your own. I was taking a
big chance, giving you to Lucille. Carolyn never would have
agreed to that one. She's terrified of Lucille. I guess you know
that by now. Lucille had—charm. Is she still a nice-looking
woman?"

Edith had to smile in the darkness, thinking of her grandfather falling for Lulu.

"She's attractive," Edith conceded.

"Well, there's nothing wrong with that. Sometimes Carolyn
gets a little funny on the subject. You have to see the good points
in Lucille, Edith, because she's part of you. You like her, don't
you?"

Edith said she was beginning to. Now that her fear had vanished, she was trying to see Lulu in a different way, not the way
Carolyn would, more the way Clarence sees Lulu. Edith does
appreciate Lulu's spirit and playfulness, but still she can't help
feeling sorry for her. Edith tries to be her daughter, but she will
never be Desert Ray, the child Lulu would have raised, and Lulu
knows it. Edith is also afraid that Lulu's marriage (if she goes
through with it) will be a simulation as well, a pretend match, a
last resort solution to the problem of, not only loneliness, but
homelessness.

Grandpop has theories on finding one's identity, that it was
important for Edith to find Lulu in order to know herself. But
for Edith, the sense of being herself came in the moment of
saving Martin's life. Edith Seagrace. The name still seems arbi-
trary to her—patched-together pieces from a grandmother she
never met and a father she barely remembers. But it anchors her
into the place that Grandpop and Carolyn made for her. And it
takes her in the direction she wants to go.

"I don't look too uptight, uptown, East Side?" Florence asks.

Edith can't imagine what Florence is talking about. She's turning in front of the mirror, pursing her mouth, looking over her shoulder, in a vampy fifties way that would make Edith laugh if she didn't realize that Florence was doing it unconsciously. Florence is serious, Edith realizes. She really wants to know if she looks all right, when she always looks perfect. As Carolyn has never asked Edith how she looks, Edith assumed this was something adult women didn't worry about, that by the time she herself was twenty-five, say, she would not have to ask whether or not she was wearing the right thing.

"Well, you are from the Upper East Side. Why should you look like all those arty people from downtown?"

"I think I'll wear the black."

Edith feels she's being unfair to Martin, standing in his room for the first time since he died, and talking about clothes of all things with Florence. She opens the French doors and steps out on the deck. Here nothing's changed. She leans her forearms on the rail and looks over the garden, admiring how the white flowers gather in the dying light, imagining that Martin is in the room behind her, and will come in a moment to join her. He was the perfect father in a way—opening a world for Edith, discovering someone in her that she hadn't known was there—discovering himself in her, the way a father might when his daughter reaches a certain age.

If he had claimed her from the beginning as his daughter, then her life might have progressed in an entirely different way. She might have moved in with Martin and Florence, gone to work at *Ubu,* maybe even taken Martin's name. She would be on her way to becoming another person—Edith Weatherstone. This is what she felt, the first time she stood here looking at this scrap of Eden hidden away from the rest of the city. She felt the pull of that life, of that person.

If Martin had known from the beginning, then he would have known how to act. Or would he? He rejected Edith once, when Lulu showed him a photo of her infant self. He rejected her again when Florence tried to tell him. He denied that he'd ever had a child. Perhaps, in fact, the possibility of being Edith Weatherstone never really existed.

She hears footsteps behind her and allows herself to imagine that it's Martin, coming to put his arms around her and say that he does want her as his child, that his actions were a mistake, part of his illness. She waits for his touch, even though she knows that the footsteps are Florence's.

"There was a bird. The first night I stayed here, I heard a bird singing this amazing song. It went on and on," Edith says.

"Oh, yes, the mockingbird. There's always one somewhere in the garden, in early summer. But not now. The mockingbird never sings his night song in the fall," Florence says.

CLARENCE IS LATE BECAUSE IT TOOK HIM A WHILE TO dress, to decide on just the right look to convey who he is and at the same time to please his friends and do credit to them. Edie is going to be amazed at his suit and tie, extremely masculine and correct. And a real diamond stud in his ear. A gift from Austin. He hasn't even told her about Austin.

Lulu picked the right date for her opening, the third weekend in September when most of the downtown galleries have their big openings. It's like the first day back at school—with everyone strolling around greeting each other. Clarence recognizes people from his bartending days at Maude's and even gets to give out a business card or two. This is what he loves about the city—the little worlds within the bigness of it, the way they overlap, the gossiping and scheming. The city is so densely populated that it maximizes opportunities for chance meetings, for reconnecting under altered circumstances.

Lulu's gallery looks good, even from half a block away. A sufficiency of milling out front. It's packed. Lulu has plenty of friends, and Larry must have brought in some more. Even Montero has, if not friends (which would be hard to imagine), connections who could be persuaded to come downtown for an opening. The disadvantage to having so many people is that everyone talks to one another and ignores the work. The litter mobile turns jerkily in a corner and no one pays it any mind. The disembodied shell of QB, his long johns, running shoes, and baseball cap, dangling from a wire frame, evokes no reaction. A few people glance at the mail collage that Clarence worked on; they ignore the table scraps in jars, the pyramid of discarded crossword puzzles. It's the kind of show that is best seen alone, one person walking through, preferably on a rainy Tuesday, when most of the world is uptown doing things.

He wonders if Lulu regrets her decision to junk the videos. No one would be standing around discussing summer travel and country houses if the videos were potently flickering on every side. It was Edie, of course; Lulu worried about how Edie would react. Clarence, standing in the entrance, watches Lulu chatting up a group of friends. She looks more art dealer than artist, prosperous, sleek in her new haircut. Well, she's a mother now, and about to be a married woman, and she's determined to play the role to the hilt. Or is the change more profound than that?

Clarence noticed a difference in Lulu even before she decided to cut her hair and scratch the videos. Her stride shortened; her gestures were not as open and free. He asked Edie if she noticed and Edie said she couldn't tell because her way of looking at Lulu had changed so radically. Edie has decided that Lulu is a victim. She can accept her better as her mother if she sees her as someone who was forced into choices she didn't want to make, but Clarence thinks Lulu is too much the master of her destiny to be considered victim. The term doesn't do her justice.

He misses Lulu now that she's gone off to live with her sugar daddy, and Clarence with his. But Lulu and Larry took him out to dinner once, to Vong's, which Clarence had been dying to try. And he loved riding around in Larry's limo. And he and Austin are invited for the weekend to the house in the Berkshires, as soon as the remodeling is complete. Clarence wonders if Lulu will still be there. Not that Larry isn't generous and loving and all that, but he's so safe. Can Lulu really tolerate all that security?

Edie waves and comes from across the room; Florence is with her. Clarence knows that Edie's a little nervous about bringing Florence into Lulu land. She's wondering how Lulu's going to behave. "Edie!" Clarence picks her up and twirls her around. She fingers his diamond stud. "From Austin, the love of my life," he whispers.

"I've heard so much about you." Florence takes Clarence's hand in both of hers, charming him instantly, although he recognizes that she is doing it to signal her status as one of Edie's mothers. But Florence is pretty and rich, so why not? You can never have too many mothers, he's told Edie.

Edith sees Lulu and Larry coming toward their little group. Lulu offers Florence her hand, but Florence goes for an embrace.

She's still very emotional from Martin's death. They look alike, in a way, as if they come from the same social set, two well-to-do women of a certain age. They could be friends who meet for the occasional lunch. And yet they were rivals—enemies even.

Edith has heard the story separately from each of the three women: Geraldine, Florence, and Lulu. Geraldine tells it as if she and Florence were co-conspirators against Lulu and Edith, and a terrible injustice was done. Florence claims she had no idea that Martin was actually involved, that she and Geraldine were only trying to help Lulu out, who was obviously not capable of raising a child. And Lulu assigns no blame. It's simply the way it happened.

Edith told Geraldine that she doesn't take it personally, that Geraldine tried to have Edith's fetal self aborted. Edith would have made the same decision. It was irresponsible of Lulu to go ahead and have a baby with no plans for supporting it. It was sheer good luck on Edith's part that she was adopted by people who had the means and the will to care for her.

Of course, if it hadn't been for Lulu's reckless, riskful courage, Edith wouldn't be standing here today. As Clarence has pointed out, Edith owes her everything.

Lulu slips an arm around Desert Ray's waist and draws her close. Their bodies match: hip to hip, shoulder to shoulder. Lulu looks at Ray and sees her baby girl. The eyes haven't changed. Lulu knows how Ray smells, the texture of her skin. "Clarence, take a picture," Lulu says, handing him her camera, and he does. Lulu will put it in a photo album, one devoted to pictures of Ray. She has already planned where the album will be kept in hers and Larry's house.

Clarence thinks Lulu's altered her personality to please Ray, but Lulu feels that she's simply allowed herself to be caught by a more mature, settled version of herself. She used to feel it stalking her, but kept running to stay free, open to possibilities. Once she found Ray, or Ray found her, she was in the perilous position of having something to lose, and she couldn't bear to risk it. She has decided to become stable, stationary, a woman who lives in one place, who allows the stuff of life to accumulate around her. She will begin to grow old now because she is no longer a single unit in time, but part of a progression. There is another version of herself filling the space of youth, and there will be another after her.

Lulu hugs Ray close again and then releases her. Ray has seen someone she knows. Her face lights up, and she goes to meet him. It's that boy, the one she was with the night Martin collapsed. "What's his name?" she asks Clarence.

"Oh, that's Ben."

"Is he a nice boy? Should I be concerned?"

"Lulu, Edie already has a mother who asks that kind of question. Between you and Edie, I think you just have to worry about your own behavior," Clarence says.

RYO YAMANAKA HAS THE FEELING THAT SHE'S COME IN at the end of the movie. It makes her profoundly uneasy. Why, for instance, is Martin's wife—no, widow—here of all places, and how does she know Lulu? Isn't that the girl who Henry was squiring around, the one who's working at *Ubu?* It's obvious now, seeing her standing beside Lulu, that they're related. Mother and daughter? And where are the video screens? Lulu completely ignored Ryo's advice. There isn't even the small screen she'd originally planned. Now Ryo is going to have to grub around and come up with another story, a conventional story. She'll have to use her wit and style to try to fool people into thinking they are reading something new.

"What happened?"

"Oh, you mean the videos? I changed my mind," the bitch says airily.

"You could have called. I planned my whole piece around you, and now I'm stuck."

"It was a last-minute decision. In the end, this seemed more interesting—reconstructing a person from the bits that have fallen away from him, the bits being small unconscious messages to the rest of the world, or to the one who makes the effort to decode them."

"I don't think she's going to be giving you a review," Larry says to Lulu, watching Ryo stalk out of the gallery.

BECAUSE HE'S TALL, CLARENCE NOTICES WHEN ANOTHER tall person enters a room. And since he's come to New York, he can spot another gay man, even one who dresses like a preppy banker—attractive, lanky, early thirties. At first the banker is only mildly curious, but before long he is drawn into the exhibit, seems to be experiencing a strong emotional connection to the work. He looks around from time to time, as if there must be someone who could explain it to him.

"This is my stuff," he tells Clarence. "She stole my stuff."

"She just took it out of your garbage," Clarence says.

"It's weird, it's like seeing a video of yourself, one you didn't know was being shot. I mean, that's my underwear hanging up for the world to see. It's—like a violation. This has got to be illegal. I should sue."

"I wouldn't take you as the type who sues. You're lazy. You throw a lot of your mail out unopened."

"Yeah, I probably won't sue, but what kind of a person would do this? Put old takeout containers in a Plexiglas box? Here's my toothbrush. . . ."

"You're taller than we thought, and more built."

"I've been working out."

"Here at the Soho gym?"

"No, at Burton's."

"Oh yeah? What's it like there? I heard it was kind of a scene," Clarence says, who has been thinking of joining for precisely that reason, but it's uncool to admit that you go to a gym for any purpose other than to work out.

WHEN GERALDINE STARTED ON HER WALK, SHE HAD NO idea that this would be her final destination. She should be more careful; being without a regular schedule could lead her into irrational acts. She stands just inside the entrance, feeling like a spectator at a play or like a ghost come back to haunt the living. Ryo Yamanaka walks right by, not even bothering to snub her. Lucille (it took Geraldine the longest time to figure out who she was) has been calling to people she spots on the other side of the room, probably everyone she's ever met in the last twenty years, and yet she can't seem to see Geraldine. Even Florence, who burst into tears when she saw Geraldine at the funeral, has looked right through her at least twice.

The way Lucille appropriates Edith, as if she has a right to her, when what did she ever do except drop her, like a cow giving birth in the field. (Years ago, when Lucille met Geraldine in the street, she'd bragged that having a baby was nothing; she'd only felt a little indigestion; she didn't understand what all the fuss was about.) Lucille pulls the girl next to her, showing her off, how alike the two of them are.

And they are. Geraldine's breath catches. *They're the same.* Physical resemblance is the least of it. The girl possesses the same talent as her mother. Is it talent or attitude? Why not call it karma, or soul? They both have the ability to attract love to themselves and to accept it as their due.

How they hold themselves for the photograph: tall, straight, triumphant. For they have triumphed. The daughter has avenged the mother. It happened as Geraldine predicted. Edith destroyed them all. Martin is dead. Florence widowed. Geraldine deposed.

No, that isn't right either, because Edith did not consciously act with these goals in mind. She was the instrument, or the one who allowed them to complete their destinies. And except for Martin, they are not really destroyed. Florence looks positively blooming. She'll find someone, or someone will find her, maybe someone who will love her the way Martin never managed to. And Geraldine isn't at *Ubu* anymore, but there is life after *Ubu*. Geraldine finally found a home, a place that gives her joy every day. And she wouldn't have done it for herself. She did it for Edith. As for Martin—maybe he found something he never would have without Edith. Martin learned to love before he died.

And Geraldine learned to love in a new way, a way that needs nothing in return. It's the kind of love one was supposed to feel for Christ, but somehow all the rest of what one learned at church got in the way of it: the confessions and penances, the whole rigmarole. Geraldine would always end up feeling guilty that she couldn't call up this selfless love for Christ. But she can for Edith. It's the part of herself she likes the best. Geraldine loves herself for loving Edith.

As if Edith could feel this love, she turns to Geraldine. Her face lights up. She leaves Lucille and practically runs toward

Geraldine, whose mouth opens in greeting, whose arms spontaneously rise from her sides, preparing for an embrace.

Geraldine looks around to see if anybody noticed, but of course no one did because Geraldine is invisible. What is that boy's name? Ben. Geraldine feels as if her own daughter went by without seeing her. And maybe Edith is in a way the child Geraldine would have liked to have had with Martin. To be fair to Edith, she was very warm at the funeral, seeking Geraldine out and sitting beside her. She did this even though Henry, acting bereft, had Florence's arm in his and clearly wanted Edith to sit with them. The man has no shame; he never once set foot in the hospital.

Never mind.

Geraldine has not come to display her wounds. She came (although she didn't plan it) as an act of good will, to show that she wants to be included. After all, if it weren't for Geraldine, Lucille might never have found her daughter; Florence wouldn't have known Martin's child. If Geraldine is careful not to resent their good fortune, they might not be so cruel as to cut her out of their circle of happiness.

LULU SEES CLARENCE LEAVING WITH SOMEONE. "OH, Larry, run and tell Clarence we're expecting him to come to dinner with us. Tell him to bring his friend."

Florence touches Lulu's elbow. "There's Geraldine. I never expected her to come."

Geraldine is standing just inside the door, as if afraid someone will challenge her right to be here. Lulu recognizes the feeling; it's one she's had for most of her life. How strange that Geraldine, who was always the insider, should be standing at the edge waiting to be recognized, and Lulu should be at the center.

It's because of Desert Ray. Lulu has found the piece missing from her being. She was crippled without Ray, and now she's whole.

"Florence, go over and ask Geraldine to come to dinner with us. Tell her I promise to stay out of the garbage, and I won't eat off anyone's plate—except maybe Larry's." It's fitting, Lulu thinks but has the tact not to say to Florence, that they should be together for once, all of Martin's women. *Martin's women.* It tickles Lulu to think of them this way. It's so funny that she looks around for someone to share it with, but there's nobody who would understand.

Edith, standing with Ben, hears Lulu's laugh, so wild and free that it makes her laugh too. "What a wonderful laugh Lulu has," Ben says. "It's amazing, how alike you are."

The laugh turns the heads of invited and uninvited guests. It interrupts Florence's conversation with Geraldine. It makes Clarence and Larry look at each other and smile. It floats out to the street and catches up with Ryo Yamanaka, although she refuses to acknowledge it. Lulu's laughter melds into all the sounds of the city, and rises with them in an indistinguishable hum, reaching even the wind-filled ears of migrating birds flying their solitary star-marked paths.

Mary Tannen is the author of three previous novels—*Second Sight*, *After Roy*, and *Easy Keeper*—and several books for children. She is a regular contributor to *The New York Times Sunday Magazine* and *Vogue*. Her short fiction has appeared in *The New Yorker* and received an O. Henry Award in 1994. Tannen lives in New York City with her husband and their two children.